CHEAPSKATES

Also by Charlie Stella
————————

Eddie's World
Jimmy Bench-Press
Charlie Opera

CHEAPSKATES

Charlie Stella

CARROLL & GRAF PUBLISHERS
NEW YORK

Cheapskates

Carroll & Graf Publishers
An Imprint of Avalon Publishing Group Inc.
245 West 17th Street
11th Floor
New York, NY 10011

AVALON
publishing group incorporated

Copyright © 2005 by Charlie Stella

First Carroll & Graf edition 2005

Library of Congress Cataloging-in-Publication Data is available.

ISBN: 0-7867-1479-4

10 9 8 7 6 5 4 3 2 1

Printed in the United States of America
Distributed by Publishers Group West

For my mother . . .
because she really did know best.

I suppose this is the first time you ever run into a bus driver . . .
—RALPH KRAMDEN *(The Honeymooners)*

CHAPTER

1

"SEE THAT?" TOMMY BURNS asked Johnny Mauro.

They were having coffee in a diner on Park Avenue South across from Union Square Park. Burns pointed at a middle-aged couple arguing outside. The woman flailed her hands in an angry fit. The man pulled up the collar of his short leather jacket and turned his back to a strong gust of wind. When he turned around again, the woman was right there waving a finger in his face. Burns shook his head at the sight.

"You see that more'n more these days, guys catching it on the street like that," he said. "I see it every day driving the car. It's the way of the modern world."

Burns was a short, thin man somewhere in his fifties. He had gray hair and piercing blue eyes. He was dressed in a wrinkled gray sports jacket over a black turtleneck. His hat and gloves lay on the table to one side.

"I imagine you see a lot, driving," Mauro said. He was still watching the couple. When they disappeared inside a taxi, Mauro sniffled, then sipped his coffee. "How's that going?" he asked.

"Serves the purpose," Burns said before sipping his tea laced with milk. "I didn't have a hook, it'd be another story. These camel jockeys all over the place now. You should see the looks on some of the people, they get in my car. Relieved I'm not wearing my laundry on my head or wearing a robe. At least I get requested a lot more now'n I used to."

Mauro was thirty-nine, average height and weight. He had a thick head of black hair and dark brown eyes. He was glancing out the window again and spoke without turning to Burns. "And they fight in the cars, the women yelling at the men?"

"Airport runs mostly," Burns said. "On the way to vacation or a business trip or whatever. They're on edge or it's that time of the month. I had this one couple last week, I picked them up from a luxury building on the East Side, near the tunnel there, and the woman is giving it to the poor SOB from the second they're in the car to I drop them off at Continental in Kennedy. How the guy didn't shove her in fronna a bus, I don't know."

Mauro smiled. "You ever get married?"

"Never once," Burns said. "I'm not the sharpest knife in the drawer but I do know when I don't belong. The civil service or a wife, either way, forget about it, not for me. I couldn't take orders from the nuns when I was a kid and I can't take them now. Uh-uh, no, thank you."

A waitress brought both men toasted muffins. Burns scraped jelly from a packet onto half of his muffin. Mauro used butter.

"I just come back and I still got no interest in it, getting married," Mauro said. "Not after this last stretch."

Burns stopped to ask, "What was it, two years?"

"Twenty-eight months," Mauro said. He bit into his muffin and chewed a few seconds. He spoke with his mouth full. "Twenty-eight months, two weeks, three days. And the last thing I wanted, I got out, was a piece of tail. Believe it or not."

"To each his own."

"I was with my girlfriend the night before I surrendered and don't you know it, she's giving me shit the entire time I don't shove something in her mouth," Mauro said. He waved the thought off. "I couldn't wait to go away."

"Still? I mean, since you're out. Nothing?"

"Last night before I go see our friend. I grabbed some kid off the streets. Twenty bucks. No muss, no fuss. It's all I need these days. I give the broad I used to see a try but she's busy, what she says."

Burns was washing down some muffin with his tea. "I hear you. I'm right with you, it comes to that, paying for it. I got me a regular works out the Tavern on Glenwood Road, not far from where you're at in

Canarsie. Black broad. Stocky, the way I like them. Thinks she's a singer. What do I care what she thinks she is? Takes care of the details. I pay her and off she goes until the next time."

"Call me jaded," Mauro said, "but who needs it anymore? Like you said, those two out there before, it's painful to watch, what guys'll do to keep a piece. Very painful."

Burns glanced around the diner and leaned in close. "How is our friend?"

"He wants to know you still do work?"

"Always. I can't pay my shylock on what I make driving, never mind my bookie."

Mauro leaned in to whisper. "It's a guy getting out in a few days. A knock-around guy used to be around Joe Sharp."

"Around somebody means he's connected," said Burns, sitting back again. "I don't need the aggravation, it isn't sanctioned. The other thing, it'll be pricey. The guy is connected, our friend already knows that."

"I was told to go no higher than ten. I hope that's doable."

Burns frowned. "Fifteen'll put the smile back on my face."

Mauro opened his hands. "I was told no higher than ten."

Burns sipped his tea.

"I can go back and ask, you want me to," Mauro said. "It's no skin off my ass to ask."

Burns shrugged. "What the fuck. A man's not supposed to enjoy his work anyway. Ten it is. Half up front."

"Good," Mauro said. "And the guy, he is and he ain't around Joe Sharp. He was, before he got sent up, but he's not now, since Sharp went away. Technically, I'm speaking. This guy went away on some personal shit, had nothing to do with Sharp."

"Technically or otherwise, the guy is connected, it's a potential headache," Burns said. "I'm fifty-two going on seventy from the cigarettes. It's fifteen minutes now I'm not smoking, but that's because of the goddamn laws they have, you can't smoke anywhere. Soon's I'm outta here I'll chain-smoke through half a pack before I'm back in the car. I'll smoke the other half before I'm over one of the bridges. The way I see it, another ten years driving, if I survive, I'm down in Florida for whatever time I have left, playing gin rummy, continental, poker, whatever game I can find I can afford. I don't need something to go wrong at this late date. I'm not half your size or a quarter your strength. I'm too old to go away. The Mandingos inside want my skinny rump, how'm I gonna stop them?"

Mauro finished his coffee and set the cup at the edge of the table for a refill. Burns waited for Mauro's full attention again. "Our friend giving me the green light or not?" he asked.

Mauro passed a book of matches across the table. "Why I'm here. I come to you first because our friend suggested you."

Burns took the matches and stashed them inside his jacket pocket. "Our friend gave you my name, that's good enough for me. You'll get me the details soon?"

"No later than tomorrow," Mauro said. "I'm waiting on another thing to see about and then we're on."

"This other thing isn't you shopping, I hope. I make a deal with somebody, I make a deal."

"No problem. You're the man. This is something else. Related but not related. I'll get you the info and the money end of day tomorrow. I'll give you a call. Where, your cell phone?"

Burns covered his mouth with a fist as he coughed. "I'm not inside here, I'm probably outside next door. Like a goddamned teenager sneaking a smoke, that's what it's come to."

"What you call it before?" Mauro said. "The way of the modern world?"

Burns toasted Mauro with his empty teacup. "Indeed," he said. "And a fuckin' shame it is, too."

"It's that easy?" Janice Barrett asked Johnny Mauro.

"You seen him take the matches, right?" Mauro said. He turned up the heat on the dashboard of her Blazer. "You're from up north, you like the cold?" he asked as an afterthought.

"So I pay you another ten thousand and you pay him from that and it's done," she said. "Is that it?"

Mauro looked over his shoulder into the back of the SUV. "Jimmy the Blond didn't give you my name, I'd swear you're taping this. How many times you wanna go over it, sweetheart?"

Janice was bundled in a down jacket, snow pants, and boots. She brushed a lock of the short blond wig she was wearing from her face as she turned in her seat.

"I just want to be sure," she said. "I don't want any misunderstandings or any trouble once this is done."

"Hey, doll, I'm the only trouble you can have," Mauro said. "And you to me."

"Half up front, half after the job."

"One more time, yes."

Janice looked at the man she'd watched through the diner window earlier. Now huddled in a doorway, he was smoking cigarettes. He tossed a butt on the floor, crushed it with his foot, and immediately lit another.

"That's three in a row," she commented. She noticed a small pile of butts at the man's feet. "A man after my own heart."

"Huh?" Mauro said. He looked confused.

Janice pointed at the man. "Cigarettes your friend smoked now."

"Because he couldn't smoke inside," Mauro said. "He's a junky it comes to smokes."

"He must be freezing out there."

"He's of age," Mauro said. "Look, hon, not that I'm not enjoying this, but we have a deal or no? You fronted me five and we're this far along. You're having second thoughts, you wanna pull out, please do so now before it gets too deep to pull out. I don't mind it, you change your mind up to this point, you come on a solid recommendation, but now's the time to shit or get off the pot. I can't live the rest of my life on five thousand dollars, and there are plenty people out there got hard-ons for other people with enough to pay they go away. Whatta you say?"

Janice reached down under her seat and pulled out a thick envelope. She handed it to Mauro.

"These windows tinted?" he asked.

"Of course."

Mauro opened the envelope and ran a thumb across the neat stacks of hundred-dollar bills. "Looks about right."

"Count it if you have any doubts," Janice said. "There's five thousand dollars there. You won't be able to call me tomorrow and tell me there was less."

Mauro counted through half of one stack. He did the math in his head, then counted the stacks themselves. "All right. Five and five make ten. The next ten on delivery."

"Delivery meaning proof of death," Janice said, all business. "I won't pay you just because he disappears. Either I see it on a local news channel, or it's verified in some other way I know it's for real. A newspaper article, or like I said, on the eleven-o'clock news."

"I can bring him to your apartment, you want. But that'll cost extra."

"I'm serious," Janice said. "I'm not giving you ten thousand dollars and forgetting about this. If you think you're scamming me, trust me, you're not."

"That a threat?"

Janice turned to Mauro. "I'm thirty-seven years old. I'm a professional businesswoman and I know enough about the streets, between being married to a street guy and knowing his friends, and from people like Jimmy, specifically, to not be played for a sucker. Trust me on this. I won't let you steal ten thousand dollars from me."

Mauro was involved in a stare-down until it was clear the woman wouldn't blink. "Okay," he said. "Fair enough. But you can sleep well tonight. I just got out myself and I need the money. Your ex'll get clipped a day or two after he's released. After which, you'd better have the rest of my money, sweet cheeks, because count on it, I won't let you steal from me, either."

Janice nodded nervously as Mauro jammed the envelope with his cash inside the waist of his pants. He pulled up his collar and stepped out of the Blazer into the brittle, cold New York night.

CHAPTER

2

"WHAT YOU THINKING ABOUT?" Reese Waters asked Peter Rizzo.

Rizzo finished his cigarette and dropped it on the cell floor. He crushed the butt with his right foot and stood up off the cot. "My money," he said. "I'm thinking about my money."

Reese, seated on the toilet, was paging through a *Playboy* magazine. A tall blonde in lavender bunny pajamas was on the cover. He opened the magazine to her picture and held it up.

"You think she'd go for me?" he asked.

Rizzo focused on the blonde's crotch. "Why not?" he asked. "She shaved? I never understood that. The whole point of having a blonde would be to see she's natural or not, right?"

"I never had a blonde," Reese said. He folded the magazine and dropped it on the floor. "Never had a white woman."

They shared a cell on the third tier of D-block, the last move inside the Fishkill Penitentiary before prisoners were released. Reese had gone away for stealing a car. Rizzo had broken a man's jaw and pleaded guilty to the assault, his second offense. Now they were two days from release.

Rizzo spread his legs, bent at the waist, and stretched both arms to touch his shoes. He held the stretching position a few seconds before standing up again. When he saw Reese staring down at the cover of the magazine, Rizzo said, "You're probably the only guy in here reads the damn thing, you know that?"

"I'm probably the only guy in here *can* read."

Rizzo stretched his arms behind his head. "We can go after it together, my money. Fifty-fifty."

"I think you best put that money behind you."

"Yeah, right," Rizzo said. "I'm too old to forget fifty grand, never mind the two-year bonus in this place because of it. I'll forget it when I'm dead."

Reese grabbed a cigarette from his pack on the stainless steel sink alongside the toilet.

"I'm getting antsy," Rizzo continued. "The closer we get to out of here, this thing with my ex, it's eating at me."

Reese put fire to the cigarette, took a long drag, and blew smoke rings.

"Impressive," Rizzo said.

"You getting nervous is all," Reese said. "You know who you are in here." He thumbed over his shoulder at the tiny window high on the wall above the toilet. "It's scary, going back outside. Brings a lot of dudes back, the fear."

"I was thinking about taking a poke at that fat hack down in mess the other day just to spend another week in the hole," Rizzo said. "Just to give myself some more time to think."

"You just thought for two years. You don't need to think. You need to get over it."

Rizzo dropped to the floor and started a set of push-ups. Reese counted to himself. He stopped counting at forty. Rizzo went another ten before stopping mid-push-up. He held himself rigid until his triceps began to shake. He slowly lowered himself to the floor and let the air he was holding out of his lungs.

"She still owes me," he said as he caught his breath. "Fifty grand. I could use it . . . as start-up cash. I could make a move. Leave the state . . . I was thinking. Go south. Go anywhere."

Reese said, "You Robinson Crusoe now?"

"Robinson who?"

Reese was cleaning himself. He finished, then said, "You got someplace to go without the money? Because you probably aren't gonna get it without holding a gun to her head. You might as well start thinking about something else."

Rizzo crawled up off the floor and removed his T-shirt. A jagged scar ran across his stomach where he'd been stabbed in a prison attack. He used the T-shirt to dry his face.

"Well, after her, I'm through collecting," Rizzo said. "If it eases your mind any."

"You a hardheaded Eye-talian," Reese said.

"What I am is a convict about to be released with two choices. I could collect the fifty grand my ex-wife stole from me, or I can go work at McDonald's. Two years down the road, my job is long gone at Il Palermo. So are my connections. I'm not about to start busing tables. I already know which choice I'm making. The question is, you wanna help me collect it, maybe go into some kind of business afterward? Or you intend to steal another car, wind up back here?"

"I already told you," Reese said. "You want to split a cab, twelve hours each, alternate shifts as long as we can take it, I'm fine with that. I was thinking about buying a medallion anyway, once I cashed out my pension from the MTA. The only good thing came from this mess was getting fired from that job. I was losing myself driving a bus. You can only get spit on so many times before you start to think you deserve it."

"Twelve-hour shifts, back and forth, until when? We croak? You think we'll make any real money doing that?"

"I think we'll make some honest money and pretty fast, we put in the time. And trust me, I've had my fill of this place or anyplace like it. I made a dumb mistake and listened to a cousin of mine I should've shoved in front of the car I drove for him. My fault. Score one for the American penal system. I'm rehabilitated. I'm not coming back."

Reese meant it, too. The fact that he was able to tolerate prison life had started to scare him six months earlier. He feared the way he had learned to cope inside.

"Except now you want to start over," Rizzo said. "And we don't have to. She owes me. The woman flat-out robbed me. I'm not saying we can't do the cab thing, but why not do it with something already inside the tin cup? We could do something real, we put enough money away. Open a joint."

"Open a joint," Reese repeated dismissively. "What, so we can wind up collecting envelopes for more of your Eye-talian friends, all those bookies and shylocks? You get back into the bar business, you asking for more trouble. Why not just leave it behind?"

"Because I'm bust the day I step out of here," Rizzo said. "We get my money, I can leave the bar business. After I get what was robbed."

"I'll tell you what," Reese said. "You want, I'll talk to her. You gonna get crazy, I want nothing to do with it. Either she'll pay up or she won't. Doing something crazy won't change things. She already served up two suckers, you and the man you broke his jaw to wind up in here. I'll talk to her, see what the deal is. After that, she don't pay, I'm out. Consider it a favor, my asking at all."

"For saving your life?" Rizzo asked.

"Something like that," Reese said.

There had been a riot between the mob guys and one of the black gangs. Reese was caught in the middle while working a laundry detail. Rizzo fought off two mob associates to protect Reese. He was stabbed the next day for fighting with his own people. After the stabbing, Reese and Rizzo were moved into protective custody together.

Now Rizzo sat on the edge of his cot. "You gonna flush or what?"

Reese reached behind and flushed the toilet.

"Technically, I should charge her," Rizzo continued. "She understands how it works, holding onto money. Technically, at a bank rate, she owes me more than fifty grand."

Reese stood up from the toilet, pulled up his pants, stretched his arms over his head, and washed his hands. He dried them with paper towels and grabbed his drumsticks from his cot. He was a tall, thin black man. He scratched at his short, recently cut hair.

"Technically, you can't go within a city block of your ex once we out of here," he said as he twirled both sticks. "Which is why I'll be the one doing the talking. You keep doing push-ups and get it out of your system, all this bile you still choking on. Because once we're outside, this thing with your ex-wife, whatever happens, happens. I'm not shaking down some woman bold enough to push your buttons. If I can't get her to reason and do the right thing, I'm walking away. I'm thinking the West Coast someplace. Maybe Vegas or L.A., or maybe San Francisco."

"What you gonna do there?" Rizzo asked. "Play drums outside one of the airports for spare change?"

"Deal, if it's Vegas," Reese said. "Maybe drive a cable car if it's Frisco. My fifteen years with the MTA might do me some good after all."

Rizzo winked at his friend. "Drive it or steal it?"

"You can't steal a cable car, you dumb ass," Reese said. "They're on tracks. Go up and down those big hills, back and forth, all day and night."

"Sounds like a blast," Rizzo said. "I'm excited for you."

CHAPTER

3

THE WIND OFF RARITAN Bay was gusting at thirty miles per hour. Johnny Mauro set his fishing pole on the floor of the dock and leaned into the wind. Except for an idle fishing boat, the Harborside Marina was empty. Mauro jammed his hands inside his jacket pocket and waited as a fat man crossed the pier.

"This supposed to fool anybody, carrying the fishing poles?" Mauro asked when the fat man was close enough to hear.

The fat man dropped his pole on the floor alongside Mauro's. He removed a short, thick, half-smoked cigar from his mouth and turned away from the wind.

"Right now, without that pole, you're consorting with a known criminal," the fat man said. "So am I."

"The fishing poles we aren't using change that?" Mauro asked.

"My lawyer tells me to do it so I do it," the fat man said. "I figure he's smarter than you, so I listen."

Both men huddled close together and crouched in the face of the wind whipping off the water. "It always like this over here?" Mauro asked. "The wind, I mean."

The fat man was "Fat" Tony Gangi, a street boss with the New Jersey faction of the Vignieri crime family. He was short and squat, at least three hundred pounds. He motioned toward a brick building across the marina.

"I'd go in there except I forgot the keys," he said. "The bathroom is locked until spring."

Mauro removed a small envelope from inside his jacket and handed it to Gangi. "Knock yourself out," he said. "I give the work to

Tommy Burns. He was nervous about the guy but I told him he was asked for specifically."

"That's already more than I need to know," Gangi said.

Mauro turned to where some construction equipment was parked alongside the harbormaster's office. He motioned with his head. "This your contract?"

"This and the other thing farther up," Gangi said. "They're redoing the waterfront here."

"Sounds like a score to me. Maybe there's a job for me in it somewhere."

Gangi cupped his right hand over his right ear. "Fuckin' wind," he said.

"I'm talking down the road," Mauro said. "After I take care of this other thing."

"We'll see," Gangi said. "Jimmy Valentine is working on something with a guy upstate New York. You don't mind living with the hicks a few months of the year, maybe you can supervise one of the sites up there. There's all kind of people watching down here." He pointed at a blue van parked off to one side of the marina lot. "My permanent chaperones," he said.

"Fuckin' feds," Mauro said.

"Jimmy's guy upstate has the safe stuff," Gangi continued. "Residential real estate. He built Jimmy's house a few years back. They're in bed together goes back another dozen years or so. This waterfront job over here is gonna draw attention like shit draws flies. You don't wanna be here, you don't have to."

"I don't wanna be anywhere near a job," Mauro said. "Except I'm gonna need one or have to go back inside, and that I definitely don't wanna do, not again."

"I'll ask for you," Gangi said. "It's the best I can do."

Mauro nodded. "I tell you about this broad contracted the work?" he asked. "She's a tough one. Stared me down as good as anybody in the joint. Gave me a warning, too."

"Yeah, well, Jimmy give her your name, so don't forget that," Gangi said. "Maybe you shouldn't be talking about her."

"You think he's getting any of that?"

"Who the fuck knows?" Gangi said. "What I just say? You should or shouldn't talk about it?"

A moment of uncomfortable silence ensued. Gangi nudged Mauro and said, "She's a looker, yeah, probably. Jimmy's not known to pass on a piece. It's what got him into a fix more'n once, a looker. If you're asking because you're interested, remember what's she's doing with you before you fall in love. Then I'd worry about whether Jimmy's got a claim on her."

"You make a good point," Mauro said.

"You're fucking-A right, I do," Gangi said. "A broad contracts a piece of work, no fucking thank you."

A powerful gust of wind sent both men hard into the railing.

"Jesus Christ," Mauro said.

"Just let's get this thing done for now and I'll ask around about that other work for you," Gangi said. "You're just out, right?"

"A few weeks."

"Getting any?"

"It's not as important anymore," Mauro said. "I can't afford to ignore business like when I was a kid."

"Tell me about it," Gangi said. "Seems like that's all we're doing anymore. Hiding from one thing or another while we try to earn. Then when you think it's all clear, you can come up to breathe, buy yourself a new car, a vacation home someplace, some cocksucker you did a thing with eight years ago gives you up and the bullshit starts all over again. I'm telling you, the day I got my stripes, I could take it back, I'd fucking run to do that. I'm a skipper going on eight years now, five out and three in. What's the fuckin' point?"

Mauro picked up his fishing pole. The hook came loose from one of the eyes and snagged Gangi's pants at the cuff.

"Don't move," Mauro said. He kneeled down to release the hook.

"Why don't you put that thing away before you hurt somebody," Gangi said when Mauro was standing again.

"I put three hundred I can't afford to give up in the envelope," Mauro said. "From appreciation. I want you to know that."

Gangi wiped his nose with the back of a wrist. "Duly noted," he said. "And I'll do my best to not spend it all in one place."

◆　◆　◆

Reese was sitting on his cot practicing triplets on a paperback of Graham Greene's *The Power and the Glory*. He was having trouble sleeping. He was anxious to get out of prison and nervous about living with his mother again. There wouldn't be enough money left in his bank account to get his own place, and he couldn't borrow what little his mother might have.

He closed his eyes and remembered how as a kid he used to worry about what he would do for work when he was an adult. Reese had always wanted to play drums. When his parents bought a house in Canarsie, he was told he could use the basement to practice. After one year, his parents rented a small trap set and Reese learned to play by ear.

He stayed with the drums all through high school and after he graduated. He played in a few bands with musicians older than himself, and eventually took a bus driver's job with the city rather than attend college. When Reese formed a band of his own, he met the woman he would eventually marry, a thirty-one-year-old singer from South Carolina. Four years later, Sarah Tyler broke his heart when she left Reese for a white piano player she'd met during a gig in Atlantic City. Reese quit playing drums with bands after the divorce.

He had lived alone ever since. His mother was getting on in years and wasn't always healthy. They were close, but Reese hadn't lived with her since he was twenty-two. Two weeks ago he had turned thirty-seven.

Reese figured he would drive a cab for work. His criminal record would preclude him from working for the city again. It would probably keep him from working most jobs.

Now he kept his eyes closed and tried to picture his mother's apartment as he played accented press rolls on the paperback: the small vestibule inside the apartment door, the kitchen straight ahead, the living room off to the right, both bedrooms behind the kitchen, the smaller one off to the right with the bathroom next to it.

Reese added alternating accents to his triplets, and Peter said, "Hey, Buddy Rich, you wanna give it a break?"

Reese spoke at the bunk above him. "You up?"

"Who can sleep with that noise you're making?"

Reese glanced at his watch. It was four-thirty in the morning. "What's the matter?"

"The money," Peter said.

"Again?"

"I can't get past it."

"You better get past it."

"I think I could kill her."

"I think you should keep that to yourself."

Peter swung his legs over the side of the top bunk and pushed himself off. He landed next to Reese. "I dream about it sometimes, killing her." He sat at the far end of the bottom bunk. "I can't get past it anymore. I want my money."

Reese set his drumsticks on the blanket. He had been through this conversation before. He was hearing it more and more often the closer they came to being released. Lately, it seemed Peter was obsessed.

"When she set me up," Peter said, "I made it easy for her because I reacted without thinking it through. She counted on my reaction. She knew exactly what I'd do."

"You need music for this song or you going from memory?" Reese asked.

Peter ignored the remark. "She was sleeping with two dudes. Not at the same time, not kinky shit, but two different guys. The one I hit was another poor bastard she was using. The other one is the guy she was protecting. Her real boyfriend at the time."

"She put it in your face she was sleeping with some dude and stealing your money," Reese said. "You made a mistake. You need to get over it."

Peter seemed lost in thought. "She must've needed him for

something, too, she didn't want me to go after him. The other boyfriend, the one she was protecting."

"So, what, now you want to go after him, get yourself another couple years back in here?"

Peter put up his hands. "I'm not hitting anybody. I'm just saying maybe the one she cares about is the one I should approach. Not threaten, just approach. Maybe the guy gets nervous, he talks her into making good on what she robbed."

Reese made a face.

"What?" Peter said.

"You smoking that glue they use in the workshop. That woman you were married to isn't getting talked into anything. You go anywhere near her and they'll violate your parole before you get the smell of this place off you." He picked up the sticks and played a drumroll on the paperback. "Just forget about it for now. Get it out your system before it eats you up."

Peter said, "Your ex didn't rob you, man. It's easy for you."

Reese tossed his drumsticks back onto the bed. His ex had ripped his heart out instead, Reese was thinking, but wasn't about to go down that road before breakfast. "There wasn't any money to take," he said instead.

Peter grabbed the drumsticks and tried to cradle one in his left hand.

"They not chopsticks," Reese told him.

Peter climbed back up to his bunk and dropped onto his back. "You say good-bye to your mullah brothers yet?"

"You mean my Muslim brothers?"

"Yeah, the Nation of Napalm, whatever the fuck they call themselves."

"Islam. The Nation of Islam."

"Well? You say good-bye to Rahib?"

It was a private joke between them. Reese had saved a member of the Nation of Islam from a skinhead gang bang with a fire hose. The Nation's leader inside the prison, Rahib Kendall-Jabbar, had let Reese know that they owed him a favor. Peter liked to tease Reese about collecting on it.

"I did," Reese said. "Why?"

"Because they owe you, man. We might use them to help us collect."

"I don't think so."

"We could pay them or make a donation or something. They could burn a cross on my ex's-boyfriend's lawn."

"Sometimes you're an idiot," Reese said.

"*Salam Malakim,*" Peter said.

CHAPTER

4

"I WORE THESE THE first time," Janice Barrett said. "Do you remember?"

She was modeling pink thong underwear in her living room. She turned her back to Jimmy Valentine and showed him her ass.

"I remember that," he said, "your rump."

Jimmy, seated in her recliner, was sipping scotch. He had been scratching off instant Lotto tickets with a quarter. A stack of losing tickets was set on an end table alongside the chair.

"I remembered it from when your father was building my place in Tappan," he said. "You brought him lunch or something. You were wearing tight shorts. You got me in trouble with my old lady."

He sipped at his scotch, then set the rocks glass on a napkin. A cigar burned in an ashtray alongside the drink.

Janice wrinkled her nose as she sipped from a martini glass. "How'd I do that?"

"I said 'nice ass' when I saw you," Jimmy said. "I was in the kitchen with my wife. She was there to pick out the cabinets. I forgot she was standing there."

"Ouch."

"She said 'fuck you' and walked out."

Janice crossed her legs and listed to one side flirtatiously. "Sorry."

"Fuck her," Jimmy said before drinking the scotch.

It had been a marriage Jimmy liked to forget. His rump remark that day had started a fresh round in an ongoing battle with the second Mrs. Valentine. A few weeks later, he had her chopped up and scattered along the Hudson River from the Tappan Zee Bridge to West Point.

Janice stood just out of Jimmy's touch. "Do you remember our first time?" she teased.

"In that closet you use for a kitchen," he said. "We kissed and I turned you around. I didn't really notice the underwear, though, tell you the truth."

Janice stepped closer, and he stroked her left thigh. He moved his hand up toward her crotch, and she stepped away.

"I could put you on a stage, you like to play this game."

Janice sat on the edge of the couch. "I didn't recognize you that day at the doctor's office," she said. "It took me awhile."

"But you saw me checking you out."

Janice giggled. "You were reading a magazine or something."

"A yachting magazine," Jimmy said. "I was thinking about replacing my boat, *Donna Bella*. You walked in the office and gave me a view when you signed in at the desk. Then you sat across from me and I saw your face, recognized it. The builder's kid, I remembered. The one with the nice ass."

Janice blushed. "Who's Donna?"

"Huh?"

"*Donna Bella*?"

"It means beautiful woman. I inherited the thing with a promotion. I replaced it since. *Donna Bella II*'s a bigger boat."

Their affair was a few months old. They were keeping it under wraps because that was the way Jimmy wanted it. He had business with her father that couldn't be disturbed. Today they were celebrating her ex-husband's imminent demise.

"I asked your father once what happened to you," he said. "Did you get married and so on. He got defensive and said you moved to the city. That was seven, eight years ago. I shoulda looked you up."

"Wow," said Janice, delighted at the thought. "That was before I got married."

"I would've done yous both a favor."

Janice laughed. She was supposed to be in a committed relationship with a coworker. She knew it was over the day she let Jimmy

Valentine have her in the kitchen. She was hopeful their tryst would become something more.

"What happens now?" she asked.

Jimmy took a long, deliberate drag on the cigar. He made her wait for a response. He looked her over and touched himself through his pants.

"Forgetaboutit," he said, running the words together. "It's not important. The important thing is you don't let your old man find out."

"My dad? Of course not."

"He's got enough on his mind."

"That thing he's doing in Croton?" she asked. "Is he working with you on that?"

Jimmy lost his smile. "My business with your father has nothing to do with any of this," he said as he pointed a finger back and forth.

"Sure," she said, sitting back on the couch. "I'm sorry."

"He's involved with some friends of mine. He needs to remember that. Enough said."

"Okay. Sorry."

Jimmy pointed back and forth again. "And you and me, we never had these conversations," he told her. "We never were involved with one another. That's for your sake. Remember that."

"Sure," Janice said. She set the martini glass on the cocktail table. "I'm sorry," she repeated.

Jimmy took his time staring her down. "All right," he finally said.

Janice felt an emotional meltdown. Her lips quivered. "Don't be angry."

Jimmy remained silent.

The guy exuded power, she was thinking. He not only looked the part, crime family *consigliere*, he also relished it.

"Please?" she whispered.

Jimmy grinned from one side of his mouth. "Who's angry?"

Janice forced a smile.

She had thought her ex-husband was connected when she first met him a few years back. It had been an intriguing relationship while they dated. After they were married and living together, the relationship quickly turned mundane. A year into her marriage, she met a wealthy advertising executive with a reputation for promiscuity. She was divorced shortly thereafter.

Walking into Jimmy a few months earlier in a Manhattan doctor's office had been fortuitous. Janice had been searching for a way to buy out the man she had left her ex-husband for. She needed a partner with financial and personal clout. Jimmy was the epitome of power. She was eager for their relationship to become more than an affair.

Except now she was a little nervous that she had mentioned her father's business with Jimmy.

"I'm ready if you are," she said.

Jimmy yawned.

"Or I can take care of you if you're tired," she added nervously.

"I think that might be the way to go today, you don't mind," he said.

Janice was up off the couch and down on her knees before Jimmy could set down his glass.

CHAPTER

5

IT WAS THEIR LAST day, and neither of them could sleep. They were permitted to exercise together a few minutes before sunrise. A light drizzle started to fall as Peter finished his push-ups. Reese had just finished his stomach work. They were both sweating and tired. Except for a lone guard standing near a door, the yard was empty.

Peter was explaining why his marriage had turned so ugly so fast. He was going through a laundry list of things his ex-wife did with money that had eroded his feelings for her.

"I'd ask her to pick me up cigarettes while she was at the store and she'd come home with a single pack instead of two or three or a carton—what I do for her, she asked me," he said. "Or when she went shopping, the grocery bill would total no more than thirty dollars. I'd go shopping and the bill was triple that at least.

"Or days when the cleaning lady came. She'd remind me to leave the money but she'd never consider doing it herself, a big fifty bucks. Enough of that shit happens, you start to notice, it's no coincidence."

Reese was wiping sweat off himself with his T-shirt.

"She made me feel stupid for buying her flowers," Peter continued. "She made me feel like a sucker to pay for dinner, and she didn't like cheap joints. The Palm, Peter Luger's, Sparks, the place I used to run, Il Palermo. She liked fancy joints. Her old man, give him credit, he sprung once a year for a meal at some joint in Westchester where he'd take us on our anniversary. I'd hate to see what he left the waiter but at least he paid the bill. She was just like her father when it came to that, too. She'd leave ten percent, not a dime more, if that much."

Reese was smiling now. "You getting yourself worked up again."

"She learned it all from her father," Peter said. "The guy once walked from Grand Central Station to Madison Square Garden in a cold rain rather than pay for a taxi. I got him tickets to see the Knicks—supposedly his favorite sport, basketball was—and he wouldn't go unless the tickets were free. He walked from Grand Central to the Garden, all the way there and all the way back, rather than spring for a cab. Don't forget, the guy is worth three, four million. We were living uptown at the time. I was in a cab and probably in my bed before the old man was near Grand Central."

"They say apples don't fall far from their trees," Reese said.

Peter was ranting and didn't hear him. "Her mother, too, from the stories she told me. She was another one, the old lady. She'd go to Atlantic City with her friends from the church and come home with the quarters they give out. Janice asked her how she did and the old lady'd say, 'I didn't gamble. I like my money.' She died when Janice was young. Probably clutching her bankbook."

"They nothing but cheapskates," Reese said.

"Except for the brother," Peter added. "He wasn't so bad, not back then. He was just a general fuck-up. You know, too much booze, fooling around on his wife, and stuff. He had a kid that kept him grounded, I think, but he was a total phony it came to his old lady. I suspect he picked that up from the old man, cheating on his wife rather than pay for a divorce and some peace of mind.

"I tell you that, the old man, until his wife died, they slept in separate bedrooms because he was too cheap to divorce her. He was a weird dude. Had his own connections, too. Did work for one of the Vignieri skippers up in Westchester. Like I said, he had deep pockets. But he'd cut his balls off before he'd pay for something he might enjoy."

Reese could sense his friend's rage building. He tried to avoid where their conversation was heading. "You need a lift later, I got one for you," he said, changing the subject.

"Huh?"

"Somebody picking me up," Reese said. "You're welcome to come along. You're welcome to come for dinner, too."

"Thanks, but no thanks," Peter said. "Which reminds me, speaking of dinner, I tell you about the thing the old man did with the cake, the Entenmann's? He'd go to the outlets and stock up on the cheapest cakes, the ones they couldn't sell or the ones with the damaged boxes, and he'd eat them for breakfast and lunch all week."

Reese laughed cautiously as Peter wiped his face.

Peter said, "The man would eat it seven days a week, breakfast, lunch, and dinner, if he could get away with it."

"I can see where you'd be pissed," said Reese, still trying to prevent his friend from obsessing. "Except these people don't sound like the type that will see the light, not in this life. You best let it be and move on. Think happy thoughts."

"Sometimes I think if I ever get cancer, diagnosed with cancer, I'll run her over on the way to chemo. How's that for a happy thought?"

Reese grinned, but it was measured. He dropped to the floor and began a set of push-ups to prevent further discussion.

Later, they were separated during the release process until after breakfast. When they met again, they were waiting to sign for their personal property. Peter was smoking a Marlboro. He offered one to Reese.

"No, thanks," Reese said.

"You pack all your books?"

"I donated them."

Peter was surprised. "All those books? You serious?"

"I read most of them twice," Reese said. "Some three times."

Peter looked up at the clock on the wall. "It's winding down, our time in here."

A prison guard set two boxes filled with personal items on a counter. He held a clipboard up and checked the tags.

"This isn't the right stuff," the guard said. He removed both boxes and disappeared behind a partition.

"You want that ride?" Reese asked. "It won't be a problem. The man's a priest, so you don't have to worry about insulting the Nation."

"The Nation of Napalm?"

"I'm telling you, Rocky Balboa, you pull that shit when you're out on the street, they'll fuck you up."

"Relax," Peter said. "And thanks but no thanks on the ride. I'm in no rush to get home. I'm looking forward to the time alone on the trains. I like the idea of taking it slow, going back to the city."

"Just make sure you go home," Reese said. "No detours."

"Sure, Dad," Peter said.

Reese gave him the finger.

✦ ✦ ✦

The back office of the Dunkin' Donuts on Smith Street in Perth Amboy adjoined the rear of the discount shop next door. Jimmy Valentine, wearing his curly blond hairpiece and using a cane, stepped into the office of the Dunkin' Donuts and knocked on the door linking it to the discount shop. Tony Gangi opened the door, and the two gangsters greeted each other with cheek kisses.

Jimmy closed the door behind him. Gangi shut the other door, and both men sat on folding chairs across from each other.

"How was the traffic?" Gangi asked.

"Horrible," Jimmy said. "Can they fit any more people on Staten Island? That expressway is a fuckin' parking lot."

"Where'd you park?"

"The post office. I got a car service. I went in one door and come out the other. I checked, both agents are still watching the front, the jerk-offs."

Gangi motioned toward the discount store. "My chaperones are directly outside. You see the blue van? That's them. They don't even bother disguising it anymore. I tell them hello and good-bye."

Jimmy lit his cigar. "What's the problem with the drywall? I got your message."

"Barrett," Gangi said. "The old man's got his pecker in a ringer because of the estimate. Says it's front-loaded. He can't accept it."

"He sign off?"

"He won't. Not unless we half it."

Jimmy made a face. "Half it? Fuck him."

Gangi lit a cigar. "I think your personal intervention might help him to see the light."

"My personal intervention right now, with all this indictment bullshit over my head, will bring nothing but attention to something doesn't need any."

"He's got issues, he says, with overloading the estimates. He says the drywall is quadruple what would be deemed acceptable."

"We need that drywall bill to lay the groundwork for the rest. We can't double up down the road."

"What I told him," Gangi said. "He said it's unacceptable. It's his name on the deed and bla, bla, bla, he wants more direct control over the situation. It's bad enough we send him convicts to cover their payroll, he said he's not about to bankrupt his reputation for the sake of a quick score. He says we should be more patient. He says quadrupling a bill will quadruple his risk."

"So, there it is. The motherfucker. Greed. He wants a bigger cut."

"He's standing strong on this. He's an arrogant piece of work when he's feeling his oats."

"Really?" Jimmy said. "I got something'll make him drop to his knees faster than his daughter."

"I was wondering you went after that."

Jimmy didn't hear the remark. "That's all this is, you know. This guy, he takes the cake on greed."

"You don't have to tell me," Gangi said. "The whole time he's talking to me last time he's out here, over at the restaurant, he's stealing things off the table. Little packets of sugar, the Sweet'n Low, the fuckin' Equal, and the swizzle sticks, you can believe it. I bet I checked him for metal, he had two or three forks when he left."

"Well, we need him to sign off on this stuff and fast. As for Mauro going on his payroll, who cares? Negotiate him out if you have to."

Gangi didn't agree. "The guy just handled that other thing, he deserves some cover, Jimmy."

"The guy brokered that other thing," Jimmy said. "Mauro made a nice touch for bringing two parties together. Speaking of which, the old man should only know what his little girl just got herself involved with, he needs a better reason to sign off on that drywall than I'll cut his fuckin' legs off at the knees."

"You sure you wanna go that route?" Gangi asked. "I mean, fathers and their little girls. You never know."

Jimmy wiped his mouth.

"He might run straight to the feds," Gangi added. "He might sprint."

Jimmy let out a breath of frustration. "All right. Keep her out of it for now. Maybe I can work something out and have the guy come to me someplace. It isn't safe, though. They got Frank Gennaro, the feds. He's hiding under a couch somewhere telling my life story on those Canarsie Pier hits. I figure I don't have much time before those ghosts come out to haunt me."

"I'll do my best," Gangi said.

"Do better'n that," Jimmy said. "Or let's get rid of him, the old miser. Sooner or later, enough has to be enough, no?"

CHAPTER

6

IT WAS TEN DEGREES outside the prison administration building. The sky was dark from threatening clouds. Reese and Peter walked with their heads down until they were standing outside the main gate of the Fishkill Penitentiary. When the gate closed behind them, both men hugged. Peter passed Reese a piece of paper.

"From your boy, Rahib," he said. "He said I should give it to you when we're outside."

Reese glanced at the folded paper and jammed it inside his pants pocket.

"Why don't you come over before you go home?" he asked after releasing his grip on Peter. "My mom is anxious to meet you, the man saved her boy from all those crazy redneck Eye-talians."

"I'd rather get it over with," Rizzo said. "Face the music and see where I stand, although I'm not expecting flowers and a parade. Last time I spoke with my mother, she put me on hold until there was a commercial. She was watching her stories."

"The door is open, you wanna come stay."

"I appreciate it."

"My mom'll put a few pounds back on your scrawny ass in the meantime."

Rizzo looked Reese up and down. "I'm scrawny?"

"Look, if you catch any flack over there, give me a call and I'll come get you," Reese said. "My mother is gonna try and play matchmaker with that woman from the church she's already decided is right for me, and I'll need somebody to get me out of it. You'd be doing me the favor."

Peter was smiling at the last bit of information. "You're probably the first guy ever got out of the joint doesn't want female companionship. I'm not so sure I should come by just yet." He spotted the taxi he had called from inside the penitentiary. He took a deep breath and pointed at Reese. "Don't forget you got that appointment tomorrow morning."

"I'll be there," Reese said.

"Okay. Give your mom my best."

Reese watched until Peter was inside the taxi that would take him to the train station. He waved as it pulled away. He stood in the cold a good fifteen minutes before the car he was waiting for finally arrived.

"Father John Ebbs pick you up outside the penitentiary and take you straight to my door," Elle Waters had told her son over the telephone the night before. "Father John is a good man but he don't like to waste his time. You be there waiting for him when he pulls up. And watch your mouth while you're in his car. I see you tomorrow and get you to eating right again. I invited Father John, too. He a big man likes his food. You best not talk yourself out on the drive home either. Save something for before and after dinner."

Recalling his conversation with his mother, Reese smiled. When he opened the door to the Ford Taurus station wagon, he saw that Father John was indeed a big man. Three-fifty to four hundred, Reese was guessing, as he slipped onto the front passenger seat and extended his right hand.

◆ ◆ ◆

Reese spent the first afternoon and evening as a free man again with his mother at her apartment in the Fairfield Housing Project in East New York, Brooklyn. Elle Waters was seventy-two years old, stout, and in failing health. She served as a Eucharistic minister at Saint Lawrence Catholic Church, a few blocks from her apartment. Tonight she was still crying because she was convinced that her prayers had been answered, her baby boy was back home.

"You eat some more of that ham before my company comes and they eat it all," she told her son.

Reese was sitting at the kitchen table. Father John had already left to say the seven-thirty Mass. Reese finished his third plate of ham, potatoes, cornbread, and collard greens. He sucked on a piece of ham bone. He wiped his fingers on a napkin, took a drink from a bottle of Budweiser, and suppressed a belch into a fist.

"I can't," he said, shaking his head at his mother. "No more. I'm lucky to walk after this."

"What they must've fed you in that place," Elle said as she cleared the table. "Well, I have pie in the oven and you best save room for that."

Reese opened his eyes wide. "Pie? Mom, I can't eat no more. Not tonight, baby. I'm about to bust."

"You shhhh yourself," Elle said as she ran hot water over a Pyrex dish. "The good Lord sent you home and I'm here to make sure you stay home. They a pack of paperbacks on the coffee table in the living room. Father John and Laney and some other people from the church give me those. You read them. Take your time about it, too. There's no hurry for them back. When you ready, we find you a good woman, and you can get on with your life. I already told you about Laney. She coming tomorrow to say hello."

Reese was smiling with his eyes closed. "Ma, you can't be doing that kind of thing, playing matchmaker."

Elle turned the hot water off and let the cold water run a few seconds. She filled half a glass and walked it over to Reese. She looked down at his smiling face and poured the water directly over his head. Reese jumped up from the chair.

"Ma! The hell you doing?"

Elle pointed a stubby finger at her son. "Don't you be telling me what I can and can't do, boy. Now sit yourself down and get ready for some pie. It's out the oven in two minutes."

Reese was wiping his face with a dish towel. He felt a sharp pain in the middle of his stomach and waved a hand at his mother.

"No more food. Not tonight, Mom. I can't. I'm about to explode. I'm in pain over here."

Elle stood at the sink and ran the cold water again. Reese saw her set the glass beneath the faucet and leaped for the bathroom. He locked himself inside.

CHAPTER

7

WHEN PETER RIZZO FINALLY made it home, he found his mother playing cards. She was a frail, seventy-four-year-old woman with white hair and blue eyes. A worn navy blue robe was draped over her pink house-dress. Her feet were covered with fluffy, open-back slippers.

Grace Rizzo sat at the far end of the table, nearest the slightly opened window where her smoke could escape without bothering the other players. She introduced her son to her friends before they played the final few hands of the night.

"This is my oldest boy, Peter," she told them. "He just got out of prison today. He's staying with me for a few days."

Peter flinched at the mention of his being in prison. He peeked at the players around the table, but they were all more interested in their cards. He gave a half nod to everyone and retreated into the kitchen.

He wasn't sure if his mother's mentioning his getting out of prison was a clear signal that she was unhappy to see him, but he knew that when she told her friends he would be staying with her for a few days she was making a declaration. He wouldn't be welcome after that.

Peter made himself a sandwich and ate cold macaroni out of the refrigerator while the game broke up. It was a little before midnight when the apartment was finally empty. His mother sat in her chair in front of the television and used the remote to change channels.

"Ma, you think we could talk a few minutes before your shows?" he asked.

"You still hungry?" Grace asked without looking at her son.

"No, Ma, I ate. I'm fine."

"There's more in the freezer."

"I'm fine."

"You sure?"

"I'm fine, Ma."

She half turned to her son. "Did you call your brother?"

"Not yet, no."

"He's doing good."

"Good for him. I'm glad."

"He's got his own place now," she said, turning back to the television. "They bought in Staten Island."

"I'm glad. He works hard. He deserves it."

"He got a promotion, too. He's a foreman now."

"That's great."

Grace looked back at him again. "You should've went into that with him, the sanitation."

"It's not for me, Ma."

"He gets a pension after twenty years. He can retire and do something else while the city pays him."

"That's great but it's not for me."

"What *is* for you, Peter?" she asked, turning to him one more time. "Jail?"

Peter frowned. "No, Ma, jail's not for me."

Grace turned her attention back to the television.

"I was hoping you were over this," he said.

"Go talk to your brother. See if he can do anything for you. I'm an old lady. What can I do?"

"Right," Peter said. "I'll talk to Paul."

✦ ✦ ✦

He walked along Shore Road until Fourth Avenue. He crossed the avenue and headed to a pay phone just outside Fort Hamilton Park. Peter glimpsed at his watch, then dialed the number Reese had given him.

"It's me," he said when he recognized his former cellmate's voice. "Sorry if I woke you."

"I can hardly move," Reese said. "My mom's stuffed me."

"At least she's happy to see you."

"She thinks it's the Lord's work, but yeah, she is. What's the matter? You sound down."

Peter was fighting back tears.

"Pete?" Reese said.

"My mother wasn't too thrilled I showed," Peter finally said through a sniffle.

"You okay, man? Where you at?"

Peter wiped his nose on the back of his hand. He took a few seconds to compose himself. "Yeah, I'm fine. I'm all right."

"You sure? I can borrow a car, you tell me where to come."

"No, forget it. I'm just walking around, thinking."

"Uh-oh."

"Yeah, I know. I think I want the interest. I think I should get it."

"Jesus, man, she ain't even agreed to pay you the principal yet."

"I think you should tell her I want the interest. I need a change, man. I need to get away from here. I'm gonna need every dime she owes me."

"You a pushy Eye-talian, you know that?"

Peter forced a chuckle. "Yeah, I guess."

"Sit on it tonight and see what the morning brings."

"I'm just telling you now so you'll know. I want what she owes me plus the interest. I went away because of her. I should get what she owes."

"Just don't do anything on your own," Reese said.

"I won't."

"Promise."

"I promise. I'll cross my heart, you want."

"I'm being serious," Reese said.

Peter remained silent.

"You okay?" Reese asked again. "For real?"

Peter couldn't talk about it. "I gotta run," he said.

"You sure you're okay? I can get a car easy enough."

Peter forced another laugh. "Yeah, I know, that's how we met, your access to cars. I'll talk to you *domani*."

"Pete?"

Peter hung up and turned into the park. He walked toward the base of the Verrazano-Narrows Bridge. Headlights crossed his path about fifty yards from the fence bordering the Fort Hamilton grounds. Peter thought it was a police car and stepped to the side to let it pass. It was a navy blue Chrysler. An old man with gray hair was driving. He motioned at Peter to come closer as he held up a piece of paper.

"You know where this address is?" the driver asked. He was holding the paper awkwardly with his left hand.

Peter froze where he stood, about five yards from the driver's door, but it was already too late. The driver braced the silencer against his left elbow to steady his aim. He fired three times in quick succession. All three bullets found their mark.

Peter barely heard the phutlike sound. His eyes opened slightly between the first and second shots. He was already dead on his feet before the third one exploded through his heart.

CHAPTER

8

"WHO'S THE CADAVER?" DEXTER GREENE asked his partner.

They were outside the Brooklyn morgue. It was a few minutes before sunrise. The cold was biting. Greene's hands were jammed inside his winter coat. His partner, Arlene Belzinger, wore a short, fitted black leather jacket and tight blue dungarees with yellow leg warmers covering her knees and thighs. Her black hair was held back with a white barrette.

"I don't know, but he's cute," Belzinger said. "They're running his name now. He has a tattoo he might've picked up in prison. A pretty big stomach scar, too."

"One of the boys?" Greene asked.

"Could be. He wasn't carrying identification, but he certainly has the look."

"Had the look," said Greene, correcting her.

"He's still cute."

"And you a sick girl."

They were waiting for a phone call. Greene stood with his cell phone in hand while his partner stretched her legs at the curb. Greene watched her a few seconds, then turned away when his phone rang.

Belzinger was thirty-five, beautiful, and tough. She had jet-black, short, straight hair and big brown eyes. Her lips were thick. Her body was tight. She stood straight and bent from the waist until she could hug her legs. She held the position a few seconds before releasing her legs and standing straight again.

When she saw her partner talking into his cell phone, she applied ChapStick to her lips. Greene ended his conversation and folded the cell phone. He was a short black man, forty years old, with an athletic build.

Belzinger said, "Anything we can work with?"

"He's out of Fishkill less than one day," Greene said as he wrote on his notepad. "He was released early yesterday."

"Mob?"

"He served time on an assault, broke some dude's jaw."

"Handsome and athletic."

"And dead."

"Nobody is perfect."

Greene finished writing and pointed at their car, parked across the street. "After you," he said.

Belzinger feigned a little-girl voice. "Ahhhh, can't I drive, Dad? Please, please, please, can't I?"

◆ ◆ ◆

Reese shook his head when he saw the woman walking her dog across Third Avenue. The last temperature reading he'd heard was fifteen degrees. He guessed it was closer to zero with the windchill.

A few minutes earlier, he'd watched a uniformed doorman walk a pack of dogs around the opposite corner and return to the same building where Janice Barrett lived.

Reese chuckled at the sight of the woman smoking a cigarette in her fur coat and sneakers. He looked up at the luxury building and couldn't imagine how much apartments might cost in there.

"She's too cheap to pay somebody to walk the dog," Peter had told him. "She makes about two hundred grand a year, she eats her weekday lunches and dinners on the company credit card, and she steals most of what they keep in their pantry for the rest of her meals."

Reese shaded his eyes from the early morning sunlight. He felt a chill from a rigorous breeze and quickly jammed his hands inside his pockets. He watched the woman smoking as the dog walked in tight circles a few times before settling on a spot and taking care of business.

When she headed back to the building, Reese intercepted her at the corner. The poodle was excited and jumped for attention.

"Janice Barrett?" he asked.

The woman stopped suddenly and tugged on the leash. The dog spilled over backward.

Reese tried again. "Janice?"

"What? Who are you?"

"A friend of Peter Rizzo."

She surveyed the immediate area at the mention of Peter's name. "Peter? Where is he?"

"He's not here."

She surveyed the area again before she focused on Reese. "What do you want?"

"Peter asked me to talk to you."

The dog was straining to get at Reese. "Stop it, damn it!" she yelled at the dog. "Talk to me about what?"

"His money."

"I'm listening."

"He'd like what you owe him," Reese said. "Fifty thousand, plus two years back interest. Bank rate, of course."

"I don't owe him a thing."

"Peter lost two years of his life. He's not asking anything for that."

"And who're you?"

"His friend."

She looked him up and down. "You another convict?" she asked. "Somebody he met in prison?"

Reese hesitated a moment before answering. "I'm a friend," he repeated.

"I was wondering whether he'd try something like this. Now I know."

"The man just did two years because of you," said Reese, getting into it more than he intended. "He's not trying anything. He just wants his money."

The woman smirked. "Or?"

"Excuse me?"

"He wants his money, he sent you to tell me, or what?"

Reese felt his muscles tense the way they would a moment before he'd have to throw a punch in prison. He said, "Peter said you could push buttons."

"He did, did he?"

Reese did his best to relax again. "Look, all the man wants is what he's owed."

The woman stared. "And I already told you I don't owe him a thing."

Reese returned the stare.

"He used to run a restaurant," she said. "Did Peter meet you there or somewhere else?"

"I'm just a friend."

A police car passed on Third Avenue. She immediately grew cocky at the sight of it. She said, "Well, friend, fuck off, because I don't owe Peter a thing."

Reese stood his ground.

She glanced at the police car again. "Are you going to let me pass now, or do I have to scream?"

Reese stepped out of her way.

"And you can tell Peter to go fuck himself," she said over her shoulder.

Reese stood in silent anger as she pulled the dog across the street. A delivery truck dropped a bundle of newspapers on the sidewalk a few feet from a delicatessen off the corner. The woman picked up the top paper from the bundle and hid it under her fur coat.

CHAPTER

9

AFTER INTERVIEWING THE FAMILY, the homicide detectives began their investigation with the defense attorney who had handled Peter Rizzo's assault case two years earlier. Neve Rosenblatt was a thirty-six-year-old Israeli American. He had been practicing criminal defense for five years. He also had served as assistant district attorney in New York four years before starting his own firm.

Greene and Belzinger found him outside the Brooklyn brownstone, where he rented office space on Eastern Parkway in Crown Heights. Rosenblatt was tall and gangly. His head showed a distinct loss of hair around the black yarmulke he was wearing. He was standing in an oversized coat at a frankfurter cart. Rosenblatt pointed at the mustard as the vendor forked a fresh roll from a plastic bag.

Greene introduced himself and Belzinger as Rosenblatt paid for his lunch. The attorney nodded before taking a bite from the frankfurter.

"That kosher?" Greene asked.

"Kosher smosher," Rosenblatt said. "I'm hungry and I love hot dogs."

"We're here about a former client of yours," Greene said. "Peter Rizzo."

The name got Rosenblatt's attention. The attorney nodded. "He should be getting out about now. This week, I think."

"He's already out," Greene said.

"And he's dead," Belzinger added.

Rosenblatt stopped chewing. He swallowed his food and shook his head. "How?"

"Murdered," Greene said. "Three shots in the chest."

"In the middle of Fort Hamilton Park sometime during the night,"

Belzinger added. "So we're assuming it was a hit. We're waiting on ballistics but there's a good chance a silencer was used. Nobody heard anything."

Rosenblatt was still holding most of his frankfurter. He looked to his right, saw a trash can, and tossed it in.

"Peter Rizzo was a decent man," he said. "No matter what you might think, he was a decent man."

"That's what we wanted to talk to you about," Greene said. "Why you did a plea instead of fighting the assault charges. We understand there was something fuzzy about it, what happened."

Rosenblatt was still trying to digest the bad news. "Peter wouldn't let it go to trial. He admitted to beating some guy up, breaking his jaw, and he said he was wrong to do it, that he hit the wrong person. He was very conscientious. A lot more so than most."

"Why'd he do it, break some guy's jaw?" Belzinger asked. "What was behind that?"

"A nightmare," Rosenblatt said before turning back to the vendor. He peeled a dollar bill from a money clip and set it on the wagon. The vendor handed him a Diet Coke. He pulled the tab and immediately took a sip.

"His wife owed him money," he said. "She made some baloney deal with him in the divorce where he agreed not to get an attorney for the sake of saving on legal fees." He stopped to sip more of his soda. "She agreed to pay him seventy-five thousand dollars but had the agreement drawn up for twenty-five. She gave him some baloney about her having to pay the taxes and he signed the papers. She gladly gave him twenty-five at the signing, what was on paper, and she screwed him for the balance. He didn't think she'd do that to him, but she did. I can't tell you how many people get screwed that way."

"How much money?" Belzinger asked.

"Fifty thousand," Rosenblatt said. "And I offered to go after her for it afterward, once he was arrested. I offered to tag on the court fees for his criminal trial, but he wouldn't have anything to do with it. He said he'd handle his wife when he got out. He wouldn't make the same mistake about hitting the wrong person."

Both detectives looked to each other.

Rosenblatt quickly waved it off. "That was just Peter talking. He wouldn't touch his ex-wife. Not because she didn't deserve it, because if ever there was a woman who deserved to get nailed, it was her. No offense, miss, but that's the truth. Wait'll you talk to her, and you should, you definitely should talk to her."

"You think she could have Peter Rizzo killed?" Greene asked.

"I think she could've done it herself," Rosenblatt said. "She's that calculating."

"What if she was in fear for her life?" asked Belzinger, somewhat defensive.

"Peter wouldn't touch a woman," the lawyer said. He stopped to count off his fingers. "He wouldn't rat on somebody, he wouldn't lean on people who didn't deserve it, he wouldn't even try to avoid prison time, there's no way he'd ever touch his ex-wife. And that's probably what frustrated him so much, that she knew all that and still wouldn't pay him. Beating that guy up was nothing more than frustration. She put that poor bastard out there . . ." He stopped to think. "Hal or Al or maybe Nate, Sokolof, I think his name was. Whatever. He was a piece of bait. She used both of them, Peter and the guy he hit."

"You're saying she set him up?" Belzinger asked.

"Set them up," Rosenblatt said. "There's no other way to say it. She told Peter she was having an affair on him. I think he could handle that easy enough, they weren't a cozy couple by then, except she put that affair in his face while she was stealing his money. You obviously never met Peter. He's not Al Capone, but he wasn't somebody you'd pick out of a crowd to push his buttons."

"He had one arrest before he went away," Greene said. "Another assault, charges dropped. Did he ever touch his wife?"

"No," Rosenblatt said. "He ran a restaurant for connected people. He sometimes collected money for them. Some bookmaker, I think. Peter wasn't a vicious guy but he liked to stay in shape, lift weights. He wasn't a leg-breaker by any means, not that I know of, but if he knocked on your door in the middle of the night and you owed your bookie money, you'd probably pay it."

"I asked you did he touch his wife," Greene said.

"No," Rosenblatt said. "Never. There's certainly no record of it and if there was, she would've used it in the divorce, trust me."

"You don't like her very much, do you?" Belzinger asked.

"Janice Barrett, that's her maiden name, she went back to it after the divorce, is definitely the person to go talk to on this. Although you might want to watch her awhile before you tip her off."

"Not that you're telling us how to do our jobs," Greene said.

Rosenblatt touched his chest and raised a hand. "Never," he said. "Hand to God."

CHAPTER

10

"I'M NOT COMFORTABLE CARRYING this," Janice Barrett told her father. She was standing behind her desk as she contemplated the Walther P1 9mm her father had just given her. She set the gun on the desk and folded her arms across her chest.

Standing in front of his daughter's desk, Michael Barrett was still wearing his heavy coat, hat, and gloves. He was sixty-eight years old, tall, and thin. His face was worn from a rough life in the construction business. He set his hat on the edge of the desk and pulled the black leather gloves off his hands.

"It isn't for comfort," he said.

Janice turned her head away from the weapon. She buttoned the burgundy sweater she was wearing and lit a cigarette.

"Can you at least not smoke?" her father asked. He was pulling his coat off. "At least not while I'm here." He folded the coat neatly over the back of the empty chair to his left.

"I'm nervous," Janice said. "I smoke when I'm nervous."

"You smoke all the time."

Father and daughter finally sat. Janice looked at the gun and leaned forward to push it across the desk.

"I can get arrested for carrying that."

"It's registered," her father told her as he pushed the gun back across the desk. "You can't get arrested."

Janice glanced at the office door to make sure it was closed. "Peter's dead," she said. "Somebody killed him last night."

"Yeah, I saw it on the news," her father said nonchalantly. "Who you think he pissed off enough to get himself killed? One of his goombah friends, I'll bet."

Janice avoided direct eye contact with her father. "I don't know, but I don't think I need to carry a gun. Not anymore."

"You're sure of that, huh?"

"Why wouldn't I be?"

"What about the guy that approached you this morning?" he asked. "Ever think the two might have something to do with each other, your ex and this black guy?"

"Of course they did. He said he was Peter's friend."

"Okay, so, you tell me. He just got himself killed after spending two years in prison. Same day he gets out, somebody shoots him. And he went away for hitting someone to get money from you in the first place. What kind of friends do you think he made in prison?"

Janice cupped her hands over her mouth. "Had, Daddy, he's dead."

Michael pointed a finger at his daughter. "Don't be a smart-ass."

"Don't patronize me."

"Who called who this morning about this black guy?"

"He caught me off guard," Janice said. "I was scared. I didn't know Peter was dead. I learned about that on the news after I walked the dog."

"Yeah, well, he approached you for money, right? What the hell else do you need to know?"

Janice didn't get it. "What?"

"It was a shakedown, for Christ sakes, what this black guy was doing. He mentioned Peter, right? He knew about the money, right? They want it."

Janice thought about it a moment. "He probably didn't know what happened to Peter."

"What's the difference? He was shaking you down. If he approached you for the money this morning, he's not going away. Why would he care whether Peter is around? He's probably glad your ex is dead."

Michael Barrett motioned at the gun with his head. His daughter moaned and grabbed the gun. She put it in one of her desk drawers and slammed it shut.

"There," she said. "But I'm not carrying it around with me. I'll bring it home, but that's where it stays."

"The point is," her father said, "I know people who can handle this kind of thing. People that owe me. I expected this as soon as you mentioned Peter was getting out. I knew he'd come looking for that money."

"What are you talking about?"

"I had somebody look into Peter and any possible friends he might've made in prison. He was a connected guy before he went away, your ex-husband, and I'm sure he made some new friends inside."

"Who did you get to look into Peter?"

"Doug Johnson, the insurance guy."

Janice was surprised at the name. Doug Johnson was the last man she had been intimate with before she met Peter Rizzo three years earlier. The affair had been a well-kept secret.

"Doug Johnson?"

"He has people who do insurance investigations he lets me use from time to time. I gave him a call after you called me. I don't like this, what happened this morning. Especially after Peter was killed."

"I think you're being paranoid."

"And I think you're too naive for words. Look, you managed to outsmart the dumb son of a bitch for fifty thousand dollars. Then he got himself sent away for two years because of it. Did you really think that would be the end of it? What, he was coming out reformed? Fifty thousand dollars is like hitting the Lotto to people like Peter. I say he was coming for his money and that black guy was part of it. I don't know how Peter got himself killed and I don't really care. I do care about this other guy, though. I don't think he's going away on his own."

"All right," Janice said. "Fine. But I'm not carrying a gun around the city with me."

Her father grabbed a handful of gummy bears from a bowl Janice kept on her desk. "Fair enough," he said before popping some of the candy into his mouth.

"In the meantime, don't you have enough going on in Croton? Alex said you were spending all your time up there and in New Jersey. What's in New Jersey?"

"My new partners. Perth Amboy, to be exact. And Croton is turning into another headache I don't need right now, so don't mention it."

"Why? I thought that was a big deal for you."

"It's a huge deal for me. For you and your brother, too, once it's completed. But my new partners are a little overanxious to cash in. They don't believe in letting real estate appreciate on its own. They're in a big rush, these goombahs."

"This isn't under our name, is it?" Janice asked. "Not Barrett Construction."

Michael shook his head as he reached for another handful of gummy bears.

"Leave me some of those," Janice said.

Michael spoke as he chewed the candy. "I set up a subsidiary. We're protected in case I have to bankrupt this thing, but I don't want my reputation going down the toilet because of it either. I'm getting old. All my friends on the county boards are dying off. And your brother certainly isn't making any friends with influence, not fooling around with those goddamned waitresses and whatever else he fools around with. Your sister-in-law's father is the only solid connection Alex has after I'm gone. Lydia may not be a rocket scientist, but she's a good enough mother. When Alex ruins his marriage, he can probably count on ruining half his business, too. As much as I try, I can't protect him from himself. You know that."

"So maybe you should give these guys what they want and get it over with," Janice suggested. "Your partners, I mean. Cash in and turn the property over. Retire from the business. You have enough now."

"And Alex?"

"Alex is a grown man, Daddy," Janice said. She took a long drag on her cigarette. Her father waved at the smoke with both hands when she exhaled.

"Don't you think it's time he took care of himself?" she asked. "If he loses half his business, he can still make a living off the other half."

"Your brother spends money a lot faster than he earns it. This Croton thing does tie up money he'll borrow on if I leave it in play, though. At least it'll slow him down."

"So, there's your answer. Do what they want and forget about it."

Father and daughter were silent while Janice crushed out her cigarette.

Michael said, "Don't forget to take that gun home. I didn't buy that so it would become a relic."

"You didn't buy that at all. It's Uncle John's. I recognized it soon as I saw it. It's one of the guns he used when he was with the state troopers. He left a few of them to you. I remember that one and the other one, the revolver."

"What's the difference?" Michael said. "Somebody had to pay for it."

❖ ❖ ❖

"What was that all about?" Brad Nelson asked. "A mid-afternoon powwow with Dad?"

Janice opened the drawer to her desk and showed her boyfriend the gun. "This. He wants me to walk around with it."

"Cool," said Brad, holding a hand out. "Give it here." He reached for the gun but Janice set it back inside the drawer. "Hey, let me see."

"It's not a toy," Janice said before shutting the drawer.

Brad was on his way around the desk. "I just wanna see it. Come on."

Janice stood up and blocked his path.

"Come on," Brad whined.

"No, damn it."

Brad recoiled with both hands raised. He was short and thin. His once blond hair was mostly gray. He wore a navy blue Armani suit.

"Jesus Christ, lighten up," he said. "I just wanted to see it."

Janice waited until he was around the front of the desk again before she sat. She immediately lit a cigarette.

"This about Peter?" he asked.

"What do you think?"

"Did you kill him?"

"That's not funny."

"Well?"

"Fuck you, Brad."

"I was joking, honey."

"It's not funny."

Brad brushed lint off his tie. "Well, why do you need the gun now that Peter's dead?"

"I don't know. I didn't need it to begin with. He's paranoid, my father."

"He's your father. I'd do the same thing, I guess. He's being protective."

Janice looked at her calendar book and remembered an appointment across town. She started to gather her things.

"Dad lending you the money?"

"I didn't ask," Janice said.

"There's not much time left on the clock, babe. I'm gonna need a partner, pronto. A week, two weeks at the most."

Janice ignored Brad as she logged off her laptop computer.

"This Boston thing isn't gonna wait much longer than that," he added.

Janice slid the laptop into the carrying case and zippered the bag.

Brad said, "I have other interested parties."

Janice used the shoulder strap on the carrying case and grabbed her purse.

"Two that have the money."

Janice walked around the desk and headed toward the door.

"Jan?"

Janice stopped at the door. "Fuck off already about the money, Brad," she said. "I'll get it."

CHAPTER

11

HIS MOTHER HAD ALREADY left for the day when Reese returned from the city. He read the note she had left him and groaned at the last line: "Breakfast in the oven."

Reese went straight to his room and slept through the rest of the morning.

When he awoke, it was early afternoon. He noticed the time and thought about prison. The inmates in protective custody would have access to a fenced-in area of the yard from one to two o'clock in the afternoon. Peter would stretch and exercise his muscles without weights. Reese would use the dumbbells and work his stomach. Sometimes the rest of the day could take forever after their time in the yard.

He rolled out of the bed when he remembered Peter. They were supposed to meet later in the day. It would be another unpleasant conversation, with him trying to convince his friend to forget about the money his ex-wife was stealing, except now that he had met the woman, Reese understood Peter's frustration.

He used the remote to turn on the television in the living room. He devoured most of the huge breakfast his mother had cooked. Afterward, he sat in his mother's recliner and coped with his second stomachache from overeating in two days.

Reese moaned as he flipped through the channels on the television until he found a local news station. He winced from a sharp stomach pain and did a double take when he saw Peter's mug shot on the news.

"The murder victim has been identified as Peter Rizzo, an ex-convict just released from the Fishkill Penitentiary," a news reporter was saying. "Police claim the victim was found by a man walking his dog. The family was then notified and . . ."

Reese was staring blankly at Peter's mug shot. The reporter's voice became white noise in the background. He no longer heard it.

When he could think again, Reese tried the phone number Peter had given him. He called a few times before someone finally answered. A friend of the family told Reese the Rizzos weren't taking calls. Reese asked about the funeral arrangements but wasn't sure he'd heard right when the woman said, "There isn't going to be a funeral."

He flipped through the channels searching for the story again. It was too late in the afternoon. The nightly news was still a few hours off. He tried calling the Rizzo family one more time. Peter's brother answered. Reese introduced himself and was quickly dismissed.

"You met my brother inside the joint?" Paul Rizzo asked.

"We were friends," Reese said.

"Just like my brother, making friends in there."

Reese saw himself frown in the hanging mirror across his mother's living room. "Your brother was a good man," he said.

"Yeah, why he was in prison."

"Excuse me?"

"Look, I'm glad Peter made friends, but we're really not interested anymore. Thanks for calling."

Reese did a double take at the telephone receiver in his hand when the line went dead.

❖ ❖ ❖

Mauro delivered the balance of the payment for killing Peter Rizzo to Tommy Burns at a pizza parlor on Fourth Avenue in Brooklyn. The streets were crowded. Both men stood in a doorway to shield themselves from people traffic.

"You have balls, my friend," Mauro said. "Fort Hamilton Park?"

"I borrowed a car and used stolen plates," Burns said. He took a long drag on his cigarette and held the smoke inside his lungs.

Mauro was juggling a hot container of coffee to keep his hands warm. "I hope it wasn't reported, the borrowed car," he said.

"Was back in the lender's driveway before they knew it was gone, I'm sure," Burns said. "You feel like taking a ride, I'm headed down to A.C. when I'm done."

"Can't wait to spend it, huh?"

"I'm feeling lucky. I woke up this morning and found I nailed the daily number. First time in five, six years. I got an old lady in my building I'll cash it through to avoid the taxes. I'll throw her a hundred, she'll take the bus down to A.C. and make her own deposit."

"Well, our friend appreciates this," Mauro said. "He already called to say so."

"Pleasure's mine. Always."

"What do you play down there, in A.C.?"

"Normally, I slow grind it at the tables. Blackjack, poker, that bullshit; Let It Ride when I'm about broke."

"But today you're feeling lucky," Mauro said.

"Thanks for reminding me."

"So?"

"Craps. I'll see how I do at that and then catch a blow job from one of the broads working the bars. I'll let her remove the rust and I'll go back down and sit the poker game. I'm getting too old to do any more'n that."

"I was there myself a couple weeks ago," Mauro said. "Harrah's. They got a bar there with live music where the escorts sit till they get a call on their cell phones. One of the valet guys introduced me. They're expensive but at least they look good. No visible scars, I mean."

Burns pointed to his mouth and said, "Nothing but lips for me, my friend. I don't care what they look like, long as they gotta sit to take a piss. Why I make them strip first. I had a friend wasn't as curious, got a hummer from a guy in drag. Nice Sunday surprise that was. That's one horror story I look to avoid at all costs."

"Speaking of lips," Mauro said, "I mentioned your name to some broad from the bar on Glenwood Road. That okay?"

"So long's you're not telling her more than she needs to know. Which one?"

"Big broad with a ring through her nose. I hadda look away from that while she went down on me but she got the job done."

"It's all we ask, they get it done."

"So it's cool, I mentioned you?"

"What's done is done. I appreciate it don't become a habit, though. You can understand, I hope."

"Sure," Mauro said. "So, you probably wouldn't want to spend the night in Atlantic City anyway, right? Or I could maybe return the favor with a broad down there, recommend one."

"It's smart I'm back here tomorrow afternoon to take a shift," Burns said. "Besides, I got a guy with some prepaid cell phones I gotta see. Let me know you're interested. He wants half a buck a unit and he's supposed to have lots."

"I can always use an angle," Mauro said. "You're back tomorrow night?"

"I hope to be. Unless I step in shit and win big enough to stay."

"Well, catch some sleep somewhere. It's a long drive back and forth, you're tired."

Burns held his hand out. Mauro took it. "All inna day's work, the drive," Burns said. "All inna day's work."

❖ ❖ ❖

Reese had a rough time of it staying home now that he'd learned about Peter's murder. After pacing the floor for half an hour, he tore the bus route map from the telephone book and headed across Brooklyn to meet the Rizzo family and find out what their intentions were regarding Peter.

He stopped in his tracks when he saw a local news van in front of the building where the Rizzo family lived. He decided against facing them now. He would try one more time by phone the next day.

Reese applied for a taxi license while he was in the area. When he was finished, he stopped at a pay phone to call his mother before taking the bus home. His mother cried at the news of Peter's murder. Reese told her he'd be home soon and asked if she wanted him to pick anything up.

"No, baby, you just come home," Elle Waters told her son. "I know you're hurting."

Reese was hurting. He also was angry. He remembered his exchange with Peter's ex-wife and couldn't shake it. Something about the woman was wrong. He wondered if she had anything to do with Peter's murder. Reese wondered if she had already known Peter was dead when he approached her.

✦ ✦ ✦

When Reese stepped off the B-6 on Flatlands Avenue, he was staring at a liquor store. A rough voice startled him.

"You don't look like you learned your lesson," the voice said.

Reese turned and recognized a friend from his bus driving days, Vincent Coleman.

"Yeah, it's me," Coleman said. "You gonna say hello or you too good now?"

Reese smiled. "How the hell are you?"

Both men exchanged hugs. Coleman was a big man at 6'3 and 230 pounds. He was fifty-four years old, with a full head of thick gray hair. They had worked out of the Jackie Gleason depot in Brooklyn together. Coleman was an alcoholic always close to getting fired. Reese liked him because Coleman was a lot smarter and cultured than people knew.

"How long you out?" Coleman asked.

"Since yesterday," Reese said. "I just come back from applying for a hack license."

Coleman made a face. "Hack license? You go crazy while you were away? They kill more guys driving cabs than they do terrorists in Afghanistan."

"I can't sing," Reese said.

"Yeah, but you can play some drums, motherfucker. What's up with that?"

"Not now I can't, not without some real practice."

Coleman pointed at the liquor store. "What you going in there for? You couldn't find enough trouble in the joint?"

Reese forced a smile this time. It was Coleman's way to be fatherly, even with a pint bottle sticking out of his coat pocket.

"I had a bad day," Reese said.

"Yeah, you looked like you lost your best friend when you got off the six. The hell you doing riding those things anyway? Don't you know city bus drivers are all drunks?"

Reese became choked up.

"What the fuck?" Coleman said. "What is it?"

They spent the next half hour catching up as they walked around the block. Reese told Coleman about prison and Peter Rizzo and what had happened the night before. Coleman mostly listened.

When they returned to the liquor store, it was time for Reese to head home.

Coleman said, "So, this Italian fella was your back inside. That it?"

"Peter and a Five Percenter named Rahib."

Coleman made a face. "Five Percenter? How'd you find them?"

"I did a favor for one and they felt obligated to me. They still do."

"I won't ask what the favor was, but you watch your ass with those people. Some crazy niggers use religion to get over. Jails are full of Muslims for a reason."

Reese let it go. They exchanged hugs and Coleman made Reese promise to give him a call during the week.

"My run starts tonight," he said. "I'm with MABSTOA now, driving the M-fifteen on South Street. I got midnight, the one on fifteen."

"I'll call you when I know what's going on," Reese said. Then he felt alone again.

CHAPTER

12

THERE WERE TWO DETECTIVES, a black man and a white woman, waiting for him when Reese showed up at the parole office the next morning. They bought him a coffee in the cafeteria and sat across from him at one of several tables arranged in rows.

The woman was a looker with a hard edge to her. Reese guessed her age somewhere around thirty-five. The man was older and looked serious. Reese answered their questions honestly, except he didn't tell them about approaching Peter's ex-wife.

"You were more than just cellmates, right?" the man asked.

"We were friends," Reese said. "Became friends. We had a couple fights with each other first, like everybody else inside."

"He saved your life," the man said.

"Yes, he did."

"And he was stabbed for his effort," the woman said.

"It was between the Italians and the brothers," Reese said. "A couple of them thought I was a gang member and grabbed me. Peter tried to tell them I wasn't, but they didn't stop. We all look alike. Peter made them stop. Knocked one of them cold and the other backed off. The Italians went after him for it. Yeah, he saved my life."

"Were you his bitch afterward?" the man asked.

Reese smirked. "You watching too many prison movies," he said. "No, I wasn't Peter's bitch. We were friends."

"What about the money his ex-wife owed Peter?" the woman asked. "Did he talk about that?"

"Constantly," Reese said. "He was obsessed with it. She robbed him and then set him up. He couldn't get past it."

"Would you?" the man asked.

"Fifty grand is a lot of money. Especially coming out of the joint with nothing to fall back on. I don't know I'd go after it, but I probably wouldn't forget it. Peter was gonna ask first. I guess he never got the chance."

"What was he planning on doing second?" the man asked.

"He didn't say. I know he wasn't planning on beating anybody up, though. He knew he was wrong beating up the guy that got him sent away. It's why he didn't defend himself in court. He was weird about things like that, doing the right thing. He did the time because he said he deserved it; hitting a guy had nothing to do with money his wife was stealing."

Peter also had told Reese that he didn't trust himself on the outside after what his wife had pulled. He had thought going away might cool him down before he did something he couldn't take back. Reese didn't mention it to the police.

"So he was an honorable convict," the woman said, more as a comment than a question.

"He was a decent man," Reese said. "A little hotheaded but decent. He wished he could take that back, breaking the guy's jaw. He was definitely remorseful, if that's what you're asking."

"We're asking did he threaten her," the man said.

"Not that I know of. No."

"What about yesterday, once he was out?" the woman asked.

"No."

"You know anything more than you're telling?" the man asked.

It was then Reese started to lie. "We didn't speak after we were released," he said. "We were planning on getting a cab together, splitting shifts. We were supposed to call each other after a few days. I called his mom's after I heard what happened on the news, but his brother answered and wasn't interested. They weren't very tight."

"So, as far as you know, there wasn't any master plan to get his money?" the woman asked.

"Not that I know of."

"Because that's a lot of money for a man to walk away from," the man said.

"Especially after he did time," the woman added.

"He didn't share a plan with me," Reese lied one more time.

They left him in the cafeteria. Afterward, Reese took his time walking to the subway. He thought hard about Peter and what had happened. If the police never found his killer, and his family chose to forget a brother and son, and his ex-wife never paid her debt, it would be as if the man had never existed—a life with no history except for two years that he had served time.

It wasn't right, Reese was thinking. It just wasn't right.

✦ ✦ ✦

Michael Barrett started his day by stopping at the Entenmann's Bakery outlet on Route 9. He selected boxes tagged for damage as his cake of the week. The cake-buying sprees were an economical alternative to eating in diners and restaurants for breakfast or lunch. He picked up six boxes of the apple turnovers for the next several days, then drove to an office park in Tarrytown.

Doug Johnson was waiting for him in one of the lots closest to White Plains Road. When he stepped out of his SUV, Barrett handed Johnson a packaged Black & Decker power drill.

"What the hell is this?" Johnson asked. He was a short, pudgy, middle-aged man with curly blond hair and fat cheeks.

"It's a power drill," Barrett said. "In case you ever have to put up Sheetrock or drill into studs to put up a picture frame."

Johnson set the power tool on the front passenger seat of his SUV. "That would be great if I did any of that," he said. "Can I take it back wherever you got it?"

In his pocket Barrett fingered two gummy bears he'd taken from his daughter's candy dish the day before. He popped the candy into his mouth and said, "It was a gift. I don't have a receipt."

"Right," Johnson said.

Barrett pointed to his watch. "Come on, what do you have for me?"

Johnson handed Barrett an envelope. "This one was pretty easy. My brother-in-law does admin up at Fishkill. He's a retired guard. You got his Social Security number, work history, and old addresses. His mother's address is in there, too, where he's probably living now that he's out. No other next of kin."

"This is the cellmate, right?"

"Reese Waters. Did eighteen months for stealing a car. He was driving a bus before that."

"He doesn't sound very dangerous."

"Except he's a convict."

"Any priors?"

"Just what he went away for. Like I said, he was a bus driver."

"And he decided to steal cars?"

"That's what he went away for."

Barrett bit his lower lip. "And they were cellmates for a while, huh? How come? I thought the blacks stayed with their own gangs in prison."

"Your son-in-law saved the guy's life," Johnson said. "Got stabbed for it apparently."

Barrett thought out loud. "Maybe that's what got him killed."

"Got who killed?"

"Never mind. What else?"

"They put them both in protective custody after that, your son-in-law and his friend."

"Protective custody?"

"You would've asked before they were released, my brother-in-law could've made it rougher. Maybe got them back into general population."

"Damn."

"Your man there kept to himself," said Johnson, pointing at the envelope. "He was a reader and a musician. Practiced drums every chance he got but wasn't in any of the bands up there because of protective custody."

"Bands? What the hell is that? They getting punished or taking auditions?"

"My brother-in-law claims it's so they don't all go crazy and cut the guards' throats."

"Well, there you go," said Barrett, thinking out loud again. "Maybe these two, since they were so buddy-buddy, maybe they made some plans together."

Johnson was confused. "What?"

"He was Italian, my son-in-law. You know how they are. They like to hold on to a grudge."

"A grudge?" Johnson asked with sarcasm. "What you do to him, Michael?"

"Never mind," Barrett said as he stashed the envelope inside his jacket.

Johnson stood smirking.

"The fuck is your problem?" Barrett asked. He hopped inside his SUV, started the engine, and put the transmission into drive.

"Right," Johnson said. "You're welcome. And thanks for the drill I'll never use."

CHAPTER

13

THEY FOUND JANICE BARRETT at the advertising company where she was a junior partner. The corner office was large and expensively furnished. Janice sat in a red leather swivel chair with a strip of black piping. Her desk was black teakwood with a thin strip of red leather around the edges. On her desk was a metal sign with the Nike slogan "Just do it."

Janice was dressed casually, in black dungarees with a white pullover top. Her nails were manicured, and her auburn-colored hair was recently styled. She was caught off guard when a pair of detectives were led into her office by one of two receptionists.

"We buzzed but you didn't answer," the receptionist said.

"I was in the bathroom," Janice said dismissively.

"Sorry," the receptionist said.

Janice motioned at the door, and the receptionist left them.

Detective Greene introduced himself, then Belzinger. They each sat in the chairs directly opposite the teakwood desk. Janice directed her glance toward Greene and ignored Belzinger.

"What can I do for you?" she asked.

"We're here about your ex-husband," Belzinger said.

Janice turned to Belzinger. "I'm sorry he's dead," she said, then turned to Greene. "We were estranged."

"I'll say," Belzinger said.

Janice turned to Belzinger again. "I didn't kill him."

"Somebody did," Belzinger said.

Janice smiled.

"Did your ex-husband contact you recently?" Greene asked.

"No," Janice said. "He was in jail."

"He could've called."

"He didn't. Never once."

"We understand you owed him some money," Belzinger said. "That that was the reason he went after your boyfriend a few years ago."

"I didn't owe Peter a penny. If you look at our divorce, he received a check for the exact amount we agreed to. My lawyer witnessed his receipt of the check. I'm pretty sure it cleared within three days of my signing it over to him."

"Except there was something about an agreement you and he had made before going to your lawyer," Greene said. "Something about saving money using one attorney instead of two. You paid him what was due on paper and beat him for the rest."

Janice opened a compact and examined herself. "I changed my mind. Regarding what we had agreed to before going to my lawyer. Peter didn't deserve another fifty thousand dollars. He knew that. Or he would've beaten me up instead of Nathan. That was nothing more than a jealous rage."

Belzinger referred to her notes. "Sokolof, right? Nathan Sokolof, the guy Peter beat up."

"You obviously already know this stuff. But if you need to hear me repeat it, fine. Nathan was my boyfriend at the time. And, yes, it was an affair. Those things happen. Peter threatened to beat Nathan up if I didn't pay him fifty thousand dollars. I would have paid, only Nathan told me not to. He didn't think Peter would follow through on his threat. Unfortunately, he did."

"And you and Nathan?" Greene asked.

"Is that really pertinent?"

"Could be," Belzinger said.

Janice turned to Greene. "We're no longer an item."

"How long after the incident did you and Nathan break up?" Belzinger asked.

Janice took her time. "Three months? Maybe four."

Greene referred to his notes again. "Is Mr. Sokolof still with the same company?"

"I think so. And he's still married, I believe."

"Well, do you two stay in touch or not?" Belzinger asked.

"We're in the same business."

"So are me and my ex but we don't speak."

"That's nice."

Greene looked to his partner. Belzinger motioned for him to continue. "Peter was killed sometime in the early morning the day after he was released from prison," he said. "He wasn't out twenty-four hours."

"Tragic," Janice said. "Really."

Belzinger said, "He was found near his mother's place in Brooklyn. They found his body in Fort Hamilton Park. He was shot three times."

"Execution-style," Greene added.

"Like a contract killing," Belzinger said.

"I don't know anything about it," Janice said. "I can't imagine who would kill him."

"Neither can anyone else," Belzinger said.

Janice didn't flinch. "I'm sorry I can't help."

Greene left his card on the edge of her desk. "Well, if you think of anything, give us a call, please."

"Of course. Is that all?"

"For now," Greene said as he stood up from the chair.

Belzinger was already standing. "We'll be back," she said. "I think you already know that."

❖ ❖ ❖

Now that he was out of prison, Reese was out of work for the first time in eighteen years. At thirty-seven, after nearly two years of working out in prison, he was in his best physical condition since high school. Yet the idea of driving again, even if it was a cab instead of a bus this time, suddenly seemed daunting.

When he returned home after his visit with his parole officer and his surprise meeting with the two detectives, Reese found his mother napping in her recliner with the television playing. Tonight she had invited over a few of her church friends, including the Jamaican woman she wanted Reese to maybe hook up with someday. Laney, he thought her name was.

Reese was uneasy about meeting a woman through his mother, especially one from church, but she had been kind enough to send him books while he was in prison, and he owed his mother at least the respect of humoring her efforts at playing matchmaker.

His mother had told him her friends would come for coffee and cake sometime around nine o'clock, and stay maybe two hours. She also had said that he could make a date with Laney for the upcoming weekend, that he might take her to a movie or for a walk in Prospect Park. Laney was a woman who enjoyed simple things, she'd said.

He looked at his mother from the kitchen. She appeared to be peaceful in her recliner, her head resting to one side and the remote on her right thigh. He checked the screen; it was *Jeopardy*, his mother's favorite television show next to *Oprah*.

He moved quietly into the kitchen and checked the coffeepot. It was still half full. He turned the heat on to warm the pot while he used the bathroom. When he came out, Reese poured himself a cup of the coffee and glanced at the clock. He wasn't sure how long his mother had been home, but it was getting late for supper. He decided he'd treat her to Chinese and found a menu from a local restaurant.

Reese ordered his mother's favorite, egg foo yong and roast pork with fried rice. He ordered shrimp and string beans for himself, and both fried and boiled dumplings. He asked how long the delivery would take and hung up.

When he heard something drop in the living room, Reese stepped inside to see what it was. His mother was still asleep. Reese looked around the room until he spotted the remote on the floor alongside his mother's foot. He felt his heart stop as he looked from the floor to his mother's face. The realization was sudden and sharp.

"Oh, Momma," Reese whispered.

CHAPTER

14

IT TOOK REESE AWHILE to finally make the call to the funeral home. He spent most of that time holding one of her hands.

When they came to pick up his mother's body, his emotions ran the gamut from sadness to anger to rage.

How could it happen?

Why would it happen?

Why now?

As they carried Elle Waters out to the waiting van, Reese was sobbing at the front window. He saw the priest pull up and stop the men from the undertaker's so he could bless Elle's body.

Father Ebbs stood at the curb and watched the van until it was gone from sight. Then he headed inside the building. Reese met him at the door.

"I'm so sorry, Reese," the priest told him.

"Thank you, Father," Reese said.

"If there's anything we can do, anybody from the church, please don't hesitate to call. Your mother had a lot of friends at St. Lawrence. She was very much loved."

"I appreciate it, Father."

"Is there anything you need help with right now?"

Reese couldn't answer.

Father Ebbs made the sign of the cross and blessed Reese and the apartment.

Reese was oblivious. He didn't see the priest leave.

❖ ❖ ❖

His mother's body had been out of the apartment less than an hour when Reese looked up the telephone numbers for Janice Barrett. He grabbed a handful of quarters and walked to the corner so his mother's phone wouldn't register the call. He dialed the home number first. Angry when he got an answering machine, he hung up without leaving a message.

He tried her work number next and was surprised when she picked up.

"Janice Barrett," she said, not at all pleasantly.

"Working late?" he asked.

"Who's this?"

"You knew he was dead, didn't you?"

"Excuse me?"

"You knew he was dead."

"Oh, you again."

"You still owe the man."

"Fuck you."

"You still gonna pay, too."

The woman hung up.

✦ ✦ ✦

"Can we talk?" Michael Barrett asked Tony Gangi over his cell phone.

"One minute," Gangi said.

Barrett was standing across the street from the Metro North tracks in Croton-Harmon, New York. He was there to meet one of Gangi's friends he would have to hire to supervise one of his construction sites. Barrett turned his back to a passing train at the same time he heard a buzzing sound over the line.

"What's that?" he asked.

"A fan," Gangi said. "We can talk, but be careful anyway. What's up?"

Barrett looked around himself before speaking.

"What is it?" Gangi asked again.

"I need a favor."

"That's rich."

"I'll be signing that thing we discussed earlier, but I'm wondering if I can talk to the guy you're sending me about doing something private for me. I have a situation I need to take care of."

A short pause followed. "The guy we suggested as a supervisor?" Gangi asked. "Him?"

"Yeah, the guy's name I added to the payroll this week. Can I say it, his name?"

"No need. You're talking tit for tat here?"

Barrett frowned. "Yes, I'll take care of it from my end, the drywall issue."

"This a piece of work we're talking about?"

"I think so."

"You think so? You should learn the dialogue before you use it."

"This a deal or not?" asked Barrett, annoyed now.

"You're a pushy cocksucker," Gangi said. "I'll give you that."

Static interrupted the connection.

"Hello?" Barrett said.

"Have him call me first," Gangi said.

"Huh?"

"Have him call me."

"Right," Barrett said. "Will do."

"And fax me the fucking drywall sign-off."

✦ ✦ ✦

Laney Brown was her name. She was an attractive Jamaican woman with olive eyes and a dark complexion. Reese had blushed the night before when she appeared at the apartment door with a casserole dish of beef and rice. She had been shocked to hear the news about his mother.

Today she had taken the morning off from teaching her eighth graders at the Starrett City Junior High School and had come by to express her condolences. They were in the kitchen, where Reese prepared a pot of fresh coffee. His eyes were still swollen from occasional crying fits that had gripped him since his mother's body was removed from the apartment late last night.

Laney set the gift she had brought for him on the kitchen table. "Open it," she said.

Reese fumbled through the wrapping paper. The small statue confused him when he pulled it from the box.

"It's Saint Jude," she told him. "Patron saint of the impossible."

"I went to Saint Jude's in Canarsie as a kid," Reese said.

"Your mother told me. You were an altar boy?"

It was true, although Reese frowned on the memory now. He had thought he'd made a deal with God the day he became an altar boy. He had thought that God would protect his family so long as he committed himself to practicing his faith. His deal had soured over time.

He was inaccurate when he told Laney, "I wasn't happy about it, becoming an altar boy."

He hadn't started to lose his faith until his father died, the year he graduated from Saint Jude. When his mother could no longer make the mortgage payments on the house and was forced to sell it one year later, Reese was pretty much finished with religion. Twenty years later, when he found himself in prison for a crime he hadn't really committed, Reese was embarrassed for ever having believed in the first place.

"Your mother used to light candles to Saint Jude at the Thursday novena," said Laney, bringing him back. "It was something I picked up and kept forgetting to give her ever since she told me you were coming home."

It was always confusing to Reese how his mother had held on to her faith through all those tough years. He smiled thinking about her now and kissed the statue for her.

"Do you need any help?" Laney asked. "With the arrangements for your mother, I mean. I can take the rest of the day if you want."

"I don't know what to do," Reese said. "How does it work, with the Mass and all? I don't have a clue."

"Your mother wanted to be cremated. No wake. She told me in case something happened while you were away."

"I'd like someplace to visit Mom."

"She wanted to be cremated."

Reese didn't appreciate being told what he should do about his mother. He told Laney, "But she's my mother, right? I'd like to see her sometimes. Visit her grave."

Laney remained quiet this time.

Reese said, "You gonna make me feel guilty now, huh? That where this is going?"

Laney rolled her eyes. Reese stared hard and waited for more.

"Well?" he finally said.

"Your mother wanted to be cremated, man. I know it bothers you, but it is what she wanted. You want to go against her last wish, so be it."

Reese gave it a moment. He didn't like the idea of scattering his mother's ashes someplace, but how could he not do what she had asked?

"You'll have to make a decision and call the funeral parlor soon," Laney reminded him. "They'll need to know what you want to do."

"Nice thing to have to decide my fourth day out of the joint."

"It isn't much of a decision, man. You already know what she wanted."

The woman was relentless, Reese was thinking. His mother couldn't have been a worse matchmaker.

"Well?" she said.

"I guess she left you behind to haunt me about it, huh?"

"Come on, man, it isn't rocket science. Do what your mother asked."

CHAPTER

15

THE DETECTIVES DROVE IN silence until they were on the Belt Parkway. Belzinger was wearing a tight wool sweater under a leather jacket. Greene had turned the heat up high inside the car. Belzinger was sweating. She struggled out of the jacket.

"What time the lawyer call?" Greene asked.

"Last night sometime," Belzinger said. "I didn't check messages until I got home. I was surprised he called me instead of you. I thought I scared him."

"Lawyers don't usually scare that easy."

"I meant as a man."

"Rosenblatt didn't like Janice Barrett," Greene said. "That's for sure. And he was upset at hearing the guy was murdered."

"I don't think I ever saw a lawyer lose his appetite over a client before. But we didn't like the guy's wife, either. I certainly didn't. I'm sure she's dirty."

Greene moved into the left lane and leaned his foot on the accelerator.

Belzinger said, "Rosenblatt said we should probably check all the father's construction projects, scan the payrolls and so on, going back at least ten years."

"We can do that from the office, have them phone it in," Greene said. "He's mobbed up, the old man, we'll learn it. You could ask John about it."

"I'd rather not, you don't mind."

Belzinger had been involved with a detective assigned to the Organized Crime Unit. They had recently split up.

Greene sucked his lips inside his mouth as he darted around a slower-moving car in the left lane.

"Rosenblatt said one of the things the mob does in the construction game is latch onto contractors with bids they can wash money through," Belzinger said. "They pad the materials and labor costs and hire their own. Sometimes they add fictitious names to the payroll. Sometimes the people they hire have as much construction experience as you or me."

"Careful there," Greene said. "I built my kids a tree house."

"Yeah, but you wouldn't consider yourself a consultant on the electricity or the plumbing."

"That what he said they do?"

"Usually. Either they're consultants or some other form of management. Supervisors, foreman, whatever title they need to make it appear kosher."

"Thumb-benders doing schematics?" Greene said. "Yeah, right. And I'm Tiger Woods."

◆　◆　◆

Reese had called the number his prison buddy Rahib had given Peter Rizzo the day of their release. Mufasa Kareem Abdul-Jabbar was supposed to be tight with Rahib and would be able to provide Reese with alibis for his parole officer should he need them. Reese had waited through eight rings before he could finally leave a message. He left his name and number and the time.

It wasn't a quarter hour before the kitchen phone rang.

"Yeah, Reese Waters," he said into the phone.

"My brother, my brother," the voice on the other end said.

"This Mufasa?" Reese asked.

"The one and only. Mufasa Kareem Abdul-Jabbar, at your service."

"Well, I'm just checking in with you," Reese told Mufasa. "Rahib gave me your number up at Fishkill. Said I should give you a call when I got out."

"Indeed he did. Man said he owes you. That means I owes you. The entire Nation owes you."

Reese suppressed a chuckle. "Cool," he said.

"You feel like coming out to meet?" Mufasa asked. "Get a little something to eat, maybe? I'm sure you can use it, you just come out the joint."

"Well, tell you the truth, I really can't right now. My mom died last night."

"Say what?"

Reese gave it a second before repeating what he'd said.

"Oh, my God," Mufasa said, his voice full of emotion. "I'm so, so sorry, my brother. So sorry."

"I appreciate it. Thanks."

"Is there anything we can do? Anything at all? My God, you just come out and your momma dies. Lord have mercy."

Reese was wondering why Mufasa wasn't asking Allah for mercy. "Yeah, it was pretty bad," he said. "I have things under control right now. I already applied for a taxi license to keep my parole officer off my back."

"You just let me know if there's anything I or anyone else in the Nation can do for you, my brother. Anything at all. For your momma or for yourself. And don't you sweat out no parole officer. They give you a hard time, you tell them you workin' for the Nation. Back those white boys down so fast they don't know to spit or wind they wristwatch."

"Well, I sure appreciate the offer, my man," Reese said. "I really do. And I'll be in touch."

"Please, brother, please be in touch. And once again, I'm so sorry about your mom. Allah have mercy."

"Thanks again," Reese said, smiling at the mention of Allah now.

"*Salom Malakim,*" Mufasa said.

"*Malakim Salom,*" Reese said.

He hung up, looked at himself in the kitchen mirror, and said, "*Salom Malakim,* Lord have mercy, whichever turns you on."

CHAPTER
16

THEY HAD BEEN SITTING in the SUV for a few minutes. A box of Entenmann's apple turnovers lay on the console. Mauro ate one of the cakes but still was thirsty. He had told Barrett that he didn't like thermos coffee, and the old man motioned toward the diner.

"They have takeout," he had said.

Now Mauro was back on the front seat. He sipped the coffee through a hole he'd torn in the plastic cap.

"You'll need a car if you're going to move up here," the old man said.

Mauro pointed to the banged-up Toyota across the parking lot. "That's how I got here. That there."

The old man was eating slivers of frosting off one of the turnovers. "I'll work with Gangi on this but I won't let you screw off," he said. "This is a business. If you're not there to make sure the workers show up, start on time, I'll fire you, make no mistake. This isn't country club work, my friend. The construction business is competitive up here. It's not like in the city. There are no unions."

Mauro patted the old man on the leg. "Look, pops, take it easy, okay? It's a job, I understand that. No need to fire me before I start."

"I'm letting you know the ground rules going in. I put you on my payroll, I expect you to work."

Mauro lit a fresh cigarette. "Right."

Barrett let down Mauro's window a few inches.

"Oh!" Mauro said. "It's fucking freezing."

"If you're going to smoke in my car, the window stays open."

Mauro took a drag on the cigarette, tossed it out the window, then turned to the old man. "Okay?"

Barrett brought the window back up.

"You're a regular hard-ass, huh?" Mauro said.

"It's a rough business," Barrett said. "You'll learn that soon enough. The good thing is they won't know you going in, as a supervisor, I mean. They'll try and befriend you and take full advantage. Showing up late and taking their time starting is the number one problem you'll have. You send one of them home the first time they pull that, dock him a day's pay, and the rest will fall in line. At least for a little while."

"I'm not looking to make friends. You won't have to worry about that."

"Fair enough," Barrett said. He again offered the open box of turnovers to Mauro.

"No, thanks. Go 'head, I'm listening."

"You spoke to Gangi, right? He filled you in?"

"Something I should do for you. He wasn't specific."

"I need somebody taken care of. A black guy. He's in Brooklyn. I need him to go away."

"Is it permanent, this move? Or he should be scared off to another state or something?"

Barrett took a bite from the turnover. "Frankly, I don't care," he said. "I can put you on a cushy site, one up near Peekskill, where you wouldn't have to do anything the first month or so, until the ground thaws. That's a bonus for getting this done right away."

"What about cash? Trust me, it's a much better incentive."

"That depends on what you're willing to do."

"You'll have to be more specific. Contrary to popular opinion, there isn't a price list."

"So long as it's negotiable," Barrett said.

"I'm listening."

Barrett took another bite of the cake. A small piece of frosting dropped off onto the console. Mauro grabbed the piece between two fingers.

Barrett said, "You already know it'll require violence, right?"

"I'm not squeamish," Mauro said before popping the frosting into his mouth.

◆ ◆ ◆

Laney had come back with potted chicken, rice, and steamed fresh vegetables. She was a stubborn woman, he could tell, but here she was doing things for him.

He wondered what her story was. All he knew so far was that she had gone through an ugly divorce two years ago and that she had been a very good friend to his mother.

Now he tried to explain to Laney what had happened and how he suspected that Peter's ex-wife had something to do with his murder.

"I went to see her and I understood why he didn't want to let go of his money," Reese told her. "She's exactly what he said she was, the exact opposite of Peter. She's evil is what she is. The Queen of Mean."

"Evil begets evil," Laney said. "Her day will come. You should move on and forget it."

Reese wished it were that easy. He had seen things inside prison that screamed for revenge, things he had never believed one man would do to another, but more often than not, there was never any justice for the victims.

"That woman set him up for that jail sentence," he went on. "First she stole his money and then she set him up to go away. Knowing he'd go, too. That's the evil part of it, more than stealing his money. She knew Peter would take the fall."

"So why did they ever get married?" Laney asked.

"She came from upstate someplace and thought Peter was something special. Being connected and all, it was new to her. And Peter was intrigued with someone like her falling for him. At first, he said, because she was so smart. It didn't last very long, though. A year or so, I think he said, before she showed her true colors."

Laney held up two fingers. "And there are two sides to every story."

"Except I met the woman and she's nasty. I'm sure she can put it on when she has to, but she's nasty at the core. Everything he said about her."

"And I'm sure she talked trash about him, too."

Reese had had enough. "Hey, what is it with you? Why you so quick to dump on my friend over this? Why you taking her side?"

"I'm not taking anybody's side, you fool," Laney told him. "I just don't see the point of wasting all this energy over it. He's dead. Fighting with his ex-wife, especially if she's the Queen of Mean, isn't going to solve anything now."

Reese grew angry listening to her. He was glad when she glanced at her watch and said she had to get to church. He walked her to the door and was surprised when Laney pecked him on the cheek before she left.

He didn't understand her. He wasn't sure he wanted to.

When she was gone, Reese loaded a plate with the food Laney had brought. He sat down at the kitchen table and ate like a hungry man.

CHAPTER

17

"I'M GONNA HAVE TO cut this short," Jimmy said. "I have an appointment with my lawyer, the cocksucker."

"Oh, okay," Janice said. "No problem."

They were having a late lunch at the restaurant-bar her ex-husband had managed. Il Palermo had since changed owners and motifs, but it was still a trendy place to be seen. The layout was simple—three adjacent rooms, and around the perimeter of each of them waiters and their assistants stood like statues at the ready. The long black marble bar in the front hosted a veritable who's who of New York celebrities.

Jimmy and Janice were in a booth in the VIP room at the rear of the restaurant. A waiter had just told them the specials. Jimmy sipped at a glass of red wine and waited for privacy.

"This black guy," he whispered. "He get in touch with you again?"

Janice was studying the expensive menu. "Just the phone call," she said over the top of the menu. "I'm not sure he'll go any farther. I didn't mention him when the police came around, though. I didn't see the point."

"Good. The less they know, the better. This spook gets pushy, I'll handle him." He pointed at the menu. "Whatta you feel like?"

Janice was smiling behind the menu. She set it down. "I think the fish special."

"Me, too," Jimmy said. He turned to the waiter standing near the doorway. *"Due speciales dei pesci, per favore,"* he called.

Her cell phone had been ringing the past half hour. She had

ignored the calls. She got another, and Jimmy said to take it while he used the bathroom. He slid out of the booth and she answered.

Janice frowned when she recognized Brad Nelson's voice. It was clipped and edgy.

"What were the police doing at the office?" he asked.

"Excuse me?"

"What were the police doing in your office?" Brad repeated. "Everybody is talking."

"You mean the receptionists are talking. Why don't you fire them?"

"I'm serious, damn it. What's going on?"

"You're also being accusatory and I don't like it."

A pause followed. Janice said, "Hello?"

"I think we need to talk," Brad said. "Tonight, if possible."

"I'll call you later," Janice told him. She could see Jimmy heading back to the table.

"What time?" Brad asked.

Janice hung up.

"There a problem?" asked Jimmy as he sat.

"Nothing major."

"Work?"

"Always."

Jimmy sipped his wine again. "I been thinking about it," he said. "You should run your own business."

Janice leaned forward and took his hand. "I think you're right."

"So what's stopping you?"

Janice wiggled in the booth and said, "Funny you should ask."

✦ ✦ ✦

Reese tried calling the Rizzo family one more time. The mother answered and quickly passed the phone to her son.

"Who's this?" Paul Rizzo asked with an attitude.

"We spoke the other day," Reese said. "I'm a friend of your brother. I was calling about—"

"The guy from prison?"

"Yeah," said Reese, with some attitude of his own before he checked himself. "Yes."

"There's not gonna be a funeral."

"Excuse me?"

"There's no money for a funeral. The city will have to take care of it."

Reese was dumbfounded. He was about to ask another question when the line went dead. He immediately called back.

"Don't hang up, man!" he said. "I'll take the body. I'll bury him."

"Yeah?" Paul Rizzo said. "Good for you."

"Who do I call?" Reese asked.

"I have no idea," the brother said, then hung up again.

✦ ✦ ✦

"I was just leaving for the day," Nathan Sokolof told both detectives.

Greene and Belzinger were standing at the reception desk at the advertising firm where Sokolof was a senior vice president. They had just had him paged when he suddenly appeared, coat and briefcase in hand, on his way out.

"I'm sorry for the inconvenience," Belzinger told him. "Is there somewhere we can talk privately?"

Sokolof sighed. He was a fat man with thick glasses and a full beard. "Follow me," he said.

He led them into an empty conference room around the corner from reception. Sokolof sat at the head of the table. Belzinger sat to his right. Greene remained standing.

"Will this take long?" Sokolof asked. "I was hoping to get home early. If I miss the next train, I'll have to wait an hour. I live upstate."

"We'll do our best," Belzinger said.

Sokolof sighed again.

"Do you know about Peter Rizzo, what happened to him?" she asked.

"I read about it, yes. I saw it on the news."

"He's the man who assaulted you, correct?" Greene asked.

"Two years ago. And he didn't give me a bloody nose. It wasn't that kind of assault, some bogus thing. He broke my jaw. It still hurts."

"Where were you when he was killed?" Belzinger asked.

"In bed with my wife. In Scarsdale, where we live. And I really hope you aren't going to ask her about that. Two years ago I told her it was mistaken identity, why that animal broke my jaw. I don't think she bought it back then, but she might be forgetting it about now. I'd rather not open an old wound if it isn't necessary."

"She probably hasn't forgot about it," Belzinger said. "Can you prove you were home without my calling her?"

"Yes," Sokolof said, irritated now. "I took the train from Grand Central and I was with two friends. You can also ask somebody on the other end. I stopped off to pick up some dry cleaning near the station."

"I see."

"Look, I didn't kill the son of a bitch. I'm not sorry he's dead, but I didn't kill him."

"What about Janice Barrett?" Greene asked. "Do you see her anymore?"

"Only when I can't avoid it. When it's business. I try my best to keep my distance from that woman. I think you can understand."

"Not really," Belzinger said. "Why's that?"

"My wife, for one thing. And I happen to know she was seeing someone else at the time. Brad Nelson."

Belzinger wrote the name down and waited for more.

"He's the senior partner where she is now," Sokolof continued. "I think I was the bait so her ex-husband didn't damage the goods."

"How do you know all this?" Greene asked.

"It's a small world, detectives. It's a lot smaller within the advertising world. People talk. She wasn't exactly careful about it once her husband was locked up."

"You sound pretty bitter," Belzinger said. "Anything else?"

"That's not enough? The guy wired my jaw. It still hurts when it rains."

Belzinger tilted her head. "What else she do?"

Sokolof blushed and turned away.

"Mr. Sokolof?" Greene said.

"Something I won't ever repeat in court, so don't think I will. For my wife's sake."

"What is it?" Belzinger asked.

"She got me to approve her Christmas bonus."

"So?" Belzinger said.

"I knew she was leaving. As a partner, I had a fiduciary relationship with the firm. I knew she was leaving and I approved the maximum amount."

"For sex?" Belzinger asked.

"Excuse me?"

"You approved her bonus so she'd sleep with you?"

"No, nothing like that," Sokolof said defensively. "I didn't know what she was up to. I was a sucker, trust me. My kid had worked for her for a while. She was sending me messages through the kid. What a nice guy I was, how much she liked me, and so on. I approved her bonus because I thought, you know . . . I was actually thinking about leaving my wife." He laughed at himself uncomfortably. "We did it two times and I thought she was falling for me."

Belzinger looked to Greene.

"She used him," Greene said. "That it? She used you?"

Sokolof swallowed hard. "She played me like a violin."

CHAPTER

18

NEIL LEHMAN ENJOYED SAILING and spent three months a year on the ocean. He was tall, lean, tanned, bald; he had a weathered look. The high-profile defense attorney appeared much older than his fifty-four years.

As a former New York city district attorney, Lehman had made a name for himself prosecuting Mafia big shots. After his attempt at running for the state legislature failed because of a questionable relationship with a minor, Lehman switched to defending criminals. Ten years later, his private practice was huge, with a client list that included Hollywood celebrities, rap stars, politicians, and several new high-profile organized crime figures.

Lehman inherited Jimmy "the Blond" Valentine's case the day that one of his law partners was killed in a carjacking while on vacation in Los Angeles. Valentine was the reigning *consigliere* of the Vignieri crime family in New York. An informant under federal witness protection had implicated Valentine in a triple execution murder. As the court date drew near, Lehman was pressing his client to take a deal the federal prosecutor was offering.

Valentine was being obstinate.

"What's on the table?" he asked Lehman.

They were in Lehman's corner office on Fifth Avenue at Forty-second Street Valentine had appropriated a brown leather couch and was scratching the foil off instant Lotto tickets with a penknife. A Cuban cigar burned in a crystal ashtray on a glass coffee table. Seated behind his desk, Lehman was smoking a dark European cigarette.

"Minimum security," Lehman told his client. "Which means house arrest with federal chaperones the next five years. After that, a new identity and location. And you get to keep your stash."

"It's almost perfect," Valentine said.

"Excuse me?"

"Why isn't it perfect? I mean, five years with federal agents in my hip pocket? What's the point?"

"They're saving face. They at least have to slap your wrist."

"For what I'd be giving them, they should blow me six times a day."

Lehman sat forward in his chair. "Maybe, but they're not going to do that. It's a great deal, Jimmy. Unless you want to stay in and do the stand-up routine, spend the rest of your life in jail, maybe get executed, you should take what they're offering before it's too late."

Valentine waved the advice off. "You guys kill me," he said.

"Why's that?"

"Because so long as I stall them, I'm out. I make the deal 'before it's too late,' I'm stuck somewhere playing with myself and half a dozen federal agents until they set a bunch of trial dates that can be stalled forever. The longer I hold out, I can skip the bullshit security. Every day without those guys in my hip pocket is a bonus."

"What else do you want? What else do you think you'll get?"

Valentine picked up his cigar. "Gennaro," he said.

"They're not going to do that."

"How do you know?"

"Because they owe him."

"For giving me up," Valentine said.

"Exactly. Why wouldn't they protect him?"

"Because they don't need him anymore. Once I make the deal, they don't need Gennaro anymore. I'll let them tape what I have in a court under oath, so we don't have to wait for their trials and all the stalling. What do they care what happens to Gennaro once I give them that?"

Lehman held his breath a few seconds. "The federal government isn't going to let you walk around until they go to trial," he said after exhaling. "No way, Jimmy. And they're not going to deal away a witness under their protection."

Valentine set down the cigar and started on a new Lotto ticket.

"Frank Gennaro can tie me to a triple hit," he said. "They can put me away forever, you said. Either in a cell or they whack me with the needle. They'll look the other way because I can give them a Jersey crew. Once they have those guys, they'll get another dozen or so back on the New York side of the river. They'll have, what, two dozen, maybe three dozen, wiseguys after that? This is the same federal government that brokered those deals with Sammy and how many other guys? Absolved them of how many murders? You still wanna tell me they can't arrange something for Frank Gennaro? Maybe they'll give me some breathing room, some more time before I have to go in."

Lehman shook his head. "Sorry, Jimmy, I just don't see it happening."

Valentine glared at his attorney. "Do me a favor," he said. "Go fucking ask."

CHAPTER
19

REESE WAS SHAKEN. LANEY had warned him about the viewing. She had been to one before. "Try not to stand too close," she had told him. "They usually only touch up one side of the face."

She held on to his arm as they left the La Polla Funeral Home. Reese had just viewed his mother. She was to be cremated later the same day.

"I'll never lose that image," he said. "I shouldn't have come."

He had leaned over to kiss his mother's forehead. Her skin was cold. When he pulled away, he could see that the eye on the far side of his mother's face was sunken. He couldn't shake the image from his mind.

Laney rubbed his back through the heavy coat as they waited at a bus stop on Flatlands Avenue.

"And that casket," Reese said. "It was so cheap."

"They're going to burn it, Reese," Laney said.

He was quiet as the bus pulled up. He got on without paying. Laney signaled to the bus driver that she would take care of it.

✦ ✦ ✦

"You going into the business?" Tommy Burns asked Jimmy Mauro.

They were sitting in a booth in the rear of the Glenwood Tavern in Canarsie. Mauro was there to buy a gun. Burns was trying to sell him black-market prepaid cell phones.

"I'm too old to change professions," Mauro said as he examined one of the cell phones. "How much these go for?"

Burns sipped scotch from a rocks glass. His free hand rested a few inches from an ashtray where his cigarette was burning. "Hundred retail. What they're programmed for. You can probably get them for eighty you look around. I'm paying forty and looking for fifty on bulk. Sixty per piece. I got lots, you're interested."

Mauro set the cell phone on the table. "When'd these things become so fucking important is what I wanna know," he said. "First it was pagers and I never could get used to them things. The three or four I had, I lost as fast as I got them. Left them on bars or whatever. I'll probably do the same with this."

"They're a part of life these days," Burns said. "Even the kids, you drive past the high school, halfa them are walking around holding one up to their ears."

"I must be a dinosaur. I still prefer a pay phone."

"Yeah, you can find one works."

Mauro held the cell phone up. "Can I take a half dozen on consignment?"

Burns grinned. "What am I, Pa fuckin' Bell?"

"I don't have enough for this and the other thing. Not today I don't."

Burns took a long drag on his cigarette. "Maybe you wanna sell a couple of these first and then come back for the other thing. Since you're not changing professions, I mean. It's not so urgent."

Mauro pushed the cell phone across the table. "Protecting myself is always urgent," he said. "The way things are, sometimes staying inside is safer for a guy like me."

"Why, you got something to worry about?"

"Maybe I'm paranoid," Mauro said. "You read the papers, guys are taking tickets like they're in a fuckin' bakery to make deals. I'm going to work upstate someplace, somewhere unfamiliar, I'll sleep better nights knowing I have something under my pillow."

Burns nodded. "I can understand that."

"Then I'll take whatever you have. Something simple doesn't jam."

"A revolver," Burns said. "A good old thirty-eight. Very reliable piece. It's also very loud, if you are thinking about doing a piece of work."

"Is it simple? I know how to aim and pull a trigger, but I'm no technician."

Burns sucked on his cigarette, then crushed the butt in the ashtray. "Simple enough. And cheap, too. Three hundred and I'll throw in a box of ammo."

"I appreciate it. I'd appreciate it more you can pass me a few of the phones to see what I can do with them."

Burns lit a fresh cigarette. "Sure," he said. "Why not? What are friends for?"

◆ ◆ ◆

Reese started drinking late in the afternoon. It had been a long time since he'd tasted scotch. His mother had kept a bottle of Dewar's for company that was more than half filled when Reese started on it. It was nearly empty when Laney told him his dinner was ready.

"I'm not hungry," he told her.

"I suppose not. But you better put something in your stomach, man, or your head is going to pound when you wake up."

"Who called before?"

"Vincent Coleman. He said he was a friend of yours. He was on his way into work. I told him about your mother." She handed Reese a glass of ice water. "Start with this and let me know when it's finished."

Reese drank half the glass and tried to stand. He felt dizzy and fell back onto the couch.

"You're out of practice," Laney said.

"My head is pounding."

Laney pointed to the water. "Drink it, man. It's your only chance."

◆ ◆ ◆

"Is Janice a suspect?" Brad Nelson wanted to know.

Detectives Greene and Belzinger had met Nelson in the company cafeteria. Each had grabbed a diet soda and sat across from Nelson at a table near the exit.

"Should she be?" Belzinger asked.

Nelson looked from Belzinger to Greene. "Am I a suspect?"

"Did you kill Peter Rizzo?" Greene asked.

"No!" Nelson yelled, then quickly glanced around the cafeteria. "No, of course not," he whispered.

"Do you know if Janice Barrett had her ex-husband killed?" Belzinger asked.

Nelson was shaking his head as he flicked a hand at the question. "No, no, no. I don't know anything. How would I know something like that?"

Greene said, "Did she ever mention trouble she was having with Peter Rizzo? Are you aware of their history?"

Nelson related the divorce story both detectives had already heard several times. Belzinger stopped taking notes before he was finished.

"What about Nathan Sokolof?" she asked.

Nelson became defensive. "What about him?"

"Janice was seeing him while she was with you, correct?"

"I guess. I know her ex went after Sokolof. Broke his jaw or something."

"That could've been you," Greene said. "The one with the broken jaw. From what we've heard so far."

"Janice apparently used Mr. Sokolof to get her husband in trouble," Belzinger said.

Nelson feigned ignorance.

Greene said, "Were you sleeping with her? Before her divorce."

"Neither of us was exclusive at the time. Not yet we weren't."

"And now?" Belzinger asked.

"Huh?"

"Are you and Janice involved in an exclusive relationship, Mr. Nelson?"

Nelson looked from one detective to the other. "Yeah, I guess so," he said. "I think so."

CHAPTER

20

MAURO HAD NEVER KILLED anyone before. He'd done some muscle work and shakedowns but usually as a backup. His past convictions included armed robbery and fraud.

When he found the address Michael Barrett had provided, Mauro parked his car across Flatlands Avenue alongside Starrett City. He walked around the block of buildings fenced in on the same avenue and stood in the shadows of a box truck parked at the corner. He smoked a cigarette while he surveyed the building where Reese Waters lived with his mother.

When Mauro was finished with the cigarette, he hefted the .38 inside his coat pocket. Tommy Burns had told him the gun was reliable and very loud, and that he would be waking a lot of people once he pulled the trigger.

He timed the private patrol car that circled Starrett City and waited twenty minutes before one passed. When the taillights turned off the avenue at the far corner, Mauro crossed Flatlands Avenue.

✦ ✦ ✦

Laney had stayed to make sure Reese didn't drink himself into a coma. She wasn't happy spending extra time there, but she was concerned about the amount of alcohol Reese had consumed in so short a time. The funeral mass at Saint Lawrence was scheduled for eight o'clock the next morning. Laney planned to return to work afterward.

She had gone into Elle Water's bedroom to take a nap when Reese started snoring on the couch. It had been a long day and Laney fell soundly asleep.

Inside, Reese snored while holding the statue of Saint Jude in his right hand. When the doorbell rang, he nearly fell off the couch.

He struggled to make his way to the apartment door. His head was pounding and he still felt a little drunk. He went to rub the sleep from his eyes and poked himself with the statue.

Reese peered through the peephole and saw a man standing with his back to the door.

"Yeah?" Reese said.

The man half turned. "Reese Waters?" he asked.

"Yeah, and you are?" Reese said. He was about to back away from the door to open it when he dropped the statue. He bent at the knees to pick it up, and the first bullet exploded through the apartment door, just above his head.

Reese dropped to the floor as the second of three consecutive shots slammed through the middle of the door. He crawled backward until he could turn the corner into the kitchen. Laney was in the bedroom doorway. He waved at her to get back. He could hear footsteps outside in the hallway, then the sound of the heavy stairwell door slamming shut.

"Reese?" Laney called.

"Call the police," he told her.

"You okay?"

"Call the police!" he yelled.

✦ ✦ ✦

"I like you in pinstripes," Jimmy told Janice.

He was standing at her apartment door wearing a short black wig. It startled her. She beamed when she recognized him.

"Hi!" she said, then went up on her toes to kiss him.

Jimmy removed the wig once he was inside the apartment. "I come at a bad time?"

Janice locked the door and said, "No, not at all. I didn't expect you but I'm glad you're here."

He went straight to the living room and took his seat in the recliner. He dropped the wig on the end table while Janice poured him a scotch. She brought him the drink before mixing herself a vodka martini. Jimmy waited until she was seated before toasting.

"*Salut*," he said.

"Cheers," she said.

They both sipped their drinks.

"Does that really work?" asked Janice, pointing at the wig. "Do you fool them?"

"Them being the agents? Sometimes. When I really want to, I do. Sometimes it's better they think I'm trying to fool them. They get cocky they see they have me once in a while."

"Do they follow you everywhere?"

"They try to."

"Did they follow you here?"

"There's a car downstairs. Why I pressed half the buttons in the elevator going to the top floor. Let them figure it out. I have another friend in this building. Some guy I know."

Janice sipped her drink again. "You live a weird life," she said.

"Exciting, though, too, right?"

He could read her with one look, she was thinking. She giggled as she blushed.

"So, tell me again about this guy approached you the other day," Jimmy said.

"He called, too, but I think he was just desperate. Nothing happened. Turns out he was my ex-husband's cellmate. My father found that out. They were probably trying to scare me into paying. I don't think he knew what happened to Peter."

"Your father?" Jimmy asked.

"He freaked out when I told him about the black guy. He even brought me a gun."

Jimmy sat back in the chair. "I hope he doesn't know about that other fuckin' thing."

"No, not at all. I could never tell him about that. He has no idea. About us, either."

Jimmy eyed her suspiciously. "I fuckin' hope not. That could create problems none of us need. He was being some kind of a hard-on with the drywall contracts, your father. We still have to work together on some other things. Imagine he learns about this."

Janice put a hand to her chest. "I swear it, Jimmy. I never said a word. Never."

Jimmy took his time finishing his drink. When his glass was empty, Janice immediately refilled it.

"And let me know if this black guy comes around again," he said. "Maybe he disappears, there's nothing else to investigate, the cops'll go back to protecting the public."

"Of course," she said.

He waited for her to return to the couch. She sat on the edge of a cushion and folded her hands nervously.

"Did he mention a number, the bone?" Jimmy asked.

Janice was confused. "Huh?"

"The black guy. Did he give you a figure?"

"Peter claims I robbed him of fifty thousand dollars but that's bull-shit. He was just crazy he caught me fooling around. He was going to extort from me. I knew he was going to do that as soon as he came out. I didn't think he'd find help in prison, though."

Jimmy was still suspicious. He lit a cigar.

"The black guy mentioned the fifty thousand," Janice continued nervously. "Plus back interest," she added, rolling her eyes. "Imagine?"

Jimmy continued staring. Janice nearly spilled her drink.

"I do like your pajamas," he finally said.

She was wearing blue and white pinstripe pajamas. She stood up and slowly turned for him.

"I'll probably like the bottoms more once they're off but I like you in stripes. They look good on you."

Janice smiled demurely. "Thank you."

Jimmy took a drag on his cigar. Janice saw there was no ashtray and raced across the room to get one. Jimmy held the cigar in his mouth until she sat again.

"You wanted to tell me something?" he asked.

There it was again, just like that, the guy taking control. It immediately brought her back.

"I have a proposition," she said. "A business proposition."

Jimmy waited.

"What you mentioned at lunch yesterday," she continued. "There's a business I can buy into up in Boston, an advertising company looking to sell. My partner here in New York wants to buy it, fifty-one percent, so he can control it. He offered me forty-nine percent but I don't have the money."

"You ask your father?"

"No. He wouldn't be interested. If it isn't construction or the stock market, he doesn't invest."

"What about your brother? You have one, right?"

"Alex has his own problems. He doesn't have money to lend."

Jimmy motioned at her to open the pajama top. She did it slowly. He motioned at her to take it off and she let the top slip off her shoulders down her arms.

She started to unhook her bra; Jimmy waved a finger. "I don't like it when the bags show," he said.

Janice was instantly dispirited. She tried her best not to show it.

"You look sexier with a bra," he said as he pointed to his own cheek. "Especially with this thing here, the mole. That makes it sexier, the lacey lingerie."

She recovered somewhat. "I can have the implants removed. The doctor said he could do it, take them out."

Jimmy motioned for her to stand up. She stood, untied her pajama bottoms, and they fell to her feet. She stepped out of them slowly. He twirled his finger and she turned for him. She was wearing a white thong.

"God bless America," Jimmy said.

Janice looked coyly over her shoulder with her back to him.

He waved at her to sit on his lap. She crossed the room till she stood directly in front of him. He set his drink on one of the recliner arms and guided her down to his lap.

"You want finance, that it?" he asked.

"I want control," Janice said.

Jimmy was impressed. He picked up his glass. "*Salut,*" he said.

CHAPTER

21

DETECTIVE GREENE ARRIVED AHEAD of his partner. Reese Waters had called him after his girlfriend had called the local precinct. Greene walked through the crowd of patrolmen on the scene and found Waters talking with detectives from the Seventy-fifth Precinct.

"I'll take this," Greene told them.

The three detectives huddled together for a few minutes, then the two from the precinct left the apartment. Greene sat on a folding chair across from Waters and a woman he assumed was the girlfriend. He presented his shield to her.

"Detective Greene," he said.

"Laney Brown," the woman said with a slight island accent.

"You okay?" Greene asked both of them.

Both nodded.

"First of all, I'm sorry about your mother," Greene said. "I understand she recently passed away."

"A couple days ago," the woman said. "The Mass is in the morning."

"I am sorry."

"Thank you," Waters said.

"What happened here tonight?" Greene asked. "From the beginning."

Waters recounted how he'd gone to the viewing of his mother's body at a local funeral parlor, how he'd come home with Laney, gotten drunk, fallen asleep on the couch. In finishing, Waters said, "The man shot through the door. All he had to go on was my voice. I dropped something and bent down to pick it up or I'd be dead."

"Pretty sloppy," Greene said. "If it was a hit."

"What do you mean, 'a hit'?" the woman asked.

Greene thumbed at Waters. "His cellmate was killed in Brooklyn the other morning. That appears to have been a hit, a contract killing. I doubt this was the same person, though."

"Why's that?" Waters asked.

Greene looked from the woman back to Waters again. He said, "You're still alive."

✦ ✦ ✦

When the woman detective arrived, Reese knew it was going to be a long night. Four Advils had somewhat cleared his head, but he was tired of telling the same story.

The woman sat on the edge of the couch alongside Laney. Reese was in his mother's recliner. Detective Greene straddled one of the chairs from the kitchen.

"You sure you didn't have a plan to retrieve the money owed your friend?" Detective Belzinger wanted to know.

Reese looked to Laney.

"Should I ask Janice Barrett?" Belzinger asked. "She can probably put you back in prison with a simple harassment complaint."

"I approached her," Reese said. "Peter's ex-wife. Peter asked me to approach her and tell her he expected his money."

"The plot thickens," Greene said.

"Except that was after Peter was dead," Reese said. "I didn't know Peter was dead. I talked to his wife a few hours after Peter was killed. I had no idea."

"And what did she say?" Belzinger asked. "About the money."

"She said she didn't owe him anything. I told her Peter lost two years of his life and wasn't asking for compensation for that, just what she owed, plus the interest."

"What about the interest?" Greene wanted to know. "Was Peter looking to shake her down?"

"Going bank rate. Peter wanted what was coming to him. What she stole from him. Nothing more than that."

Belzinger said, "And he was killed for it instead. Is that what you're saying?"

"Look, he didn't get paid, not a nickel, and he did get killed. If you don't think she's guilty of something, that's your problem. Me, I met the woman one time for less than five minutes, and I can guarantee you she had something to do with what happened to Peter."

"So we might as well arrest her," Greene said.

Reese rubbed his face with both hands. "You do whatever you want. But that woman is the only one who even knows I exist, and somebody just tried to kill me, too. Maybe it's just a coincidence. I doubt it."

Greene looked to Belzinger before turning back to Reese. "What about up at Fishkill? When you were assaulted by some of the mob boys and Peter came to your rescue."

"What almost got him killed the first time," Belzinger said.

"We already went over this the other day," Reese said.

"Unless you think his ex-wife was behind that, too," Greene said.

"And, what, the mob got nothin' better to do now, almost two years later, than to come after me and Peter?" Reese asked. "I'm home but a few days now, and all I see in the papers is the mob is on the run with bigger problems than what happened upstate two years ago. Tell me you don't really believe it's the mob, detective."

Laney interrupted the conversation. "And like you said," she told Greene, "If it really was the Mafia, Reese would be dead."

Reese grabbed one of Laney's hands and squeezed tight. "Yeah!" he said with emphasis. "What's up with that?"

Greene looked to Belzinger.

Belzinger said, "She makes a good point."

CHAPTER

22

"THERE WAS A REPORTED shooting at the Fairfield Houses in Brooklyn early this morning," the radio newscaster said. "Detectives were on the scene just a few minutes after the incident and report that no one was injured. Ten-ten WINS has learned that the likely intended victim, Reese Waters, was a cellmate of a man murdered just a few days ago in Fort Hamilton Park in Brooklyn, Peter Rizzo."

Mauro's first response after learning that the old man had fed him a hot target was anger. If he had known that the guy he had shot at the night before was Peter Rizzo's cellmate, he not only would've contracted the work to Tommy Burns, he also would've charged the old bastard an extra twenty grand for the effort.

His next thought on the subject was that his botched job could be a blessing in disguise. Learning that Reese Waters had been Peter Rizzo's cellmate gave him newfound leverage for renegotiation. Mauro could now turn standing around in the cold waiting for workers to arrive at a construction site into a no-show job. He also could impress on the old man how all this raised his expectations regarding cash compensation.

Mauro was carrying half a dozen of Tommy Burns's prepaid cell phones. He was supposed to call Barrett before heading up to Westchester. He decided to drive up without warning the cheap bastard instead.

✦ ✦ ✦

Alex Dale Barrett poured himself a glass of ginger ale from an eight-ounce bottle and squeezed a wedge of lemon over the glass. He yawned at himself in the wall mirror to his right and sipped the soda. He had just finished having sex with his girlfriend, Christine Molloy, a forty-five-year-old diner waitress from Croton-on-Hudson. Alex was thirty-eight years old, a little paunchy since he'd stopped smoking, and showing his first serious signs of balding. He turned his head from side to side in the mirror as he searched for new signs of hair loss.

"Yikes, it's cold in here!" Christine yelled from the bathroom doorway.

Shivering, she pulled a bathrobe around her shoulders and sprinted across the hotel room to jump into bed. Alex wasn't prepared for the gymnastics and spilled some of his soda on his chest.

"Sheee-it," he said. "Are you crazy?"

Christine quickly dabbed at the soda spill with a napkin. She dispensed with the napkin and began to lick his chest. Alex pulled away.

"Christ," he said. "Take a Valium or something. I need some time here."

Christine bit her lower lip to shape her best seductive smile. She was still attractive despite the hard life she'd led. Except for a few blotches of cellulite on the backs of her legs and rump, some stretch marks around her nipples, and a few faint acne scars, she continued to turn heads, especially when her very large breasts were held together with a bra.

Licking her lips as she spoke, she told Alex, "I was hoping to speed your trip, baby."

Alex sat up in the bed and looked at his watch. "I'm supposed to meet my father today for lunch. I blew him off the last few days."

"The old miser," Christine said. "Guess who's buying?"

"He'll pay if I let him take me," Alex said. "Some cheap buffet or one of the vendor wagons on the street, or the Entennman's factory on Route Nine. I hate when he does that." He tapped at the paunch his stomach had become. "I'm gaining enough without that shit."

"Then you take him to lunch," Christine suggested. "Back to my diner. I'll serve you both and we can really piss him off."

"Yeah, right," Alex said. "I don't think so."

Christine reached for his crotch.

Alex pushed her hand away. "Would you give it a break a minute?"

Christine lit a cigarette. She said, "Debbie, the day cashier, said she saw your father pocketing the cookies at the register; whole handfuls at a time, she said."

Alex took another sip of his soda. "Yeah, so? You think that's a scoop? He's up to something, the old man. Something to do with my sister."

Christine wrinkled her nose at the mention of Alex's sister. "Oh, missy prissy, her shit don't stink, does it?"

"I know they talk during the week. Janice calls him from work. And my father mentioned her a few times the last two weeks in connection with Peter, her ex-husband. And then the guy got killed soon as he was out of jail. And my father's being real secretive again. I know he's been in and out of the city a lot lately. And out to Jersey, too."

Alex stopped to inhale the smoke from Christine's cigarette. "And I don't trust either one of them," he said before grabbing the cigarette to steal a drag.

"You can have it, you want."

Alex quickly handed the cigarette back. "No, no way. I shouldn't have done that. He can smell it on me. He'll break my balls all day if he smells smoke on me."

Christine took a last drag on the cigarette and crushed it in the ashtray.

"Anyway, I have to see him this afternoon," Alex said. "Then I'm off to the site, and I guess I'll have to show up for my anniversary dinner tomorrow night."

"What you get her?" Christine asked.

"Earrings."

Christine adjusted her breasts underneath her robe. "Don't forget the flowers. A woman expects flowers on her anniversary."

"Right."

"Will I see you tomorrow?"

"I'm not sure. I haven't thought about it yet."

"You can meet me at the diner after lunch. I get a break at two."

Alex was lost in thought. "Huh?"

"We can do it in the old office."

Now he was confused.

Christine let him see some more of her breasts. "In the old office, hon. Where I used to, you know . . ." She pushed her left cheek out with her tongue as she guided a fist toward the opposite side of her face.

Alex looked stunned.

"What?" Christine asked.

Alex slowly opened his eyes wider.

"Whaaaaaat?" she repeated, drawing it out.

"My father ever saw you do that," he said, "he'd pull a gun and shoot you. Right on the spot, he'd shoot you dead."

Christine rolled her eyes. "Which is why I wouldn't even consider giving him head, honey, the miserable curmudgeon."

CHAPTER

23

REESE MANAGED TO FALL asleep for a few hours before he had to get up for his mother's funeral Mass. He spent time with the family photo album and cried as he looked at pictures of his parents.

A recurring nightmare he lived with while in prison, and one that he'd kept to himself, involved losing his mother before he was released. Most times, the dream came as a result of conversations about family with Peter. The first time he learned that Peter had never had family visit him even once in Fishkill, Reese dreamed his mother had died in a fire. Another time, after he discovered Peter's birthday had come and gone without so much as a card from home, Reese dreamed that his mother was lost in the woods alone.

He set the photo album down when he felt angry again. He was still stunned from the sudden loss of his mother. All he could think about were his private deals with God so long ago.

After two cups of coffee, Reese noticed that the police had left a patrol car parked in front of the apartment building. The detectives had said they would call again as soon as they knew something, but Reese wasn't so sure he wasn't a suspect himself. At least that's the way the brother detective made him feel.

Laney had stayed the night and was cleaning in the kitchen. She told him he was right to be cautious about the police. "With all that's gone on in this city," she said, "a black man has to be especially careful."

"Not to mention one with a prison record," Reese said.

He was standing at the living room window. He could see the exhaust from the patrol car.

"You should talk to a lawyer, man," Laney said. "The brother detective was especially suspicious of you, I think."

"Or it was a good-cop, bad-cop routine," Reese said. "I'm not sure it wasn't."

"He wasn't playing with you," Laney said. "He didn't believe you."

"He's a cop and I'm a bad guy just out of the joint."

Laney made a face.

"What?" Reese asked.

"You're being a little too considerate to these people," she said. "You're innocent. Somebody shot through the damn door last night. I was here with you. We were both scared to death. Don't make excuses for that detective."

Here she was, being contrary again. Reese had to grin.

"What's so funny?" she asked.

"You're a tough one," he said.

Laney set her hands on her hips. "One of us better be."

✦ ✦ ✦

Reese's first experience with death had come when his father died at a construction job. Reese was fifteen and had just come home from working his paper route. His mother was crying fitfully at the kitchen table. She hugged Reese hard when she told him his father was dead. It was a moment he would never forget, how her voice had cracked from the raw emotion behind those five painful words. "Oh, Reese. Your daddy died."

It was the same for him later, inside the church. Reese could barely contain his emotions. Laney stood alongside him and pointed out Elle's church friends. An administrator from the hospital where his mother used to visit with AIDS patients said a few words. Reese broke down and sobbed during the speech.

Elle had requested that her ashes be spread on the small stretch of lawn behind Saint Lawrence, even though it was against the law. Father Ebbs performed the honors privately for Reese and Laney once they were alone. The anger rose in Reese again, and his body was tense until he sobbed openly. He unconsciously made the sign of the cross when they were ready to leave.

When they returned to the apartment, Vincent Coleman was waiting outside the building. He was holding a bouquet of flowers. The two men exchanged a heartfelt hug on the street.

"I'm real sorry," Coleman told Reese.

"Thank you," Reese said.

They went inside the apartment, and Laney put on a fresh pot of coffee. Reese and Coleman sat in the living room. Reese told his old friend what had happened the night before.

"That why the car is outside," Coleman asked, "from last night?"

"For my protection," Reese said.

"They know anything?"

Reese smirked. "One of them thinks I did it, shot through my own door."

"Say what? One of the cops thinks that?"

"The brother does," Laney said. She took a seat next to Coleman on the couch. "I'm not sure about the woman but the brother detective is definitely suspicious of Reese."

"Suspicious of what?" Coleman asked. "The man was nearly killed last night."

"I'm not sure he believes me," Reese said.

"Then that's some bullshit," Coleman said. "NYPD bullshit."

Reese closed his eyes and saw his mother again. He saw her sunken eye and remembered kissing her cold forehead. He saw her ashes being spread. He opened his eyes, saw her recliner, and punched the arm of the couch hard.

"I can hang around, you need me," Coleman said.

Reese leaned forward and rubbed his temples.

"Reese?" Coleman said.

He had closed his eyes again. This time he was seeing Peter in a casket. He felt his teeth clench.

"Reese?"

Reese punched the couch again. "The man did two years, his family didn't come to see him once!" he yelled. "He did time and they didn't come once!"

Coleman looked to Laney. Laney held a finger to her lips.

Reese said, "He did the right thing and that bitch had him killed!"

Reese pounded the couch with his right fist until he was exhausted. He let his body slump on the couch and caught his breath. He apologized when he was calm.

Coleman noticed the empty bottle of Dewar's on the floor alongside the kitchen garbage pail. "You kill that?" he asked.

"Huh?" Reese said. He looked back at the bottle.

"I'm impressed," Coleman said. "It's not the same as a wine cooler, Dewar's."

"You going?" Reese asked.

"Unless you need me to stick around."

"Go on, I'm fine."

Reese stood up to exchange another hug with Coleman. Laney let him out of the apartment.

Reese still felt cheated. He had spent less than two days with his mother before she was gone. He wanted to scream out at the God Elle Waters had worshiped with so much of her energy.

How could God take her now?

And what about Peter? How could God put the man through two years of prison just to kill him the day he gets out?

Laney was watching him in silence. She could see his rage building again. "You okay?" she asked after a while.

"Not really, no," Reese said.

"What is it?"

Reese felt his teeth clenching again and didn't respond.

"The cremation?"

"No," he said. He could feel his right hand ball into a fist.

"You can still bury the urn. Father Ebbs said you can put it where he spread the ashes."

"It's not that," Reese whispered.

"What then? What is it?"

"Peter."

"Peter's gone, Reese. You have to let it go."

He looked up and glared at Laney.

"He's with God now," she said.

"He's in a morgue in Brooklyn is where he is."

Laney didn't respond.

"I can't let it go," he said. "I can't leave it like this."

"You have to, man. For your own sake."

"Bullshit. I'm going to do the right thing. I'm going to get his money."

CHAPTER

24

THEY WERE ON THEIR way to talk with Janice Barrett again. Greene was sipping coffee as he drove. Belzinger was eating a sesame bagel stuffed with cream cheese. She wiped her mouth with a napkin after each bite she took.

They had argued about Reese Waters as soon as Greene picked her up. Belzinger was convinced the ex-convict was telling the truth. Greene thought he was lying through his teeth. Both detectives were silent as Greene drove across the Brooklyn Bridge into Manhattan.

As he turned onto the ramp for the FDR Drive, Greene said, "The least you can do is cut some wind or belch or something. Anything to end this impasse."

"Women don't fart," Belzinger said.

"Even bisexual women?"

"Only sometimes."

Greene hit the accelerator and they were on the FDR heading north. "I don't want to fight you on this," he said.

Belzinger was watching the fast-flowing water of the East River. "You can't tell me you believe the bus driver is involved in Rizzo's murder."

"I'm telling you the man just got out of jail for a reason. That you shouldn't be too sold on his story."

"And I'm thinking there's a lot more to the Janice Barrett angle. Aside from her sparkling personality, I mean."

"You think she killed her ex-husband?"

"I think she might've had something to do with it."

"She's a bitch, I'll give you that, but that doesn't mean she had the guy whacked. She seems too smart for that."

"Unless she thinks she's smart enough to get away with it."

"You think she went after the bus driver, too? She isn't that smart or cocky."

"I don't know. Those bullet holes in the door were pretty convincing to me."

"And the man already told us one lie. He did talk to your girl."

"And he admitted it."

"Maybe because he was afraid Janice Barrett would admit it first."

Belzinger turned to her partner. "And why's that? Because he shot through his own door?"

"You see the man who shot at them?"

"Nobody saw him."

"Exactly."

Belzinger faced front again. "That doesn't mean it was Reese Waters."

"Doesn't mean it wasn't."

◆ ◆ ◆

"I was working the B-thirty-five," Reese said. "I had the pick based on seniority so I took the ten on thirty-five. Tenth bus out of the depot after midnight. I started at four in the morning. My first break came at eight-thirty. I'm back in the swing room, my cousin shows up with an emergency. Needs me to drive a Monte Carlo from in front of the depot to Church and Nostrand. He's all bug-eyed about it, tells me it's an emergency, he's gonna lose his job if he don't get both cars to some dealership."

Reese stopped to wet his lips. He was walking Laney to the junior high school in Starrett City. It was cold and windy. Laney was bundled up with earmuffs, a scarf, and heavy mittens. Reese wore his heaviest winter coat, a black skullcap, leather gloves, and sunglasses. Laney's eyes began to tear from the wind. Reese handed her his glasses.

"Thank you," she said.

"Ronnie was a slick guy," Reese continued. "Always was. I was wise to most of his tricks but not what I got myself into that day."

"The car was stolen," Laney said.

"Both cars. Except it was a scam being run from one of the police precincts. Admin people there working with a few cops and some chop shops. They have internal affairs and the FBI watching them the last six months or something. My cousin picks these people to do business with."

Laney covered her mouth to shield a grin.

"You have no idea," Reese said. He tried to light a cigarette, but the wind was too strong. He fit it back into the pack.

"Anyway, Ronnie had a friend was supposed to drive the car he asked me to take. Ronnie thought the dude was sick but the police had already picked him up. He drove both stolen cars to the depot, one after the other, but he was running late and asked me to take the one his friend was supposed to have. I'm still in my uniform, mind you. I'm on break. But at this point, with all the people involved at the precinct already, cops and all, they just assume I'm one of the regular crew out ripping cars off."

Laney couldn't suppress a smile. "I'm sorry," she said.

Reese smiled with her. "It is pretty funny, you think about it. Sometimes, anyway."

"So they arrested you, too."

"I didn't drive but ten feet from the depot. Lights flashing, cars surrounding me. Two dudes with guns drawn, one wearing an FBI jacket. I about shit my pants. Excuse me."

Laney was laughing now. "I was picturing it, what you said."

When she got herself calmed a bit, Reese continued.

"Ronnie somehow manages to avoid the roadblock and takes off about eighty miles an hour."

"Oh, no," Laney said, trying to hold it together. "Your mother said he had an accident."

"Got himself killed is what he did. Killed my alibi, too. He runs his stolen car head-on into another thirty-five bus run, the number twelve on thirty-five."

Laney couldn't help it. She was crying from laughing.

CHAPTER

25

THEY ATE APPLE TURNOVERS in Michael Barrett's SUV. The old man started on his second turnover after sipping coffee from his thermos cup.

"You'd save yourself a lot of money if you spent more time at your sites," he told his son.

Alex Barrett was picking at the icing on his turnover. "I have things to take care of," he said. "Marissa, I have to bring her to school Tuesdays and Wednesdays."

"She could take the bus you're already paying for in taxes."

"She doesn't like the bus. The kids call it the 'loser cruiser.'"

Michael Barrett licked at the apple filling in his turnover. "You're paying for the bus and you're losing money not supervising your construction sites," he said. "Your bulldozer operator showed up forty minutes late the other day. Then it took him another fifteen minutes to get settled. At forty-five dollars an hour, that'll add up fast."

Alex looked away from his father. "So, I'll tack it on the price of the house."

"That's not the point. It's a good time right now. You should make the best of it. Real estate is fickle. It won't stay good like this forever."

"Right," Alex said with no enthusiasm. He was watching a group of high school girls outside a delicatessen.

"Yeah, well, the way you spend, you better start paying more attention to your business than young girls."

Alex closed his eyes. "Jesus Christ," he said.

"Sorry to bore you."

Alex turned to his father. "What is it you want with me today? You have something to say, so say it. We both don't want to be here, right?"

Michael turned away from his son. He bit into a piece of the turnover and wiped his mouth with a paper napkin. "I hired somebody to supervise your sites," he finally said.

"Excuse me?"

"I put him on your payroll for now, at the Yorktown site, but that was to clear him with the county board. I'll be pulling him off there for the lot in Peekskill in a few weeks. His name is Johnny Mauro."

Alex looked askance at his father.

"What?" Michael said. "What's the problem? It's not like you can't use him."

"This one of your New Jersey friends?"

Michael avoided eye contact with his son. "What's the difference?"

"I'm curious," Alex said. "Humor me."

"It's for one of my friends from New Jersey, yes."

"The one you tied up all that money with, right? Just so I couldn't borrow off it for my own projects."

"Or maybe it was so you couldn't buy another new pickup you don't need. Or so you don't build another sauna you won't use. Or so your wife doesn't go out and buy another new living room set you already own."

"Or maybe it was to pay back the mob for whacking Peter Rizzo," Alex said.

Michael turned in his seat. "I hope you're not walking around repeating that bullshit," he said. "I hope to Christ you're not."

"So that's it. This Mauro guy killed Peter."

"No, that's not it. Like usual, you don't know what you're talking about. I had nothing to do with that. That was from something that happened in prison. He was stabbed in there and they finished the job when he got out. I had Doug Johnson look into it for me."

"Yeah, well, maybe Doug should give the New York City police a call, he figured it out so fast."

"Maybe you should watch your mouth."

Alex exaggerated a yawn as he glanced at his watch. "Speaking of my construction sites, I need to get there before somebody takes an extra few minutes to piss."

Michael started the engine. "You think you have it all figured out," he said. "But you don't. You don't have a clue."

◆ ◆ ◆

Mauro was lost in a town called Chappaqua. When he stopped at a gas station there, an attendant gave him directions to Yorktown Heights. The attendant also told Mauro that former president Bill Clinton had moved to Chappaqua because his wife needed a New York address to run for senator. Mauro was impressed.

"They can do that kind of stuff, move around like that?" he asked the attendant.

"I guess so," the attendant said. "Especially they got money. Look at O.J."

Mauro wasn't sure what the connection was, but when the attendant started talking about how high the price of owning a home in Westchester had gone, he paid more attention.

"One year houses went up to half a mill a unit, average," the attendant said. "Something like a fifty-thousand-dollar jump over one year, you can believe it. I'm lucky to afford the rent I'm paying now. I figure that'll all change too soon enough."

"So construction is still good up here?"

The attendant laughed. "Good? It's a lot better than good, mister, you own the property. It's like sitting on miniature oil wells."

"Miniature oil wells, huh?"

"You bought a house up here ten years ago for a quarter million, you kept it in decent shape, you can pro'bly sell it for a million and a half now. You tell me."

Mauro thought it was good luck that he had been lost and needed directions.

CHAPTER

26

EARLY ONE MORNING, AFTER the guards looking for contraband had tossed their cell, Peter told Reese, "You ever get into it again after you're out, go see my lawyer."

Legal fees had cost Reese more than half his life savings before he was forced to plead guilty. Sitting in prison had left him suspicious of lawyers.

"Rosenblatt is a genuine guy," Peter had said. "No bullshit. He's not in it for the money."

"Yeah, right," Reese had replied.

"I'm serious. Rosenblatt is one of a few people in this life I trust. He was straight up with me. He told me he could probably get me off if we went to trial. I wanted to plea."

It had been Peter's way. He had assaulted someone—the wrong guy, it turned out—and there were no mitigating circumstances. He had hit a guy, broken his jaw, and he shouldn't have. The fact that his lawyer might get him off was irrelevant.

Reese also had been guilty, but he really didn't know the car he had driven was stolen. Nobody within the legal system had cared much that it was a mistake. He had pled guilty to avoid a longer sentence. His lawyer had cost him almost four thousand dollars, after which it was good-bye and good luck, Mr. Waters.

Knowing Peter might've won his case had been frustrating to Reese. Getting into arguments over it had been worse. Peter would go on about doing the right thing. He could be relentless.

Today Reese was anxious to speak to Peter's lawyer. The police car was still parked in front of the apartment building. The detectives had advised Reese to stay indoors a few more days, but he was antsy sitting around the empty apartment. It was depressing without someone there.

His mind drifted back and forth between his mother and friend as he watched the clock. Laney hadn't been gone very long, and he missed her, too.

He was thinking he'd need legal advice sooner or later. He looked up Neve Rosenblatt's number in the Yellow Pages and jotted down the address.

◆ ◆ ◆

Belzinger flashed her badge at reception and asked the two women working the desk not to announce them. The receptionists grinned at each other.

They found their way down the hall and entered Janice's office without knocking. The junior partner was applying lipstick at the time. She was startled and gasped when the door opened.

"Sorry," Belzinger said. She pulled her notepad from her back pocket and sat in the same chair she'd used the other day. Greene took the chair alongside her.

Janice had started a cigarette before the detectives arrived. She took a drag on it now.

Belzinger looked up from her notebook and said, "Do you mind not smoking?"

"I'd rather not waste it," Janice said.

"It's against the law."

"It's my office."

"It's against the law," Belzinger repeated.

Janice cut off the tip of the cigarette with a scissors. "They're too expensive to waste," she told Greene.

Belzinger folded one leg over the other and sat at the ready, pen in hand. Janice was dressed in a smart dark suit. Her laptop was packed on her desk. She put away her lipstick and zippered her makeup bag.

"Can I ask a question?" Janice asked.

"Sure," Belzinger said.

"How did you get past reception?"

"We asked them not to announce us."

"I see," Janice said. She looked at her watch. "I have to give a presentation. Will this take long? Is it important?"

"Why we're here," Belzinger said. She took her time checking her notes.

Janice fidgeted until she looked at the time again. "Detective?"

"Why didn't you tell us about your conversation with your ex-husband's cellmate?" Belzinger asked. "I believe you were walking your dog at the time?"

Janice affected a smile that quickly turned to a smirk. She remained silent.

"Ms. Barrett?"

"I forgot," Janice said. "And I didn't know he was Peter's cellmate. If I did, I would've been more frightened."

"You forgot you met with him or you forgot to mention it?"

"Both. He also called me the night Peter was killed."

"And?" Greene asked.

"And nothing. I hung up on him."

"You're sure it was him?" Belzinger asked.

Janice shrugged.

"Was it a prearranged meeting when you met?" Greene interjected.

Janice turned to him. "Excuse me?"

"Did you plan on meeting Reese Waters?" Belzinger asked.

"No. I never saw him before in my life. I just said I didn't —"

"I see," Belzinger said. She started drawing boxes in her notebook.

Janice fidgeted again. "Is there anything else?" she asked Greene.

Belzinger held up a hand as she again acted as if she were referring to her notes.

"I really do have a presentation to give," Janice said.

"Can you tell me some more about the conversation?" Belzinger asked. "The one with Reese Waters, the man you didn't know was your husband's cellmate."

Janice huffed. "I can't remember."

"Try," Belzinger insisted.

"I have an appointment," said Janice, fully annoyed now. "I don't have time for this."

"What time is your presentation over?"

"I don't know," Janice said through a moan. "Four, five o'clock or so, maybe later."

Belzinger drew a smiley face in her notebook. "Okay, then," she said as she pulled her card from a holder in the notebook. "Call me as soon as you're finished. You can meet us at one of the precincts here in Manhattan afterward. Whichever precinct is convenient."

Belzinger was getting up from her chair when Janice said, "Look, all the guy said was he had a message from Peter about the money. He wanted his money and the interest it had accumulated while he was in prison. I told the guy I didn't owe Peter a dime. Then I found out later that Peter was killed the night before."

"Did he harass you?" Belzinger asked. "You said he called."

"Huh? No, not really. I think he was trying for Peter's money."

"How did you leave off with him?"

Janice huffed again. "I told him I didn't owe Peter anything. That was it."

Belzinger took her time again. A second before Janice was about to stand, Belzinger asked, "Did you steal your husband's money?"

"I always felt sorry about that," Janice said with no emotion. "I shouldn't have agreed to the amount we discussed before going to the lawyer. I felt sorry for him at the time. Then I realized it was a mistake, the figure I agreed to. It was too high. I didn't steal his money."

"What about his going to prison?"

"That was all his fault. Even his lawyer said he shouldn't have pled the case. He would've been better off fighting it first."

"It seems to me you could've stopped everything that happened."

Janice pointed to her watch. "I really don't have time for this now, a lecture."

"Did you have your husband killed?" Belzinger asked.

"Of course not."

"Did you send somebody to kill Reese Waters?"

"What? No. Why, did something happen to him now?"

The women stared at each other.

"Is there anything else?" Janice finally asked.

"Unless you can explain why we should believe you," Belzinger said, "I guess not. Not right now."

CHAPTER

27

MAURO EVENTUALLY FOUND MICHAEL Barrett at the construction site in Yorktown Heights. When he stood alongside the SUV, Mauro noticed that the old man was eating apple turnovers again.

"Don't you get tired of those?" he asked.

The old man licked frosting off his fingers. "I guess you opted for plan B last night."

"I guess you forgot to mention who the guy was."

"What's the difference?"

"About twenty grand."

Barrett contorted his face. "Maybe in your dreams."

Mauro stared until he had the old man's attention.

"What?" Barrett asked. "You're not serious, I hope."

"The guy was hot," Mauro said. "He just got out the joint the other day. His partner was whacked the day before. You involved with that, too?"

"Not at all. Of course not."

"Just a coincidence, huh?"

"I guess so."

"Yeah, well, I'll assume it wasn't. I'll also assume you're a smart fuck thought he could take me for a dumbski going after this guy last night. Like I need that kind of pressure, a police investigation."

"I hope you're not really expecting more money for a job not done."

Mauro cocked his head to one side. "You're a fuckin' comedian, that it?"

Barrett didn't answer.

"Yeah, I expect more money," Mauro said, "and you'll pay it, too. A lot more."

"You think so?"

Mauro was glaring into the old man's eyes now. "I'm pretty fucking sure, yeah."

Barrett tried to return the stare but couldn't. "You want to come back in the morning? I have to see a few people on the county board about your work permit, and I need to head up to Poughkeepsie before five. I can take you to meet my son in the morning."

"Why can't I tag along now and get it over with?"

"Technically, you're not allowed on the construction sites without the permit first."

"I'm gonna wanna talk with our friend in Jersey," Mauro said. "'Specially if you think we're all even after last night."

"Call who you want," Barrett said, "but you'll have to come back tomorrow. Or you can spend the night up here if you want. Go to a movie or something and take a room someplace. We can get this other thing done in the morning."

Mauro thought about it a moment. "I'm still calling our friend," he said.

"That's your business. There's a movie theater straight up the road about five miles. A Motel Six another mile past that."

"The Motel Six have a bar?"

"I would think so, yeah. There are plenty around if they don't."

"You picking up the tab on this night in the woods?"

"You're the one didn't call," said Barrett, pointing his finger. "You were supposed to, remember? I could've told you to drive up tomorrow but you didn't call."

"You don't like reaching into your pockets much, do you?"

"Not when I already paid for something I didn't get."

Mauro clenched his teeth and decided to let it go for now. "What time we meeting tomorrow?"

"How's six-thirty? Call my cell at six and I'll tell you where to go."

"That's a little early, ain't it?"

Barrett picked up another apple turnover. "That's the business."

"Speaking of cell phones, I got some prepaids I'm looking to move," Mauro said. "They come with a hundred hours of prepaid calls, like calling cards. You use them up and toss the phone afterward. I'm looking for eighty apiece but you can have them for seventy-five and charge whatever you want. They go for at least a buck apiece legit, what they're programmed for."

"Not interested," Barrett said.

"Of course you're not."

Barrett bit into his turnover. Mauro pointed at the cake. "Seriously," he said, "don't those make you sick after a while?"

Barrett ignored the question as he shifted into gear.

◆　◆　◆

Tommy Burns pulled into the lot alongside the Armory Restaurant in Perth Amboy and parked so he was facing the water. Tony Gangi was waiting for him outside the restaurant's side entrance. The two men walked along the water toward the Raritan Yacht Club.

"What's up?" Gangi asked.

Burns stopped to light a cigarette. He turned his back to the wind coming off the water and cupped his hands around a lighter.

"A mutual friend," Burns said after lighting the cigarette. "He come to me the other day about a piece he claims he needed."

Gangi continued walking. He waited for more. "This a quiz?"

"It's purely self-interest," Burns said. "I'm wondering was I cut out. I'm wondering if you know about it."

Gangi looked over his shoulder at the familiar blue van parked on Water Street. "Since when I have to clear things with you?"

"Never," Burns said. "Unless I did something wrong I don't know about."

"You telling me you think Johnny Mauro took on something you should've been given?"

"If the guy shot through a door and missed his mark, I am. If you wanted something done right was botched."

"Everybody's a greedy fuck these days, huh?" Gangi said.

Burns said, "Work is scarce enough without guys don't know what they're doing taking on jobs."

Gangi sneezed.

"Bless," Burns said.

Gangi sneezed again. "Fuck me," he said, then wiped his nose with a handkerchief.

Burns said, "All I'm saying is one day I'm paid for a job well done and the next thing I know, the guy brokered the work is asking me to get him a piece, he claims, to protect himself. Then I read in the papers how a guy shoots through a door at a guy was the cellmate of the guy I took care of a few days earlier. I'm thinking if I was cut out, you'd know about it. Or did our mutual friend cut me out?"

Gangi turned toward the van again and waved at Burns to keep walking. "You should take this up with Mauro," he said, "because I'm not interested in the story, tell you the truth. Not on your account or his."

"I'm asking was it sanctioned? Because if it was and our friend missed, I can take care of both problems. One for free, if the guy was supposed to broker through me inna first place. He did that, cut me out, it'd be my pleasure."

Gangi stopped with his back to the van. He waited for Burns's full attention. "It was sanctioned, I wouldn't tell you anyway," he said. "And that's all you need to know."

CHAPTER

28

REESE WAS STILL NERVOUS about the police. Laney had convinced him he should be. He stood outside Neve Rosenblatt's office on Eastern Parkway a few minutes before three o'clock. He was still deciding whether to take it further.

Thunder cracked loudly as rain began to pour from the dark sky. Reese reached into his front pants pocket and touched his Saint Jude statue. Another boom of thunder sent him hustling inside the law office.

Ten minutes later he was sitting across from the man who had represented Peter.

"You were shot at?" the attorney asked.

Reese explained everything leading up to the shooting. He also explained how he was afraid the police thought he had something to do with Peter's murder.

"They have a patrol car outside my mother's building," he told Rosenblatt. "They advised me to stay inside but I couldn't stand it anymore. I'm not sure if they're trying to play me or protect me."

The lawyer was seated behind his desk. He moved up on his chair. "And your mother died," he said. "Again, I'm very sorry."

"Thank you," Reese said.

"He never should've gone away. You know that, don't you? Peter never should have done time."

"The man was principled like nobody I ever met."

"Obviously, you were a good friend to him."

"He saved my life," Reese said. "We were good for each other. We had each other's back. The last couple of weeks before we got out, though, I started to worry about him. I think he might've been afraid to come out. Like maybe he knew something."

"You think she threatened him?"

"I don't know. He was upset about the money. The closer we came to getting out, the more of an issue it became. He wasn't going to let it go."

Rosenblatt bit his lower lip. "I asked him once if he wanted me to come up and visit. I thought if we stayed in touch, he might change his mind and I might appeal. At least I could've challenged their divorce. Then it would've been in the court's hands."

"I think Peter felt safe inside. I think he adapted. He knew coming out would put it all back in his face, what she did to him."

"It's a tragedy, is what it is, the shit that woman put him through," Rosenblatt said. He moved back on his chair. "And you should be home grieving, 'for both of your losses."

"I'm through grieving," Reese said. "Somebody is trying to kill me. I'm not waiting for it to happen. I've been waiting for things to happen to me my entire life."

"Right now, if somebody is trying to kill you, it might be safer to grieve."

"I'm tired of playing it safe. I need to get in control of my own shit."

"There may be things in motion now that are out of your sphere of influence, Reese. You should think about the consequences."

"I could do nothing and be a better target next time. I could do that."

Rosenblatt went silent.

Reese said, "A friend thought I should talk to you because of this thing with the police, so I came. Peter said you were a good man. I'm sure you are. I want to bury my friend. I owe him that. I intend to get it done before the city does it for me, except his family, his piece-of-work brother, won't take my calls. He hung up on me twice already."

Rosenblatt tapped his pen on a legal pad. "He once told me he wouldn't be able to get his family into court if we went to trial."

"Sounds about right," Reese said.

"Can I do anything? Do you want me to call?"

"I'm going back there today. I almost went two nights ago but decided to wait. I'll bury Peter. I don't see why they wouldn't let me."

"Some people . . ." Rosenblatt said.

A long silence ensued. Rosenblatt seemed lost in thought.

"What is it?" Reese asked.

Rosenblatt moved up on his chair. "I called the police and told them where to look for certain information that might be mob-related. Janice Barrett's family was in the construction business in upstate New York. Her father built some big-shot Mafioso's home a few years back. I think they've been in bed before, the Barrett family and the mob. I think they still do business together. They could've worked something out regarding Peter. I have no idea why they would want you, though."

"The woman is evil," Reese asked.

"I agree. And some people can't bear the thought of losing. The money she kept from Peter might represent more than the face value." Rosenblatt set the legal pad on his lap and said, "Tell me about your conversation with her again. You approached her, right?"

"I tried," Reese said.

"You're lucky she didn't yell 'rape!'" Rosenblatt said without looking up from the pad. He made a note on the pad. "Then what?"

"She was curious who I was. She was looking around."

"Scared shitless, probably. Good, she deserves it."

"She said she didn't owe Peter anything."

"But we know better."

"She tried to act tough. She likes to stare people down."

"Maybe she knew he was dead."

"She was scared when I first mentioned his name, but she grew cocky fast enough. I thought about it the next day. That woman knew something."

"Okay, let's assume so. What else?"

"She kind of dared me. A cop car pulled up off the corner and she told me to tell Peter to go fuck himself."

Rosenblatt looked up from his notes. "Did you contact her again?"

"No," Reese lied.

"Good. And you told the police this, right?"

"Not the first time. Last night."

"Why didn't you mention it the first time, your meeting with her?"

Reese was embarrassed. "I was afraid to tell them."

"Sometimes it's smart to be afraid," Rosenblatt said. He set his legal pad on the desk and moved up in his chair again. "And sometimes the math is simpler than we make it," he added as he listed off his fingers. "Her family definitely had ties to the mob and at least one Mafioso big shot. Peter was almost killed inside prison, right? He was definitely killed by a professional the day he got out. It probably adds up to the mob."

Reese said, "What happened inside, at Fishkill, when Peter was stabbed, that was the mob, guys around the mob, but that was a long time ago."

"And they would've got him in Fishkill if they were really after him," Rosenblatt said. "You were both in protective custody, but how protective was it really?"

"We were outside the general population."

"You were in a cellblock with others in the same boat. Some of those came in after you and Peter. They could've been plants just as easily, if the hard guys really wanted you."

"You're saying her family, then? Because of the connections?"

Rosenblatt pointed at the windows in his office. "The saying out there is that everybody knows somebody. Imagine you're in the construction business for thirty years or so and very successful at it. That's a traditional mob stronghold, construction, without building a Mafioso's house. Chances are . . ." He let his thought trail off.

"He said they were cold, her family," Reese said. "Emotionless, Peter called them. He said it was like eating dinner with mannequins whenever they got together."

"Forget them for now. How are you set with your parole officer? You find work yet?"

Reese told the attorney about filing an application with a cab company, but didn't mention the offer from Mufasa's Nation of Islam connections.

Rosenblatt took notes. "Let me see what I can do and I'll give you a call next week sometime. Maybe I can find something for you to do here, serving papers or something. At least speak up for you with your parole officer."

"I appreciate it," Reese said.

"In the meantime, I think you should listen to the police on this, Reese, whether you're a suspect or not. Stay home. There's no point in provoking trouble."

"I'm not staying locked inside that apartment. I just spent two years inside a cell and wasn't home a few days before my mother died. I'm not locking myself down."

"Just don't look for trouble," Rosenblatt said. "Or I can't help you. Nobody can."

CHAPTER

29

"CAN WE TALK?" MAURO asked Fat Tony Gangi.

"Sparingly," Gangi said.

Mauro was using one of Tommy Burns's prepaid cell phones in the parking lot outside a local bar in Elmsford, New York. He stood with his back facing Route 9-A for better reception.

"This *fanuke* upstate had me go after a hot guy last night without telling me," Mauro said. "I'm not happy about that."

"Yeah, he already called complaining about you," Gangi said. "I feel like a referee. I'm not happy about that."

Mauro glanced over his shoulder when a pickup pulled into the lot a dozen yards away. He turned away and started to lose reception.

"Hello?" Gangi said.

"Yeah," Mauro said, his back to the road again. "I'm just calling to fill you in. The situation requires change. I'm not happy with it, and I'm negotiating up. I already told him."

"Yeah, and he told me and so did somebody else. And now you're telling me again. You feel you covered enough bases yet, or you wanna call CNN, too?"

Mauro was confused. "Somebody else who?"

"What's the difference? I don't need to hear any of it."

"Just so long's there's no problem," Mauro said.

"Hey, it wasn't my problem to start with. Keep it between yourselves."

"Right."

Gangi killed the connection first. Mauro turned the power off on his cell phone. "Yeah," he said, "and thanks a lot. You fat fuck."

◆ ◆ ◆

The first time Michael Barrett worked with mobsters was more than twenty years ago, when he learned that his accountant had defrauded him of more than sixty thousand dollars. It was a quick and profitable exchange. Michael opened and operated a drywall company for a Westchester Mafioso. His accountant disappeared and was never heard from again.

Over time, Michael's association with the mob ebbed and flowed according to circumstance. When he needed them, Michael provided the mob with a temporary business where they could launder money, pad construction bills for materials and labor, and put friends on legitimate workbooks. When they needed him, the envelopes were stuffed with extra cash.

Michael's arrangement had always been based on maintaining minimal contact with underworld figures. The less he had to do with them, the better off their business ventures. It was a relationship that had worked well until now.

Lately, Michael had been thinking about retiring. He was also anxious to sever his ties to organized crime. His association with the Vignieri crime family had become dangerous. The key figure he was working with had become a regular feature in the daily newspapers. Jimmy Valentine was expected to be indicted on federal RICO statutes, and Michael wasn't so sure the Mafioso wouldn't cut a deal to stay out of jail.

Nor would it help if an investigation turned up the two-time loser the Vignieris had sent him to put to work, Johnny Mauro.

As soon as he learned that Reese Waters was still alive, Michael was anxious to erase a bad mistake. Mauro wasn't the type to go away on his own. The gangster had already implied that he wanted more money for a job he hadn't completed. Michael wasn't about to be extorted by a two-bit thug.

He knew he had to get rid of Mauro. He also knew that he would need permission before he did anything to facilitate resolving the problem. He had worked with the Vignieri people long enough to understand the silly protocol. There were chains of command and rules and procedures to follow to getting things done.

As he filled the SUV tank with economy gas, Michael was thinking it was convenient having Mauro nearby overnight. If all went well, he could take care of things early enough in the morning to salvage the rest of his day. Maybe the mobster was carrying enough cash to pay for the anniversary dinner the next night.

✦ ✦ ✦

Reese took the B-63 to Bay Ridge. He made it to Grace Rizzo's apartment in just under an hour. He was surprised when he found her doing a crossword puzzle.

"Ma'am, I'm a friend of Peter's," Reese told her at the apartment door. "I'd like to take care of his burial."

Grace Rizzo wore a pink robe and slippers. She was holding the crossword book and a pen.

"Where do you know Peter from?" she asked, her manner curt, unwelcoming.

Reese hesitated. "The penitentiary, ma'am."

"You were there, too?"

"Yes, ma'am."

"You're the friend?"

"I was his cellmate, ma'am. Yes."

"You spoke to my younger son, right?"

"Yes, ma'am."

"We can't afford to bury Peter."

Reese remained silent.

Grace Rizzo looked past Reese down the stairs. "Paul is on his way over here now," she said. "What do you want?"

"I need a release for Peter's body. I need you to sign something giving me permission to bury him."

The door at the bottom of the stairway opened. Reese could hear footsteps on the stairs. He turned and saw a younger version of Peter except for the portly build and baldness.

"Paul?" Reese asked as the bald man approached the top of the stairs.

"Who're you?"

"He's the one who called," Grace Rizzo told her younger son.

"Wait here," Paul said as he ushered his mother back inside the apartment. He left the door open but quickly returned to block the doorway. "What is it you want?"

Reese did his best to avoid a confrontation. "I was telling your mother just now," he said.

"Tell me."

Reese took a deep breath and continued to avoid eye contact with Paul Rizzo. "I just want to bury your brother. Maybe cremate him, if the burial is too expensive."

"We're not paying for it."

"I understand that," Reese said. "But the city says I need permission from the family to take possession of the body."

"Go 'head. You have my permission."

He stepped back inside the apartment and started to close the door when Reese used a foot to block it. "I need something in writing," he said. "I have to present the morgue with a notarized statement that you're releasing your brother's body."

Paul peered back at his mother in the kitchen and slammed the doorframe. "The fuck can't even die without making a mess!" he said.

Reese had had enough. He stepped into the apartment and bumped chests with Paul.

"Look, motherfucker," Reese said, "I want to take care of your brother. I don't know what your problem was with Peter, nor do I care. He was a good man. He was a decent man. I want to do the right thing here and I don't need to hear any more of your bullshit."

Paul turned to his mother as she reached for the telephone.

"Should I call the cops?" Grace asked.

Paul turned to Reese, "Should she?"

CHAPTER

30

DETECTIVES GREENE AND BELZINGER met for a late lunch at Christina's Italian Restaurant on Second Avenue. Greene had ordered lobster ravioli, Belzinger a small chopped salad. Greene finished taking a call and folded his cell phone. He grabbed a fork and speared the last of his ravioli.

"Well, we learned Peter Rizzo was affable," Belzinger said.

"Yeah," Greene said. "Everybody liked him so much, somebody whacked him."

"Or had him whacked. What about our witness in Fairfield? What did the uniforms find out?"

Greene wiped at the marinara sauce in his plate with a chunk of Italian bread. "Please, what a joke. A stocky white guy was seen leaving the scene."

"A stocky white guy? That's all?"

"According to Mary Lou Washington," Greene said. "She has Alzheimer's."

"Great."

"And she's nearsighted."

Belzinger sprinkled balsamic vinegar on the salad. "He was white, though, right? She could tell at least that much, I hope."

Greene dipped his bread into the sauce again. "If she wasn't sleeping when she saw him. The kid took the report said she claims she was up late from indigestion. She heard the shots and went to her window. Her apartment faces the avenue. She said she saw a man running across the street toward Pennsylvania Avenue. He turned up toward Starrett City. She also slept through another pair of uniforms ringing her bell the night of the shooting. Who knows?"

"Maybe the boys subcontracted to a rookie and he lost his nerve," Belzinger said.

"It definitely wasn't a pro. Pros don't shoot through doors. And if they do, they don't miss. Not from that close."

Belzinger ate another forkful of salad and pushed the plate away. "And you think I should give John a call?"

"If it isn't going to be a problem."

"I'd rather not."

"That's twice you said that. I'll try him later."

"Thanks."

Greene snickered. "You sure put a bug up Janice Barrett's ass."

"And she didn't flinch."

"What we were afraid of."

"She did exactly what we figured. She forgot. She forgot talking to Waters and she forgot to mention it to us."

"Well, we know something's wrong about her."

"Yeah, but she's not going to fess up. Not in this life."

Greene sipped at a soda.

"Can we get surveillance on her?" Belzinger asked.

"Not without evidence. Unless you feel like spending time in her hip pocket."

"I'd feel better protecting Reese Waters."

Greene snubbed her concern for Waters. "In the meantime, Ballistics says it was a silencer used on Rizzo."

Belzinger wiped her mouth with a napkin. "We thought as much."

"Up very close," Greene said. "It was no rookie."

"You sound sold on the boys."

"On the Rizzo hit, yes. And it could've been somebody making his way with Reese Waters. Like you said, somebody who lost the nerve and fucked up."

"Or what you really believe, still believe, that it was made to look that way," Belzinger said.

Greene grabbed the check. "My turn."

"She's dirty, Dex," Belzinger said. "Janice Barrett."

"Maybe," Greene said before he pulled two twenties from his

wallet. "But until we find the guy who missed last night, so might your bus driver be dirty."

◆ ◆ ◆

"They want you on the street," Neil Lehman told Jimmy Valentine.

Jimmy was sipping espresso in his lawyer's office. Lehman was seated behind his desk with two folders open on his lap. He scanned them before continuing.

"They'll toss Gennaro from the program on a marijuana violation, but they want to keep you on the streets as long as possible. They want to take the Vignieris down from the top."

Jimmy wiped his mouth as he listened

"It's not like winning Lotto," Lehman said. "Actually, it's a bit of a quandary."

"You ever spend a couple years in the joint?" Jimmy asked.

Lehman disregarded the question. "I won't ask you how you plan to get to Gennaro. Mostly because I suspect I can't know. I can probably be disbarred."

"There are worse things than being disbarred, counselor."

"I hope that wasn't a threat."

"Come on, I don't have all day," Jimmy said. "What else they say?"

Lehman paused a moment before referring to one of the two folders. "You get to walk when it's done as long as you don't engage in acts of violence and you preapprove any and all mob-related activity with the federal prosecutors. And they specifically wanted me to mention a name. Janice Barrett."

"That supposed to rattle me, the fact they watch everything I do?"

"The federal prosecutor told me to tell you to watch your step, Jimmy, and that's what I just did. Her ex-husband was killed this week after spending two years in jail, and they can't protect you if local authorities can make a strong enough case."

"I was banging that broad a few months before her ex-husband got out," Jimmy said. "I had my reasons for that relationship. Now they've changed. Tell you the truth, and you can pass it on to whoever feels the need to know, it's about an investment I'm thinking of making."

"You shouldn't be too bold."

"What else?" Jimmy asked.

"An amount of cash equal to your current net worth will be deposited in a secure account for your use once you're pulled from the street," Lehman said. "If they find hidden money, they'll confiscate it."

Jimmy laughed. "That what they call an extraction, when I'm pulled from the street?"

"It isn't as big a victory as you think. The particulars leave you very vulnerable. They're already outlining them by bringing up the woman, Ms. Barrett."

"Yeah, and spending the rest of my life in the joint is more vulnerable. What are the particulars?"

"There are stipulations going into the program that make it very easy for them to throw you out. As I said, Gennaro is being tossed for selling marijuana to an undercover agent. Five joints, to be exact. If they could ever tie you into the murder of Ms. Barrett's ex-husband, that would be more than sufficient cause to remove you."

"It's still a beautiful thing," Jimmy said. He pulled an instant Lotto card from his pocket. "'Specially it puts Gennaro on the street again."

"They can put you on the street the same way."

Jimmy exhaled noisily as he scratched at the card with a fingernail.

"The point is," Lehman continued, "they can violate your deal for any contrivance. One day they're letting you get away with murder, literally, because they need your testimony, and the next day your protection is removed for smoking a joint. The thing you have to remember is that once they don't need you anymore they don't need you anymore. Like Gennaro, they won't care what happens to you. If a bigger fish comes along—if Angelo Vignieri decides to flip, for instance—you might become the bait."

"Yeah, that's very dramatic," Jimmy said. He frowned at the losing Lotto ticket and tossed it on the floor. He finished his espresso and set the cup and saucer on Lehman's desk. "So they want me to run things with them looking over my shoulder. It's either that or I go away for-ever. That it?"

"Pretty much, yes."

"So," Jimmy said, "what's the fuckin' quandary?"

CHAPTER
31

JANICE LAID OUT TEN pairs of her Jimmy-Choo shoe collection on her bed; she was reorganizing her closets. It was getting late, but she was still hoping for another surprise visit from Jimmy Valentine.

Brad Nelson showed up instead.

He was there because he was horny and he wanted an explanation, he told her. Janice told him she wasn't in the mood for either.

"We need to talk," Nelson said once he was inside the apartment. He headed straight for the couch.

Janice sat in the recliner. "I'm tired," she said. "And I'm getting my cramps."

Their relationship had been based on business since its inception three years earlier. Rumor on the street had it that Nelson built his client base by sleeping with it. Janice saw no downside in that as long as she owned shares in the same company.

Now she was considering new options. Since she'd met Jimmy Valentine, her relationship with Nelson had become tiresome. The opportunities their liaison once presented had since become buyable. Jimmy had given her his blessing and promised her the finance she needed to buy into the business. Janice no longer needed Brad Nelson.

"Can I have a drink?" he asked.

"You know where it is."

"Gee, thanks," Nelson said. He sprung up off the couch and made himself a vodka tonic. He noticed that the bottle of Chivas Regal was half empty. He held it up.

"Company?"

"What do you want, Brad?"

"I want to know what's going on. Everybody does. At work, I mean. First I was told the police came to the office looking for you. Then they came and interviewed me. Now I'm told they've been back to see you again. Why?"

Janice clenched her teeth. "They're investigating Peter's murder. What did they want you for?"

"To talk about you, mostly," Nelson said when he returned to the couch. "They implied I knew about the stunt you pulled on Sokolof."

"You did."

"Bullshit," Nelson said defensively. "I didn't know you would have him beat up."

"I didn't have him beat up. Peter did that all on his own."

"They implied that you knew he would."

Janice lit a cigarette. "What else did they want?"

"Well, if we're exclusive, you and me. Are we involved."

"Are we?"

"Why aren't you seeing me anymore? We haven't had sex in three weeks."

"Four weeks."

"Whatever," Nelson said. He gulped his drink down. "What's going on?"

"I think you can figure it out."

"Oh, so we are through. Too bad I didn't know. I could've told the cops that."

Janice glared through the smoke she exhaled.

Nelson got up to pour himself another drink. He picked up the Chivas bottle and said, "A scotch drinker?"

"Brad, I'm really tired."

"Should I hang around and kick his ass?"

Janice laughed.

"What's so funny?"

"You're a little out of your league."

"Oh, really? Why, what is he, another restaurant goon? You dating a bouncer, Jan?"

She rolled her eyes. "You're such a doofus."

Brad was stunned. "A doofus? Really? I guess you don't want to buy into the Boston office anymore, huh? Your bouncer boyfriend give you inside dibs on a macaroni shipment off the docks or something?"

Janice broke out laughing.

"Fuck you!" Nelson yelled.

Janice pointed at the door. "Please," she said through her laugh.

"Maybe I will," Nelson said. He poured himself another drink.

"Please," Janice said. "Before I wet myself."

Nelson downed another drink without moving from the bar. He guzzled a fourth one directly from the bottle while Janice curled on the recliner in hysterics.

"I'm going," he finally said.

Janice was still laughing.

"I am the fuck out of here," he said as he stormed through the living room.

"Good-bye," Janice said.

Nelson tripped over the umbrella stand inside the doorway and crashed headfirst into the door. Janice jumped off the chair to see what had happened and had to cover her mouth to stop from laughing when she saw Nelson holding his forehead.

"You think everything is so funny, huh?" Nelson said.

"I'm sorry," Janice said through a giggle.

Nelson gave her the finger.

"Good-bye, Brad," Janice said through her laughter. "Have a good night."

◆ ◆ ◆

A slight, well-dressed man holding his forehead was rushing through the lobby when Reese stepped up to the front desk.

"Good evening, sir," the concierge said to the man holding his head.

"That bitch is fucking crazy!" the man yelled as he pushed his way through the revolving doors.

Reese could see the large bump and purple bruise on the man's forehead. The concierge rolled his eyes. Reese asked him to please call Janice Barrett and tell her that he was waiting to see her in the lobby.

The concierge called the intercom number and relayed the message. Five minutes later Janice Barrett came down wearing her full-length fur coat, black leather gloves, sweatpants, and sneakers. She carried a pack of cigarettes.

"Outside," she told Reese.

Reese followed her through the revolving doors. Once outside, she cupped her hands around a lighter and lit a cigarette.

"Let's make this fast," she said.

"I want to make a deal," Reese said.

"About what?"

"Peter's money."

Janice stared at him. Reese didn't flinch.

"I just came from his family's place in Brooklyn," he said. "They won't release Peter's body to me."

"What do you want from me?"

"I thought you might call them for me, so I can bury Peter."

"You want me to call those losers? Yeah, right."

"Just the brother, then. Can you call him?"

"The garbageman? I don't think so."

"How'm I supposed to get the body?"

"Duh, pay them," she said. "That's what he's probably waiting for you to do, make an offer. Paul is a first-class piece of shit."

Reese was taken aback at the suggestion. "Pay them?"

"Pay them," Janice repeated. "They're a pair of snakes, his mother and brother, they'll take the money."

Reese was lost for words.

Janice was close to finished with her cigarette. She shivered underneath her fur. "Anything else? It's too fucking cold to stand out here."

"A deal," Reese said. He pointed back inside the lobby. "We can talk in there."

"No, we can't. What deal? Hurry up."

"Instead of the whole amount you owe, would you pay for his funeral? It'll cost three grand to bury him and half that for cremation."

"You're fucking serious?"

"Yes. I am."

Janice tossed her cigarette at his feet. "How about I make *you* a deal?"

Reese returned the hard look while he waited.

"You ever come near me again, if I ever see you again, it'll be the last time," she said. "How's that for a deal?"

"You got somebody better than the guy last night?" Reese asked. "Because whoever that was, he didn't get the job done."

Janice's eyes became narrow slits. "And that's how you can tell that it wasn't me," she said. "Or you wouldn't fucking be here."

CHAPTER

32

"FAT" TONY GANGI SPEARED a few rings of fried calamari and shoveled the fish into his mouth. He chewed voraciously before swallowing and reaching for a bottle of beer. It was late. Except for the help, the restaurant was mostly empty.

Gangi waved when he spotted Michael Barrett. The old man snaked his way among the empty tables and sat on the bar stool alongside Gangi.

"You hungry?" Gangi asked.

"You paying?"

"Sure," Gangi said. He reached for a small bar menu and handed it to Barrett. "They're pretty good with the clam sauce, red or white."

Barrett looked the menu over until he found the salmon special. He pointed to it for the bartender. "Medium-well," he said. "No potatoes. Green beans, if you have them."

"Got it," the bartender said. "Anything to drink?"

"White wine."

"Pinot Grigio?"

"That's fine."

Gangi soaked a piece of bread in the spicy tomato sauce. He ran the bread across the plate and scooped up slices of garlic. He ate the bread before reaching for his beer again. He turned to Barrett and set the bottle down.

"What's the problem?" he asked. "I thought this was all settled."

"Mauro. He screwed up and now he's extorting me."

"How's that?" asked Gangi, reaching for another piece of bread.

"He missed, for one thing. He didn't get it done. Now there'll be an investigation we don't need."

Gangi stopped before biting into the bread. "What do you mean 'we,' *kemosabe*? That was between you and him."

"Because if Mauro gets picked up and he turns, he's going to turn on everybody, not just me."

"Yeah, well, what would you like me to do about it now?" asked Gangi, clearly annoyed again.

"I know I don't want him on my payroll," Barrett said. "Not now, I don't."

Gangi reached for his beer again.

"Especially if he thinks he can shake me down after screwing up," Barrett continued. "The guy takes work on and falls short and now he wants to shake me down."

"He pressed you?"

"He implied he was pressing."

"Implied or he pressed? There's a difference."

"He pressed. He specifically pressed me."

"You didn't bother telling him who the guy was last night," Gangi said. "He called me, too. A couple minutes after you called the first time. I feel like a fuckin' crisis counselor."

"What's the difference who the guy was?" Barrett said. "He didn't get it done."

"The first point you make."

"And aside from his screwing it up and bringing an investigation into the picture, something he wants to blame me for, he already has a record. He's a two-time loser."

Gangi scratched at his head. "He did time. So what?"

"Twice. There's that three-strike law now. I don't even know the county board won't red-flag him for that alone, his past convictions, once they research his name. He gets tied into last night somehow, with the parole thing and so on, he can make a mess of things."

Gangi held up two fingers. "Your second point."

"If he gets into trouble for something else, selling drugs or whatever else he does, if he gets caught doing anything at all, he has something on both of us he can deal. I don't know about you, but I'm not comfortable with that."

"Yeah, so?"

Barrett fidgeted.

"Well?" Gangi said.

"We can eliminate the problem. Neither of us wants him hanging around. Or you would've put him to work over here in Jersey. It was business. He served his purpose. Now he's more dangerous to us than any good he'll do."

Gangi stopped to glance around the restaurant. The bartender was on the phone at the far end of the horseshoe bar.

"I won't whack the guy because he's ambitious," Gangi said. "Another guy already come to me with basically the same problem. Greed. This guy thought Mauro was cutting in on his action. He was anxious to eliminate the competition."

"Somebody we'd have to pay?" Barrett asked.

"Somebody you'd have to pay. Except for all the attention I have to give this bullshit, it's none of my fuckin' business."

Barrett fidgeted again. "I'll do it," he said.

"You looking to earn your button now?" Gangi said. "I thought you had more sense than that. You can't, you know. Technically, I mean. You're not Italian."

"You might think you're being funny."

Gangi turned on the stool. "Hey, fuck you," he said. "Enough with your mouth already. You're on thinner fucking ice than you might think, my friend."

Barrett checked himself. "Sorry. But look, I'm interested in protecting myself. So should you be. Once he's gone, there's one less problem to worry about."

"And what about me?" Gangi asked. "You gonna whack me, too, someday?"

"Be serious."

"Oh, I am, don't worry. Because if you think for a second that I feel safe with you holding any of my secrets, you're a bigger fucking hick than you look. I'm doing business with you, you cheap fuck, because you're as greedy as the rest of us. You have an in to property we can't touch otherwise. You help us clean dirty money. And you're not doing it for charity, pal."

"I'm a businessman," Barrett said. "I'm not ashamed of that."

"No, and neither am I," Gangi said. "Except I also have the power of life and death and don't you ever fucking forget it." He stopped to scrape up the last of the tomato sauce with the bread. "And then there's our other friend, the one in all the newspapers lately. He's got his own problems right now with the federal government and every-body else looking to carve him up and send him away. He didn't speak up for Mauro in the past, so you're lucky even bringing this to me. You understand that?"

Barrett shook his head.

"I didn't think so," Gangi said. "It means Mauro isn't spoken for. Jimmy isn't his sponsor. I'd have to bring Jimmy your idea if he was. The rules. Only I wouldn't mention it to you, see? If Jimmy was Mauro's sponsor, you'd be the one in the shit. Something would happen, only you wouldn't know what the fuck it was. You'd just be dead."

Barrett avoided Gangi's stare.

"So you want to take care of Johnny Mauro, be my guest," Gangi said. "It's no sweat off my balls. Just make sure nothing goes wrong on your end or then I gotta start worrying about you. In case you ever wondered how the big boys do it, by the way, you miss on a piece of work, a hit, you become the next piece of work. *Capische?*"

Barrett cleared his throat. Gangi waited until the old man nodded.

"Good," Gangi said. He stood up off the stool and pulled a wad of cash from his front pants pocket. He peeled off a fifty and a ten and slapped them on the bar.

"I gotta run," he told Barrett. "Enjoy the free meal."

CHAPTER

33

LANEY WAS WAITING FOR him outside the apartment building when Reese returned home. He was surprised to see her there and wondered if there was a problem.

"No problem, man," she told him. "I thought you might want company tonight."

Reese said, "Or you checking to see I'm still alive?"

"Let's go, man, I don't have all night."

He wasn't sure how to take her, but he led the way inside. He showed her a Chinese take-out menu before picking up the phone receiver. Laney told him she wasn't hungry. He called an order in for himself and noticed that his statue of Saint Jude was still on the kitchen table. He turned it to face him where he sat at the table.

"How was your day?" Laney asked. "Did you see a lawyer?"

"Peter's family wouldn't sign the papers I need to take his body," he said. "They damn near called the police on me. Maybe they did. I got out of there."

"And the lawyer?"

"Huh?"

"What did the lawyer say?"

"He means well. He wants me to stay home and hide."

"Staying home while somebody is trying to kill you is a good idea."

"I want to do the right thing. I can't stay home and do that."

Laney said, "I can help you pay for a cremation if that's what you want to do."

Reese shook his head. "I appreciate that, but you don't owe Peter fifty thousand dollars. And I still need his people to sign over his body."

"You're going after the money? I was hoping you got that out of your system."

"Huh?"

"You're going after your friend's money, what the woman owes?"

Reese was lost in thought a moment. "He used to tell me how bad things were at home but I didn't believe a family could be that way. His mother was doing a crossword puzzle when I got there. Didn't look like she was grieving. She was like ice, too. And Peter's brother, I almost hit him. He's an asshole."

"And the woman?" Laney asked. "The Queen of Mean."

"Huh? Oh, I thought I might be able to get her to pay the bill for a burial or a cremation if she won't go for a casket. I gave her a chance to do the right thing."

Laney was dumbfounded. "Are you crazy?"

"After talking with Peter's lawyer, what he said about her family and the mob, it had to be her that had Peter killed. I'm not going to let her off the hook now."

"You better let the police handle it."

"I'm not involving myself with the police as long as they think I'm a suspect," Reese said. "What's the point?"

"To save yourself," Laney said. "Damn it, man, your mother said you could be thick, and she wasn't kidding."

Reese pushed his chair away from the table. "You know what, Laney? You're a little too pushy sometimes."

"Because I'm trying to help you," she said. "For your mother's sake."

"Yeah, well, I can handle myself, okay?"

"Apparently not."

"Excuse me?"

"You're looking for trouble, Reese. You're getting sucked into something that can't be good for you. Let it go. For your mother's sake, just let it go."

Reese stared at her a moment. "I'm going to the restaurant

tomorrow," he said. "Where Peter worked. I'm going to see if somebody there can help me get his family to release the body."

Laney held her hands up. "Don't tell me any more," she said. "This is dumb. I didn't think you were dumb."

"His wife told me I should offer Peter's family money, that his brother would take money to release the body."

"Then do it," Laney said. "At least you won't get yourself killed that way."

"I don't have enough to pay a bribe. Not if I'm going to pay for his funeral or a cremation. And it's wrong, Laney. It's bullshit."

"Well, you shouldn't go to the restaurant. You shouldn't go anywhere near these people anymore."

"I used to tell Peter to 'let it go' all the time."

"And now he's dead," Laney said.

"I'm not going to die."

"You almost died last night," she reminded him.

✦ ✦ ✦

Belzinger waited in the car parked outside Foley's to avoid her former boyfriend. Greene found Detective John DeNafria at the bar inside. He was a muscular man of average height and weight. He was sitting at one end of the long bar, directly across from the bathrooms. He was sipping whiskey from a rocks glass. He appeared to be drunk.

DeNafria had worked on the Organized Crime Task Force for the past ten years. Greene ordered a Diet Coke and explained why he was there. DeNafria listened without turning his head.

When Greene was finished, DeNafria said, "There a rush on this?"

"I'm afraid there might be," Greene said. "If it's mob-related. Somebody took a shot at Rizzo's cellmate the other night."

DeNafria half turned to Greene. "The Fairfield Houses thing in Brooklyn?"

"That's the one," Greene said. "Across the street from Starrett City."

"I'm on a leave," DeNafria said. "I was sitting a desk after that

Luchessi thing on the Canarsie pier and I couldn't handle that very well, so I listened to the department shrink and took a leave."

"To drink?"

DeNafria took another sip of booze. "More or less," he said afterward. "My wife made it official. I'm a divorced dad almost six months now."

"At least she didn't try to kill you," Greene said.

"That's still up for debate."

"Yeah, well, she didn't shoot you or have someone do it for her. That's what we're looking into right now. A woman might've offed her ex. At least Arlene thinks so."

DeNafria toasted Greene with his drink. He downed what remained in the glass. "How is Belz?"

"Impossible as always."

"I chased her away, too," DeNafria said. "It's a gift I've developed, chasing women out of my life."

The bartender refilled DeNafria's glass with Dewar's scotch. Greene pointed at the drink as DeNafria picked it up.

"This a new habit?"

DeNafria paused before sipping his drink. "You know who taught me this?"

Greene ignored the question. "Look, I have a man may or may not be on somebody's hit list. We're assuming the thing in Fort Hamilton Park was a mob hit. We don't know what this other thing, at the Fairfield Houses, was. Arlene thinks the alleged victim is clean. I'm reserving judgment."

"Must make for interesting banter."

"We have divergent views."

"He a punk, the guy almost bought it?" DeNafria asked. "Because I don't help punks anymore. Something else I learned from Alex Pavlik."

Greene huffed. Alex Pavlik was his ex-partner with homicide. Pavlik had been transferred to the Organized Crime Task Force and paired up with DeNafria before he was forced into retirement.

"One more time," Greene said. "Arlene thinks he's a decent guy. I'm not so sure. He just came out of Fishkill upstate. Did two years for robbing a car. His lawyer gave Arlene a call and tipped us off to some information in upstate New York, a family construction business that puts mobsters on their payroll. The lawyer got us a name needs checking, but I can't do it."

Greene pulled a card from his wallet and pointed to a name he had scribbled earlier. He said, "Can you look into this guy or not?"

DeNafria squinted to read the card. "How come Belz sent you?"

"Because she was uncomfortable probably. Frankly, seeing you do this, so am I."

"Sorry to disappoint," DeNafria said. He downed half of his drink.

"Jesus Christ, John."

"The Rizzo thing in Fort Hamilton and the shooting at the Fairfield Houses," DeNafria said. "Are the boys behind it? If so, who and why?" He glanced at the card Greene had handed him. "And I should ask around about this Johnny Mauro and any other names might end in a vowel. That what you're looking for?"

"That's more than enough, but yeah, and we're on a tight schedule," Greene said.

"Should I call you or Belz?"

"Me first."

"Sure," DeNafria said.

Greene slapped a ten-dollar bill on the bar and pulled a finger across his throat at the bartender.

DeNafria sniggered. "You cutting me off?"

Greene took the glass from DeNafria's hand and downed the remains himself. "As of right now," he said. He pointed to the bartender. "Coffee, black."

"Not even cream?" DeNafria joked.

"Not even cream."

CHAPTER

34

THE FIRST THING REESE thought was that the man looked more like a car salesman than a radical Muslim.

He met Mufasa Kareem Abdul-Jabbar on the corner of East Ninety-fifth Street and Avenue M in Canarsie. Mufasa was standing next to his ride, a navy blue BMW 545 with cream leather interior. The Muslim was wearing a black cashmere overcoat and expensive-looking threads underneath. Reese could tell the shiny shoes were Italian cracked leather.

When Mufasa realized who Reese was, the two men exchanged handshakes and a hug.

"The Nation must be doing right by you," said Reese, glancing at the BMW.

Mufasa said, "Those Rahib's wheels. Mines are in the garage. The smaller model, the three twenty-five."

"I'm on foot," Reese said. "But God bless anyway."

Ten minutes later, Reese and Mufasa were sipping coffees in the BMW at the Canarsie Pier.

"You really a deacon?" Reese asked.

"I'm whatever the situation requires. What about yourself? You really a bus driver?"

"I was. For fifteen years before I went away."

"How'd you stand it?"

"It isn't so bad. You need to check yourself early enough so you don't let the public piss you off too much. It's like everything else, I guess. Good days and bad. It was better than hauling Sheetrock, I tell you that much."

"There's a brother with us upstate now was driving a bus," Mufasa said. "Killed his old lady when he found her cheating."

"Some handle it the wrong way, that kind of thing."

Mufasa sipped his coffee. "He used to tell us how people sometimes spit at him when he was driving."

"Sometimes they do. That's when the job becomes a test. Cops can find a reason to smack a guy spits at them. Bus drivers don't have the same option."

Mufasa was caught up in thought. "I said to him, a man spits at you on a bus and you keep your cool, but your woman strays and you kill her? That mean your job more important than your woman?"

"And what he say?"

"Fool said he never thought about it that way."

Reese smiled. He finished his coffee and motioned toward the water. "I used to go crabbing there when I was a kid."

"Rahib, too," Mufasa said. "My uncle used to take me along with them before he was killed in a liquor store robbery. That's when my cousin first turned to Islam."

"Your cousin?"

"We cousins, Rahib and me. You didn't know that?"

Reese shook his head.

"Why I'm looking out for his things," Mufasa continued. "His wheels, for one thing. His woman, too, but I don't touch the bitch. She too crazy to fuck with."

Reese said, "Excuse me for saying, but you don't seem as devoted to the faith as Rahib. I mean, in the joint, Rahib took the stuff serious."

Mufasa smiled. "My cousin said you an observant nigger. I'm what I said, whatever the situation requires."

Reese remembered something. "Wait a minute. Where does the Kendall come in? Rahib Kendall-Jabbar."

"Rahib kept his slave name on principle. I couldn't wait to get rid of mines. Smith, believe it or not. Lawrence Michael Smith. But Rahib pissed a lot of the hard-core brothers off keeping the name Kendall."

"And Kareem Abdul-Jabbar?" Reese asked.

"I love the Lakers, man. And before Magic ever come along, or I'd go with a slave name, too. I took Mufasa from *The Lion King*. Saw it twenty-six times."

Reese chuckled.

"It was one reason we broke away and formed our own thing," Mufasa continued. "We had to. You know about the Five Percenters?"

"Hard-liners," Reese said. "From back in the sixties, right?"

"They mellowed with time, too, but they definitely more hard-core than most. Rahib is more hard-core than myself, but I like to think I'm a fit between the two, the Nation and the Five Percenters."

"Whatever the situation requires?"

Mufasa slapped Reese on the knee. "You are an observant nigger."

✦ ✦ ✦

Janice paged Jimmy Valentine and waited with her cell phone in hand for his return call. She ignored several calls from numbers she didn't recognize until she grew bored and listened to messages.

There were back-to-back frantic calls from Brad Nelson. He was shocked at how she had started an affair behind his back and concerned about their future business relationship. He was giving her twenty-four hours to come up with the cash for her share of the Boston business or he would take on new partners.

Janice disregarded his threat and forwarded to the next message. She was surprised to hear her brother's voice.

"Janice, it's Alex," the message started. "I need to talk to you. I know you and Dad talk, and I know something is up. He's breaking my balls with work. He's hiring his Jersey friends on my sites. Guys I don't want anything to do with. Give me a call or come early tomorrow night and we'll talk before dinner."

She was confused by her brother's message. They'd had a placid brother-sister relationship, mostly because she didn't get involved with Alex. Once she had moved to the city they met at family gatherings only. She started to dial his number and stopped. She called her father instead.

Michael Barrett yawned on his end of the line after Janice said hello. "Hey, what's up?" he said.

"What's going on with you and Alex? He called here before and said you're giving him a hard time."

"Hard time, my ass. I told him to show up at his sites and supervise. I asked him to stop spending his money. I should've told him not to screw around with that bimbo from the diner, especially this week, but I didn't."

"He's still seeing that older woman?"

"Of course. I think just to piss me off."

"Does Lydia know?"

"I don't think so. Or why doesn't she throw him out?"

"She almost did a few years ago."

"That was from the booze. Now she drinks, too. What a pair."

Janice huffed. "I need to ask you a question."

"Ask it."

"Did you have anything to do with that thing in Brooklyn? Not Peter; the other one—his cellmate."

There was a pause on the line. "What thing in Brooklyn?" her father asked. "I don't know what you're talking about."

"Can you talk?"

"Think about what you're asking me."

"Shit," Janice said.

"Is anything wrong?"

"No," she said. "Except for Alex," she added.

"Alex is Alex. You should know better."

Janice improvised. "I'm trying not to fight with him because of their anniversary. I'm afraid to call him back. He said you hired somebody from Jersey or something for one of his jobs."

"It's a favor, the guy I hired," her father said. "So far he hasn't showed up either. Another mystery guinea from the city. The late, great Johnny Mauro, whoever the fuck he is."

Janice snapped to attention. "Mauro?"

"Johnny Mauro. Some guy from New York that come up once, I sign him to the payroll, and now he doesn't show for the job. I'll fire him tomorrow morning, he's not there again, and that'll be the end of that problem."

Janice was silent.

"Hello?"

"Yeah, I'm here," Janice said.

"You coming to dinner?"

"Yes, of course. What did you get them?"

"A piece of property. Not that he cares."

She was still stunned at hearing Johnny Mauro's name. She continued to extemporize. "Is he really fooling around again?"

"He never stopped."

"He thinks we talk," Janice said. "Alex thinks we talk behind his back."

"We do. We are now."

"He thinks we conspire or something. He doesn't trust us."

"Because we watch out for him. Is that so wrong? Somebody has to do it."

Janice looked at her watch. "Right," she said. She was genuinely nervous now. She lied about another call.

"I'll see you tomorrow," her father said. "Let's just hope the happy bride is sober through the meal at least."

"Good-bye," Janice said.

"Yeah, see you tomorrow night."

When she was off the phone, Janice said, "Johnny Mauro? Holy fuckin' shit."

✦ ✦ ✦

Lydia Barrett changed into her new light blue teddy. She applied lipstick and sprayed perfume on her arms and neck. She stepped into navy high heels and searched the house for her husband. When she found him, Alex was in the kitchen, eating a doughnut.

"You sober?" he asked without looking up.

"Yes," Lydia said. She did her best to stand straight without the support of the doorway. "Do you like this? I bought it today. It's supposed to be for tomorrow night, but technically it's our anniversary now. It's past midnight."

Alex looked up at his wife, then poured himself milk. He saw her heels and made a face.

"What?" she asked.

He pointed from the shoes to her teddy. "They don't match."

Lydia slipped out of the heels and kicked them into the living room out of view. "There."

Alex drank his milk.

"I'm not drunk," she said. "And it is our anniversary."

"You taking your pills?"

"Yes."

Alex wiped his mouth. "He's giving us property I don't want. For our anniversary."

"That reminds me," Lydia said. She made her way to a notepad on the wall alongside the kitchen telephone. "Doug Johnson called to say he's waiting on some title for insurance. He'll bring it over soon as he gets it."

"Huh?"

"Doug Johnson called. He said—"

Alex waved her off. "I don't want more property," he said. "Not from my father."

"Sell it."

"I can't. You know I can't."

"Then leave it be until he dies. Then sell it."

Alex turned to his wife. "They're doing something together. Janice and Dad. Something to do with that Croton thing."

Lydia set her hands on her hips. "Do we really need to talk about them now?"

"Something is going on. I'm waiting for her to call back. I left her a message."

"Your sister? Oh, great. That's great, Alex. Talk about a mood-killer."

Alex snapped his fingers. "Peter was killed just like that. He got out of prison and he was killed the same day. And I know my father ran into the city to see Janice the next day. And then he told me about this guy he hired. Some Italian guy."

Lydia folded her arms across her chest.

"That doesn't bother you?" he asked.

"Not at all, except I feel sorry for the guy having been married to your sister."

"And what about the Italian guy? Like I need some mob guy I don't know to supervise my work sites."

Lydia heaved a sigh.

Alex pushed his nose to one side. "It's a favor for his friends in New Jersey," he said.

"Well, then, that sounds like something you don't want to stick your nose in, doesn't it?"

Alex bit a fingernail. "Something is up."

"What's up, Alex? What do you care, as long as you don't have to deal with those people? It's your father's headache. Leave it alone."

"The guy is supervising my site. How's it my father's headache?"

Lydia was tired of it. "Hello? Excuse me?"

Alex stood up and began to pace across the room. "Her ex-husband was killed the same day he got out of prison," he said. "Then my father and this Italian guy . . . and now she don't return my calls."

"Maybe she's not home."

"And he's always going back and forth to Jersey lately. All the time."

"Who cares, Alex? I don't."

Alex narrowed his eyes. "Something isn't right."

Lydia leaned against the doorframe. Alex looked at his watch.

"I called her two hours ago," he said.

"Alex?"

"Huh? What?"

"Are we going to fuck tonight or not?"

CHAPTER

35

IT WAS STILL DARK in the dense area of the Poughkeepsie woods where Michael Barrett had taken Johnny Mauro. The sun had yet to climb high enough in the sky to clear the evergreen trees. Barrett left the engine running and kept his lights on as both men stepped into the frigid early morning air.

The first thing Mauro noticed was the thickness of the evergreens. "It's all wilderness up here," he said.

They were half a mile from the nearest paved road. Barrett took a bite from an apple turnover and pointed a flashlight down the dirt road they had just taken. "We'll clear about a quarter acre," he said. "And pave this road with gutters on both sides."

Mauro coughed from the cold air invading his lungs. He pointed to the turnover and said, "You hijack a truck or something?"

Barrett thumbed over his shoulder toward the car. "There's more in the back, you want."

Mauro snubbed the offer and rubbed his hands together. "When's this all happen? They even have running water?"

Barrett smelled alcohol on Mauro's breath. "You drink?"

"There something else to do up here?"

"Well, I hope it isn't a habit. If you're going be around heavy machinery, you can't be drunk. We can get fined."

Mauro rolled his eyes. "Not a problem. The motel I stayed, their espresso machine was broke this morning. I sipped a little scotch instead."

Barrett started toward a blue tarpaulin on the ground between two big rocks. "Over here," he said.

Mauro took a drag on his cigarette and followed. "What's that?"

"Here's where we'll start the clearing process. From this spot here." He was pointing at the tarpaulin again. He spun to point in the opposite direction. "The front of the house will face back that way, see?"

Mauro was too cold to care. He shivered a few times and turned toward the tarpaulin. "I didn't know better, it looks like a setup, that thing laying out flat like that."

Barrett pulled the revolver from his jacket pocket, took two steps closer to Mauro, and shot him twice in the chest.

◆ ◆ ◆

Reese had spent the rest of the night with Mufasa Kareem Abdul-Jabbar to avoid going home. In the morning, when Mufasa dropped him off, the deacon explained how Reese could use the Nation of Islam's clout to his benefit, especially because he could read and was so articulate.

Reese wasn't really interested in becoming a con man, he told Mufasa, although he did have one particular scam in mind.

"We cruising with about thirty members," Mufasa told him. "Ten are in different joints around the area. Rikers, Ossining, and a few up in Fishkill, where you were. One's in Pennsylvania, in Greenhaven. Another couple are on parole and keeping their shit clean. There's about six I can call on a moment's notice. An even dozen I have time to put it together."

Reese was thinking ahead to how he might use half a dozen members of a splinter group from the Nation of Islam to get Peter's money.

Mufasa said, "Rahib told me what you did for him and some of the brothers inside. Saved their dignity and whatnot. He wants to help you out in any way he can. He also wanted to extend that offer to join hands with us. You educated and cultured, Reese. You can teach a lot of brothers things they never learn otherwise. They'll respect you coming out the joint. You'll have their ears."

"I'm not good at joining things," Reese said. "I could barely hold a jazz band together."

"You with us, you won't have to job-hunt for long. Technically, we a religious-based operation. Your parole officer would have to swallow it."

"You said you can get six guys together," Reese said. "That right?"

"Whenever you need the brothers," Mufasa said. He was smiling now. "The Nation is at your service."

Or a version of it, Reese was thinking.

He told Mufasa about his situation with Janice Barrett minus the fifty thousand dollars. Mufasa frowned at the story about the woman.

"Bitch took the man's money, probably had him killed is what you're saying."

"And all I'm trying to do is collect enough to bury him," Reese said.

"How much you need to do that?"

"Twenty-five hundred."

"You got it."

"Huh?"

"From Rahib. I write you the check now, you want. Or we take a ride and I get you the cash. You tell me."

Reese waved both his hands. "No, no, no," he said. "Don't get me wrong here. I appreciate it, but I can't take money from you or Rahib."

"Why the fuck not?"

"Because it ain't right. The woman needs to take care of this. She owes the money."

"She owes him twenty-five hundred?"

Reese checked himself from lying. "More," he admitted. "But that's all I need to bury him."

Mufasa said, "She owes him more, she should pay it all."

Reese kept silent.

"Well?" Mufasa said. "How much the bitch owe?"

◆ ◆ ◆

When he left Foley's, Detective John DeNafria had gone straight home and slept through the night. He woke up groggy, with a headache. He downed three Advils with a glass of ice water and tossed out a half-empty bottle of scotch.

DeNafria looked at the bank calendar on the wall in his bedroom; he crossed out the days since his divorce. It had been six months since he received his final papers. He ripped the calendar off the wall and replaced it with a picture of his son.

He spent the next several minutes going through his apartment and collecting pictures of his ex-wife. He piled them inside a plastic grocery bag. When he was satisfied he had them all, DeNafria took the bag out to the curb with the rest of the garbage.

He went back to his apartment to retrieve his badge, gun, and cell phone. He sat behind the wheel of his car and found the business card Dexter Greene had given him the day before. He dialed Central Communications with the Organized Crime Task Force. He was cordial with a voice he recognized when the woman answered.

"Buon giorno, Donna, this is John DeNafria," he said. "I need some information on a guy named Johnny Mauro."

CHAPTER

36

"YOU PAGED ME LAST night?" Jimmy asked.

Janice was caught off guard. "Huh? Oh, Jimmy, hi. Yes, I'm sorry. Can you talk?"

"Yeah, but easy does it, okay?"

"Right," Janice said. "You told me to call you if that guy came around again."

"Who, the spook?"

"Yes."

"Fuck. Where'd he come, to the office?"

"No, here at the building, where I live."

"What happened?"

"He wants to make a deal."

"I'll give him a deal."

"I don't think it's anything to worry about," Janice said. "I'm not scared."

"You got an address?"

"No, but he was the one in the papers the other day. On the news, too. I would think they printed his name."

"Huh?"

"His name was in the papers the other day," Janice repeated. "Yesterday. That thing in Brook—"

"It's all right, I'm on a fugazy line."

"Huh?"

"Just tell me who he is."

Janice gave him Reese Waters's name, then told him about the Fairfield Housing shooting she'd learned of from the police.

"Okay," Jimmy said when she was through. "We visiting your boy later today?"

"Brad?"

"He's not my boy."

"Sure," she said. "I can't wait."

✦ ✦ ✦

Reese waited for Vincent Coleman on the corner of Pennsylvania Avenue and Croton Loop. After they exchanged hugs, they started walking toward the shopping center, and Reese told his friend what had happened the day before.

"I'm off tonight, you need company," Coleman said after hearing the details.

"Laney thinks I should hide under my couch," Reese said.

"What about the cops?"

"I didn't talk to them."

"They watching you?"

"I don't think so."

"You best know before you do anything."

"I'm trying to get my friend's body from his family," Reese said. "His ex-wife told me I should offer them money. Imagine?"

"Nothing surprises me, boy. Remember, I have a few years on you."

"I don't have the money to bid anyway. I barely have enough to get him cremated."

They walked in silence awhile before Reese said, "I want to get that woman, the ex-wife, to pay for what she did."

"You miss the joint that much?"

"She's running a game. She's putting it on. I don't buy her routine."

"She threatened you, maybe you should."

"It's bullshit," Reese said. "She's talking trash."

Coleman stopped Reese. "She's in bed with the mob, she can afford to talk trash. If that lawyer told you her family is connected, you best heed the advice. Those people don't play."

"She's just a woman."

"Yeah, one who robbed your connected friend, got him sent up the river, and pro'bly got him killed the day he come out."

Reese started to walk again. "No," he said, "I'm talking about flesh and bones. She's no superwoman."

Coleman grabbed Reese by the arm and looked him in the eye. "You about to do something?"

❖ ❖ ❖

Wearing a long black wig and PSE&G coveralls, Jimmy Valentine arrived at the sit-down in Hoboken. He removed the wig in the basement bathroom while a Hispanic man helped him out of the jumpsuit.

"Tony here?" Jimmy asked.

"Mr. Gangi upstairs," the Hispanic man said.

Jimmy stepped out of the coveralls. "Go get him," he said.

He stood in front of the bathroom mirror to comb his hair, then wet his face with cool water. He made use of the toilet before taking his place at a card table and lighting a cigar.

Tony Gangi appeared at the top of the stairs with a fresh pot of espresso coffee and a bottle of anisette. Jimmy waved to him.

"I saw your outfit from my mother's living room upstairs," Gangi said. "Very chic."

"It was like four hundred degrees in that thing," Jimmy said. "Cold as it is outside, I had to drive with the windows open."

Gangi was in the basement now. He leaned over to kiss Jimmy on the cheek. He set the coffeepot and liqueur on a tray on the card table, then made his way to a cabinet for cups and saucers.

"That van outside," Jimmy said, "does it ever leave?"

"The only florists in America keep a truck parked in the same spot three months at a time," Gangi said.

"They're probably scooping us electronically."

"Jorge'll go outside now and use the snowblower in front of the house. You can't hear nothing with that thing going."

"Good."

Gangi sat at the table and poured espresso into demitasse cups.

"What's on the agenda?" Jimmy asked.

The snowblower's engine roared outside. Gangi leaned in close to Jimmy and said, "Some good news for a change. That therapist broad, the one with her hooks into one of the female agents guarding Frank Gennaro? She accepted the first payment, fifty grand. We owe her the next fifty after Gennaro is released."

Jimmy was impressed. "This the one swings both ways, likes designer drugs?"

"The same," Gangi said. "Lucky for us, she's a sexual deviant with expensive habits. She sees the agent twice a week for muff diving sessions. One of our people procures her drugs."

"It's a beautiful thing," Jimmy said. "And I think I can find the next fifty we owe her. What's next?"

"The Newark harbormaster. But he'll be here later. That okay?"

"Who's sitting for him?"

"Ruggiero from Jersey City."

"Another jerk-off. Can we do anything in the meantime, to get it out of the way? I have to be back in the city."

"A few things," Gangi said. "Nothing pressing. How's it going by you?"

Gangi poured anisette into both coffees before both men lifted their cups and toasted one another. "*Salut,*" they said.

Jimmy set his cup down. "It'll get a lot better when we get Gennaro," he said. "Hopefully this broad'll come through."

"*Salut,*" Gangi said again.

"I would've thought they take me in already," Jimmy said. "Except they haven't. They leak all this bullshit to the papers about a secret informant, the mystery man, and we all know it's Gennaro, but nothing happens. What am I gonna do, sweat it?"

"What's the point?" Gangi said. "I sweated everything they claim they have on me, I'd be a much thinner guy."

Jimmy grabbed a book of matches and lit his cigar.

"Aldo Vignieri wants to know can you bring this Croton thing in New York to a close anytime soon?" Gangi asked.

"Before the feds pick me up?"

"You know Aldo."

"I wanna drive around in that fuckin' hot jumpsuit, yeah, probably. Except I don't think Aldo wants me out in the open right now, especially with something this big. Especially with Angelo sweating it out in the joint."

Gangi sipped his espresso.

"You're talking to the builder," Jimmy said. "How does it look to you?"

"He finally signed off on the drywall, but you don't wanna know what that took. Honestly, I can't tell his nerves are getting to him or he's growing a pair."

"Tell me what it took anyway," Jimmy said.

"There's a before and after. I sent Johnny Mauro up there for work at one of his construction sites, after he took care of that other thing with Tommy Burns. Mauro needed something legit for his parole. Like we figured, the old man would put him on a payroll up there somewhere."

"Yeah, and?"

"This was still before I become a fuckin' crisis center," Gangi said. "The old man is calling me, Mauro is calling me, and then Tommy Burns drives up here out of the fucking blue."

"Tommy? What the hell for?"

"Claims Mauro bought a piece from him and then took on work for the old man, the botched job in Brooklyn's in all the papers. The cellmate of the other guy."

"Motherfucker," Jimmy said. "That twat told the old man."

"Huh?"

Jimmy was seething. "That twat told the old man."

Gangi waited.

Jimmy was clenching his teeth. He shook his head and said, "Nothing. Go 'head."

"You okay?"

"I'm fine. Go 'head."

"Burns feels cut out, you can believe it," Gangi said. "Wants to know did I sanction it."

"Let me guess. Tommy wants to whack Mauro, too."

"Bingo. Except I chased him away. I got enough headaches without refereeing these clowns."

"So, that was before. Then what?"

"The old man whacked him," Gangi said.

Jimmy was stunned. "He what?"

"The old man whacked Mauro. Frankly, Mauro's taking on business he can't handle, it works in our favor, what the old man did. But it's also a clear sign the guy isn't handling our arrangement anymore. Like I said, either he's paranoid or he's growing a pair at the wrong time."

Jimmy was still trying to digest the news. "That old bastard whacked Mauro?"

"He said he was gonna," Gangi said. "Came to me to ask permission. I didn't see a problem with it."

"He's covering his bases," Jimmy said.

"Either that or he's putting it right in our faces, what he has in his pocket."

"And Mauro is gone? We know this?"

"I ain't heard from him. The old man said he would take care of it. He was worried that Mauro's name on his kid's payroll would attract attention."

"When was this? When did he approach you about Mauro?"

"Yesterday."

Jimmy poured himself another shot of anisette.

"What do you think?" Gangi asked.

Jimmy was staring at the drink. "I think Barrett is a man has grown out of his shoes. Either he knows what we did for the daughter or he feels a need to back us off. He's gonna hold what he done to Mauro as leverage, leave a note in a box or with one of his kids just in case. I have the daughter pretty good but who knows about the son."

"What about Burns? You did a stretch with him, no?"

"A long time ago but he's always been solid. Tommy is stand-up. As stand-up as a guy can be these days."

"You think the son knows where Mauro is?"

"I don't know," Jimmy said. "But I can try and find out from the daughter, that's for sure. Maybe teach her a fuckin' lesson the same time."

Gangi pointed a finger. "Be careful with that one. Any broad contracts a hit makes me nervous."

"Get the old man to sign off on the plumbing," Jimmy said. "Let's get what we can while we can."

"We need him after that?" Gangi asked. "The kid takes over by default, no? The son, I mean."

Jimmy was concentrating. He sipped his drink and took another drag on his cigar.

"Jimmy?" Gangi asked.

Jimmy downed the drink. He said, "If we don't need him, we don't need him."

CHAPTER

37

IT TOOK JOHN DENAFRIA more than two hours of driving among construction sites before he finally located one of the Barrett men, in Yorktown Heights. A group of construction workers was just going on break when a laborer told DeNafria that the man sipping coffee alongside a new SUV was the son, Alex Barrett.

DeNafria stopped at the passenger window of the SUV to read the sticker price. He whistled loudly when he saw the numbers. Alex Barrett spilled the rest of his coffee on the cold, hard ground and waved at DeNafria.

"Can I help you?" he asked.

DeNafria thumbed at the SUV. "I hope that thing gives a back massage for that price."

"You're right, it should."

DeNafria pulled a pack of cigarettes from his jacket pocket. "You couldn't pay me enough to do this," he said. "Out in the cold like this, working with your hands? They don't print the kind of money it'd take to get me to do this."

"It isn't easy," Alex said. "Can I help you?"

DeNafria presented his badge.

Alex did a double-take at the badge. "Uh-oh. What's this about?"

"Is your father around?"

"Not today, no. Why?"

"Is John Mauro here?"

"What's this about?"

"I'm with the Organized Crime Task Force in New York City," said DeNafria, laying it on. "A John Mauro was recently signed to your construction payroll, for this site, I believe." He referred to a blank page in his notebook. "This is Yorktown Heights, isn't it? Mr. Mauro is a supervisor here?"

"Ah, yeah, this is Yorktown, sure," Barrett said. "But I haven't seen Mr. Mauro. I haven't met him yet. He is supposed to be on the site today but he might be clearing his paperwork."

"Can you tell me where he'd do that?"

"I don't know if he is. I have no idea."

"When do you expect your father back?" DeNafria asked.

"Later, I guess. Tonight is my anniversary. We're meeting for dinner."

"And where will that be, sir?"

"Huh?"

"The name of the restaurant."

"Tony Stazione, but it's not over here. It's in Elmsford, closer to the city."

DeNafria stayed with the routine. "And what time is your reservation?"

"For seven-thirty."

"And your father will be there?"

"He's supposed to. He's taking us out."

DeNafria gazed around the site. "Thank you, sir," he said.

He went to his car and used his cell phone. He took his time and was sure to let Alex Barrett see him with the phone to his ear. When DeNafria finally pulled off the construction lot, he observed Alex Barrett, now sitting behind the wheel of his new forty-thousand-dollar SUV, taking quick drags from a cigarette.

DeNafria said, "You are the weakest link."

✦ ✦ ✦

"If you're looking for work, buddy, you'll have to come back later, when one of the owners is here," the bartender said. "I just started last week."

"I'm looking for someone who might know a friend of mine used to work here," Reese told the bartender. "His name was Peter Rizzo."

The bartender shrugged. "Never heard of him," he said. "Like I said, I'm only here a week myself."

The bartender felt like talking. He said, "It's why I have the shit shifts, because I just started last week. They gave me days. The off days, you know. I need the experience, so I pay my dues, although I caught a break this week and picked up a couple of lunches and a dinner. That was sweet."

"My friend used to manage the place," Reese said. "He was here a little more than two years ago. He definitely worked nights."

The bartender shook his head. "Sorry."

Reese nursed his soda. He set down a five-dollar bill for the Coke and thanked the bartender. He was about to leave when he remembered Peter mentioning how much his wife used to like the restaurant, too. "Because it was expensive and she didn't have to pay," Peter had told Reese.

Reese pulled a twenty from his wallet and set it on the bar alongside the five. He asked the bartender about Janice Barrett and described her from memory, including a mole on her cheek.

"The mole on this side?" the bartender asked. He was pointing to his left cheek near his chin.

"I think so."

"She about thirty-five or so, maybe older but looks younger?"

"About."

The bartender leaned forward to whisper. "There's a woman in here the other day with a mole like that," he said. "She was with some big shot the owners fall all over you just mention his name. Jimmy somebody. Wigs, I think. Middle-aged stocky guy. He's some big-shot mobster or something. He was wearing a wig, if that helps."

"Thanks," Reese said.

The bartender palmed the twenty along with the five. "Don't mention it."

✦ ✦ ✦

Michael Barrett was standing over the makeshift grave he had dug with a pick and shovel. He rolled the tarpaulin-covered body into the grave and shoveled the dirt back into the hole. He used loose brush to cover the grave. It was hard work. He groaned as he hefted his tools into the back of his SUV.

He wasn't looking forward to the anniversary dinner tonight. Aside from picking up the tab, Michael also would have to ignore his drunk daughter-in-law while digesting the unappreciative thanks he'd get from his son for giving him title to a two-hundred-thousand-dollar lot.

He picked at one of the last two apple turnovers when he was behind the wheel again. He sat there a full five minutes and tried to relax. He was finally breathing normally when his cell phone rang. He answered on the second ring. He frowned at the sound of Tony Gangi's voice.

CHAPTER

38

"SO WHAT'D YOU LEARN for eight dollars a drink?" Coleman asked Reese.

They had met across Second Avenue. Reese turned to look back at the high priced Italian restaurant.

"I learned to order Coke, was the first thing," he said.

"How much they charge for that?"

"Never mind. But I did learn she eats there, Peter's ex. With some big shot. A Mafia big shot."

"That'd be enough for me," Coleman said. He unscrewed the flask he carried in his deep coat pocket. A middle-aged woman with a full head of gray hair gave him a dirty look.

"I have a job." Coleman waved the flask at her. "I only do this for fun."

Reese guided Coleman around the corner. "Man, try to calm yourself. This is the Upper East Side. You and me don't belong here unless we're making a delivery."

"I could deliver my foot up her ass," Coleman said.

Reese ignored him. "She eats there with some Mafia guy and the police aren't watching them," he said.

"The police are playing with themselves," Coleman said.

"Jimmy Wigs, the bartender said his name was."

"Wigs!" Coleman unfolded the *Daily News* he had jammed in his back pants pocket. "The man's in here couple times a week at least," he told Reese as he handed him the newspaper. "He's with the Vignieri people. Upper management, too, I'm not mistaken."

Reese was paging through the paper with gloves on. He stopped at the Metropolitan section when he saw a headline that read: MOB FEELING THE SQUEEZE.

Reese read the article and saw the name Jimmy Valentine with a list of aka's, including Jimmy the Blond, The Blond, Jimmy Lotto, and Jimmy Wigs. The man in the picture was stocky and apparently wearing a thick, wavy blond wig.

"Says here he's the *consigliere*," Reese said. "Like Robert Duval in *The Godfather*, right?"

"Like he can push a button and you're gone," Coleman said before taking another drink from his flask. "He's on the executive board. You don't want to fuck with this dude."

"How come the police don't know this?" Reese asked. "How come they're not all over this?"

"Because they got you, my brother. Black man's a lot easier to prosecute."

Reese was looking through the article again.

"Or they already have the guy," Coleman added. "Like the article says. He's about to go down anyway."

Reese was instantly resentful. "And what am I, some bonus the police get for free?" He folded the paper and handed it back to his friend. "Come on," he said.

"Where we going now?"

Reese grabbed Coleman's arm. "Back to our roots."

◆   ◆   ◆

"I can't believe we're doing this," Janice told Jimmy Valentine.

They were in a Starbucks coffee shop down the block from her office. Today Jimmy was wearing a curly black wig. He sipped at a coffee and quickly wiped his mouth with a napkin.

"I told Brad about you this morning," she said. "It was just like you said. He wanted to know who my partner was. I could hear him gag over the phone when I told him."

Jimmy glanced at his watch. "He gonna be up there? I can't come back later."

"He's supposed to, yes," said Janice, suddenly unsettled at Jimmy's demeanor. "Is anything wrong?"

Jimmy gaped at her a few seconds, then guided her back to the restrooms. They stepped inside the men's room. Jimmy locked the door. "You tell your father about us?" he asked.

Janice was stunned at the question. "What? No! No way."

"You tell him about that other thing?"

Janice went pale. "No, Jimmy, I swear I didn't. Why? What happened?"

Jimmy continued staring.

Janice panicked. "He came to my office after I told him about the black guy and he brought me a gun, but that was it, I swear. I don't know if he did anything on his own. I was worried when I heard he hired the guy I met, your friend."

"When did you hear that?"

"Through my brother," Janice said. "He called me and told me he was having trouble with our father over work and that my father hired Johnny Mauro. I called and asked my father, and he said he hired some guy but the guy didn't show up yet, and then he said the guy's name and I almost died. I didn't say anything, though, I swear. I didn't say a word to my father. I can't. I had no idea he hired Johnny Mauro. I heard it from my brother first, and then I asked my father if he did that other thing in Brooklyn the other night. The one with the cellmate."

Jimmy sipped at his coffee. "You're starting to confuse me," he said.

Janice was going dry. She quickly wet her lips. "The guy I told you about, Peter's cellmate in jail. He was shot at the other night. He's the guy who came to see me. The black guy."

"Keep going."

"I think my father had Johnny Mauro do that thing in Brooklyn. The one where somebody shot through a door and missed? But I had nothing to do with that. I never told my father a thing about any of this. He thought the black guy was trying to extort from me. Over Peter's money."

Jimmy spilled the remainder of his coffee into the toilet. Someone knocked on the door. Jimmy ignored the knock.

"How much money did you clip from your ex-husband?" he asked.

"Nothing," Janice said. "I swear it. He claims I robbed him of fifty thousand, but that's not true. I told you that. I gave him everything we agreed to in the divorce papers."

Someone knocked on the door again. Jimmy continued to ignore it.

"You're telling me your father doesn't know anything about us?"

"I swear it, Jimmy, he doesn't."

"And your brother? What about him?"

"Nothing. Not a word."

The knocking became louder. Jimmy clenched his teeth and opened the door a crack. A small man with tinted glasses was holding a brief-case. He looked up at Jimmy. "Are you finished in there?" he asked.

"One minute," Jimmy said, then closed the door. He turned to Janice. "Your father just caused all kinds of problems over in New Jersey," he told her. "He made a headache for me Advils won't cure."

"What did he do?" asked Janice, almost pleading now.

"Never mind. What's done is done. Now we gotta figure out a way to take care of it. I thought you told him something. You say you didn't."

"I swear it, Jimmy. I swear I didn't say a word."

The knocking started again.

Jimmy turned to the door and had to stop himself from opening it. "All right," he told her. "We're gonna go up to see your boyfriend now and take care of this business thing you want. I'm gonna be your partner."

Janice tried to smile and almost cried. Jimmy put a finger to her face. "But if I find out you said a fucking word to your old man, or to your brother, or any other fucking combination of screw-ups, I'm gonna take that fucking business from you and give it away to some Arab parking cars. You understand?"

"Of course," Janice said. "But I didn't say anything. I'd never say anything."

The knocking grew louder. Jimmy opened the door and narrowed his eyes at the small man. "You're an impatient little fuck, aren't you?"

The small man huffed as Jimmy and Janice started to walk out of the restroom together. They were a few feet from the door when the small man yelled, "Next time, flush!" then quickly locked himself inside.

CHAPTER

39

THE DETECTIVES HAD DECIDED to try the restaurant where Peter Rizzo had worked before he went to prison. They spotted Reese Waters outside and pulled up to the curb on Seventy-first Street. Greene turned up the heat inside the car as Belzinger cracked her window open to smoke.

"Interesting," Greene said. "I didn't think a bus driver just out of prison would find the Upper East Side all that intriguing."

Belzinger was silent.

"Where you think he's headed?" Greene asked. "Or you don't want to know?"

"Why don't we wait and see," Belzinger said.

"I wonder who's the drunk he's with?"

"He looks older. And he doesn't look like muscle."

"He looks like a bum."

They watched Reese and the other man cross Second Avenue and head west. Greene pulled away from the curb when he had the light. He hugged the parked cars on his left until he found a spot next to a fire hydrant. He pulled half into the spot and slumped behind the wheel as he watched Reese Waters approach Third Avenue.

✦ ✦ ✦

Reese made the call to Mufasa Kareem Abdul-Jabbar from a pay phone up the street from where Janice Barrett worked. When he was finished with the call, Coleman poked him in the arm and said, "You get tight with those fundamentalist motherfuckers inside? That what that call was?"

"No," Reese said, "I did a favor and they owe me."

"They owe you, huh? They owe you, you collect on it, they own you. Use your nappy head."

"I know what I'm doing."

"Oh, right, I forgot. You know what you're doing. I'm the one just got out the can."

Reese ignored the remark and turned north on Third Avenue. When they were directly across from an office building on Seventy-third Street, Reese led Coleman inside an apartment building vestibule.

"That's where she works," said Reese, pointing across the street.

Coleman was getting cranky. He had worked the midnight shift the night before and hadn't slept yet. "Yeah, so? Now what?"

"I'm waiting on her. Right here."

"At least we're inside," Coleman said. He opened his flask and took a quick sip of the vodka.

"You got anybody at Jackie Gleason tonight?" Reese asked.

"Huh? The depot?"

"You got anybody there can do you a solid?"

"At Jackie Gleason? Of course, but what the hell for?"

"For me," Reese said. He was standing close to the door to watch the street. "I'm not going home tonight."

"You can come by me," Coleman said.

"No, I don't want to involve you."

"You already did, motherfucker."

"No, I want to be somewhere nobody can find me."

"The depot? You crazy."

"I'll stay in one of the buses parked for the night."

"You will, huh?"

"Can you do it or not?"

"Course I can," Coleman said. "You wanna sleep on a bus instead of a couch, the hell do I care?"

"Thanks," Reese said.

Coleman leaned against a wall and allowed himself to slide down until he was sitting on the floor.

"Now, remind me what the hell we're doing here again?"

"I'm waiting on the woman, Peter's ex-wife."

"For what?"

"To scare her."

Coleman chuckled. "How you gonna do that?"

Reese looked down at his friend and said, "You'll see."

◆ ◆ ◆

"You know who I am?" Jimmy Valentine asked Brad Nelson.

Nelson was sitting behind his desk and fidgeting with the remains of a tuna sandwich when Janice and Jimmy entered his office. A square gauze bandage was taped to his forehead. He nearly choked at the sight of Valentine.

"What is this?" he asked Janice.

Valentine sat in one of the two chairs facing Nelson's desk. "A business meeting," he said.

Janice closed the office door and sat in the other chair.

"Janice?" Nelson said.

"Relax, Brad," she said. "Jimmy is lending me the money for the Boston office. But we want fifty-one percent. We'll pay you for it, whatever you think is fair."

"Within reason," Valentine added.

Nelson wiped his mouth with a napkin. Janice pointed to his chin, and he swiped a piece of loose tuna onto his desk.

"I don't want to give up fifty-one percent," he told them.

"You already have fifty-one percent of this place coming to you as soon as it's sold," Janice said. "What's the big deal about Boston? What's wrong with forty-nine percent of that office?"

"It's not what I want. You know that. I offered you the partnership based on forty-nine percent."

"So we're changing it," Valentine said. He lit a cigar.

"Please don't smoke in here," Nelson said.

Valentine stared at Nelson as he took a drag.

"Yeah, right," Nelson whispered to himself.

"You asked me for a million based on a two-point-three deal,"

199

Janice said. "We'll give you one-point-four and you put up the million. How's that?"

"Why not buy it outright?" Nelson said. "If you suddenly have that kind of money?"

"Minimize the risk," Valentine said. "There's no guarantees in this life, pal, except death."

Nelson swallowed hard. "Do I really have a choice?" he asked Janice.

"No," Valentine said.

"You don't lose anything," Janice said. "It's not like you're getting robbed, Brad. And I won't run the Boston business into the ground, you know that much."

"Can I speak frankly?" Nelson asked her before looking at Valentine.

"Why not?" Valentine asked.

"I'm afraid of you," Nelson told him.

"Most people are," Valentine said.

Nelson looked to Janice. When she remained silent, his mouth dropped open.

"What?" she asked. "What's the problem, Brad?"

"Is that it? I'm afraid and that's tough shit for me?"

Janice looked to Jimmy.

Valentine took a long drag on his cigar. "All we're doing is negotiating," he said. "What would calm your nerves?"

"If I didn't have to deal with you on this," Nelson said. "Speaking frankly, I don't want any problems with the law if something happens. I don't want to live in fear the rest of my life."

Valentine turned to Janice. He said, "You were sleeping with this guy?"

CHAPTER

40

THE DRIVE BACK TO Brooklyn had been uneventful. DeNafria was working against the clock and off the record. He sat on a bar stool and watched Joseph "Joe-Joe" Luchessi holding court in the Canarsie Lounge, the same nightclub once known as the Bamboo Lounge and made famous in the mob movie *GoodFellas*. Luchessi was the wiseguy son of the gangster DeNafria had shot and killed on the Canarsie Pier, less than two miles away.

It was midafternoon when Luchessi's crew split up. A few minutes later, a teenage girl carrying schoolbooks entered the lounge and joined the gangster. They kissed long and hard before the girl sat beside him at the table.

DeNafria kept his head down at the bar to avoid eye contact with Luchessi and sipped at a club soda while he pretended to be reading a newspaper.

The bartender brought the girl a cherry Coke. When he returned to the bar, DeNafria made his way through the dining room. He removed the sunglasses and gray wig he was wearing and took a seat across from the gangster.

Luchessi shot him a look of disdain. "What do you want?"

"I take it you know me," DeNafria said.

Joe-Joe's father was the second person DeNafria had killed during his police career. The first one, a young black kid who had shot at him first, almost cost DeNafria his badge and his freedom a few years earlier.

Luchessi turned to the girl. "Why don't you head upstairs now," he told her. "I'll be up in a little while."

The girl grabbed her schoolbooks off the table and left the club through a side door on Avenue N.

"She's a little young," DeNafria said.

Luchessi looked up at the ceiling.

DeNafria banged the table hard. "I need a favor," he said.

Luchessi smirked. "You're joking, right?"

DeNafria had gone through a rough time after he killed Benjamin Luchessi on the Canarsie Pier. He still wasn't sure if the mobster had been trying to run him and his partner over or just scare them out of his way.

Now he glanced at his watch and saw it had been nearly twenty hours since his last drink.

"Tell me you're joking," Luchessi said.

"I can issue fines in this place for that girl just walking in here," DeNafria said.

"Issue them."

"What she's doing upstairs is an entire other charge. I could call vice for that, I'm guessing. Probably child welfare services, too. Maybe the rape squad."

"She's studying," Luchessi said. "There a law against that?"

"Her mother know she's here?"

"You'd have to ask her mother."

DeNafria scratched at his beard stubble. "Johnny Mauro," he said.

Luchessi played dumb. "Who's he?"

"He's a name I got."

Luchessi didn't respond.

"Mauro went away two weeks before you were made," DeNafria said. "He just came out about a month ago. He was around your father. Apparently you were seated at the same table with him a couple dozen times at wiseguy social functions. You know, the First Communions, the graduations, the weddings, and so on. Do I really need to go through this?"

"I don't remember him," Luchessi said.

"I need to arrest you first?"

"For what?"

"Passing drugs off to a minor."

"What drugs?"

DeNafria pulled a vial of pills from his pants pocket. "Think about it," he said. "Or take your pick. Ecstasy? Crack? Cocaine? Your call."

Luchessi shifted uneasily. "This is bullshit, man. This is harassment."

"Not really. I'm a cop and you're a bad guy. Who you think they'll believe?"

"Cocksucker," Luchessi said.

"I'm asking for a favor," DeNafria said. "I'll owe you one after this. I promise. Isn't that how it works in your thing? Favor for favor between friends?"

"Except you're no friend of mine, asshole."

"Fair enough. Between assholes then."

Luchessi shifted again. "He's with another crew now, Mauro."

"With who?"

"Over in Jersey."

"Jersey?"

"What I just say?"

"Who's he with?"

Luchessi looked at the ceiling. "It's part of a restructure thing. I don't know."

"He stepping up?"

"I don't know. I haven't seen him since he's out."

DeNafria sat back in his chair.

"We done?" Luchessi asked.

"I got all day."

"What else do you want?"

DeNafria looked hard into the gangster's eyes. "I don't know," he said. "You tell me."

❖ ❖ ❖

Reese stood alongside a newspaper stand on the corner of Seventy-third Street and Third Avenue. He held a *New York Times* folded open in front of him as he watched a lobby about twenty yards farther west across the street. He checked the time; it was a few minutes after four o'clock. When he looked up again, Reese could see Janice Barrett.

She was wearing the full-length fur coat and carrying a black shoulder bag. A stocky middle-aged man with black curly hair stood alongside her inside the lobby. He wore a full-length black coat and was holding an unlit cigar. The two talked a few minutes before they embraced. The stocky man exited the lobby and headed east on Seventy-third Street. Reese wondered if the stocky man was the Mafia big shot.

When he turned toward Janice again, he saw her unfold a cell phone from her shoulder bag. She started to dial, stopped, then stepped outside the lobby. She put the cell phone back inside her bag and lit a cigarette. She took a few drags before she retrieved the cell phone again.

Reese remained in the shadows of the newsstand and watched.

✦ ✦ ✦

"Those were definitely feds following the dude with the curly hair," Greene told his partner.

"You wanna take a drive and see where they go?" Belzinger asked. "I'll wait behind."

"You wanna get us fired?" Greene said. "Our careers'll do better, we sit tight here."

They were watching from the car, about forty yards from where Janice Barrett worked. A black Chevrolet Impala had just passed them as it slowly followed the man with the curly hair. Belzinger spotted the older black man standing in a vestibule directly across the street from the office building lobby. She pointed to him.

"What's he up to?"

Greene leaned forward to see. He said, "I don't know, but if he shoots a few holes through the lobby doors, don't say I didn't tell you so."

CHAPTER

41

"YOU REALLY WHACKED HIM?" Tony Gangi asked Michael Barrett.

They were standing in a small parking lot near the harbormaster's office in Perth Amboy. Gangi was wearing a Giants Stadium jacket and a blue wool skullcap. Barrett wore his heavy down jacket, a hat, and gloves. The wind blowing off the water was chilling.

Barrett looked in both directions in the parking lot, then turned his back to the wind. "Yeah," he said.

"I'm impressed," Gangi said.

"I'd rather we not discuss it anymore."

"Fair enough."

A gust of wind moved the old man. "Jesus, it's cold. Doesn't help standing out here."

"Maybe you should calm yourself down, have a drink," Gangi said. "It's what most guys do after their first piece of work, have a few."

"I was wondering are we spending the night outside."

Gangi thumbed over his shoulder. "We can get a shot of cognac in there but I need a favor first."

"Another one?"

"Oh, what you did up there was your idea," Gangi said. "This is business. I need an estimate on a basement job. Right up the street here."

Barrett rubbed his gloved hands together. "Your guys can't figure this out?"

"My guys aren't here, the ones can do this kind of thing. It's a guy lets us park in his driveway during the day. He needs work in his cellar. I don't wanna rape him, though. Make a profit, yeah, but don't kill the guy."

"Jesus Christ," Barrett said. "Do I at least get a fifty for this estimate? I charge two hundred flat, no matter how small the job."

"I won't charge you for the drink afterward. How's that?"

"I'll pay for the drink. But I'll take fifty for the favor."

Gangi pulled his wallet from his back pocket. "You don't disappoint," he said. "I'll give you that."

Barrett plucked the fifty-dollar bill from Gangi's right hand. "Thank you. Where's the basement?"

Gangi pointed to two stocky men standing near a portable shed in the parking lot. "Those guys over there'll take you," he said. "It's good, they're the ones gonna do the job."

◆ ◆ ◆

Lydia Barrett was drunk when Doug Johnson stopped at the house to leave an insurance title for a new property. Her hair was wet from a shower. She wore a short, white terry cloth bathrobe and canvas mules. The robe was open except for a loosely tied belt. Johnson felt awkward when she invited him inside for coffee. He noticed that she was naked under the robe.

"I really only have a few minutes," he said as he followed her into the spacious kitchen. "The place looks great," he added.

Lydia crossed the kitchen to the cabinet where she kept the coffee mugs. Johnson ducked to see below the bathrobe when she reached up into the open cabinet. He caught a glimpse of her ass and glanced at his watch.

"Where's Alex today?"

"Who knows?" Lydia said.

She returned to the table with two mugs. From the table she grabbed an open bottle of vodka, capped it, and slid it inside the freezer.

Johnson was standing there, smiling at her. Except for her short, squat legs, he found her attractive.

"Sit," she told him.

Johnson noticed a light blue teddy hanging over the back of a chair in the foyer and pointed to it. "Looks like somebody was having fun."

It took a few seconds for Lydia to focus on the garment. "Oh, that. That was nothing but a waste of time, effort, and money."

She poured both cups of coffee and sat in a chair alongside his. She crossed her legs, and the terry cloth robe opened.

"It's my anniversary today," she said.

"Happy anniversary."

"Mr. Cheap Face, Michael, is taking us all out to dinner in Elmsford again. How I hate doing that."

Johnson motioned toward the teddy hanging on the chair. "Was that Alex's present?"

Frowning, Lydia slumped in her chair and exposed one of her breasts without knowing it. Johnson didn't bother to tell her.

"Alex is a nervous Nellie," she said. "He's oblivious to me."

Johnson leaned closer to lend support and touch one of her hands. "Poor thing," he said as he glimpsed down the robe and spotted the start of her blond pubic hairs.

Lydia asked, "Is it true you're a big cheat?"

Johnson was caught off guard. "Ah, well, that depends," he said. "It depends on what you consider cheating."

"Let's quit the bullshit." Lydia pulled his hand down to her crotch. "He'll be home to shower in another hour or so."

◆ ◆ ◆

When Janice reached the curb, Reese crossed the street. He waved to her when she looked up. Cigarette smoke flared from her nostrils.

"I'll fucking kill you myself," she said. "I swear it."

Reese held up a hand. "Try not to go through the whole routine all at once," he said.

Janice's jaw tightened.

"I'll give you one last chance," he said. "To make a deal."

Janice remained silent.

"You still owe the man, and I need some of his money to pay for his cremation."

Janice stepped to the side and looked up the street. "I'm calling a cop."

Reese turned to wave at Vincent Coleman. "Don't do that," he told her, then motioned across the street. Coleman returned Reese's wave.

"You see him?" Reese asked.

Janice didn't respond.

"You don't have to say anything. I know you saw him."

Janice glared at Reese again.

"You got that down pretty good, huh, the angry stare?"

"What the fuck do you want from me?"

"Twenty-five hundred dollars. You already know why."

Janice took a hard drag on her cigarette.

"Now, I'm gonna give you a phone number," Reese said. "Then it'll be up to you to contact me to take care of this debt you still owe. Then I won't bother you anymore. Neither will my friend over there, the one I know you saw. There are a few more friends you don't see."

Reese handed her a piece of paper with Laney's cell phone number. She jammed it inside her coat pocket without looking at it.

"You wanna be careful with that," Reese said. "I don't get that call, anything happens to me, or my friend over there, or anybody else we're with, some other brothers are gonna make an X-rated movie with you as the star. You understand what I'm saying?"

Janice showed teeth.

"Say it," Reese said.

"Yes," she said. "I understand it. It's called extortion."

"That's cute coming from you," Reese said. "You think about it, it isn't unreasonable."

Janice waved at an empty taxi.

"You have a nice night," Reese said.

Janice pushed her way around him. She said, "Get the fuck out of my way."

◆ ◆ ◆

When Janice Barrett shoved Reese Waters to the side and walked to the curb, Belzinger's eyes opened wide. "She didn't look intimidated to me."

"There's no love lost between those two," Greene said. "Maybe he's shaking her down."

"Yeah, right."

"We don't know he's not."

"I do. I know he's not shaking her down."

Greene smiled. "Because you and her were catty with each other?"

Belzinger flipped Greene the bird.

"Nice," Greene said.

"There's no way this guy is working with that woman," Belzinger said. "No way."

"Because it's not like he's a convicted criminal."

"Shhhh," Belzinger said.

Reese Waters was still standing outside the lobby. Janice Barrett was inside the cab and on her way.

"You want to pick him up?" Greene asked.

"No," Belzinger said. "Not yet."

CHAPTER

42

"EXCUSE ME A MINUTE," Jimmy Valentine told Tommy Burns.

They were seated in a booth in the VIP room at Il Palermo. Jimmy had just removed his wig and was combing his hair with both hands when his cell phone rang. Tommy fidgeted with his car keys.

"Oh, take it easy," Jimmy said into the phone. "Calm the fuck down."

It was Janice on the line, and she was excited.

"You want I should give you a minute?" Burns asked.

Jimmy held up a finger. "Just one. Thanks, Tommy."

He waited until Burns was out of the room before speaking into the cell phone again.

"What's going on?"

"That guy, he came to my office," Janice told him. "He must've just missed you. He met me outside the office with another guy and they threatened me."

Jimmy rubbed his forehead with his free hand.

"Jimmy?" Janice said.

"Yeah, I heard you. What he say?"

"He wants the money."

Jimmy bit at the inside of his lower lip. "How'd he threaten you?"

"He told me his friends would rape me. He said they'd make a movie and I'd be the star."

Jimmy suppressed a laugh.

"I'm scared, Jimmy. I wasn't before, but now I am."

"I'll take care of it."

"I'm going to my brother's anniversary dinner tonight and I'm afraid to go home."

"I'll take care of it."

"Can you come over tonight?"

"Not tonight, no. We'll talk again tomorrow."

"Can I see you tomorrow?"

"I'm not sure."

"Please, Jimmy."

"All right, I'll see what I can do."

"Please."

"I said I'll see what I can do."

"I love you," Janice said.

"Right," Jimmy said and killed the connection.

He looked up and saw Burns standing with his hands in his pockets near the archway. He waved him over. Burns slid back into the booth opposite Jimmy.

"Everything okay?" Burns asked.

"Never," Jimmy said. "When's it ever?"

"Anything I can help with?"

"Couple things, maybe. That black guy Mauro missed, for one."

Burns grinned. "I had a feeling. That what the phone call was?"

"Huh? Oh, no," Jimmy said. "That was some broad I'm getting sick of. Which is another thing I gotta talk to you about."

❖ ❖ ❖

"What you say to scare her?" Coleman asked Reese.

They were walking south on Second Avenue. Reese said, "I told her you were a hit man for the Nation of Islam."

"Yeah, then how come she shoved you?"

Reese turned and touched the flask in Coleman's coat pocket. "I don't know, maybe she saw this."

They crossed Seventy-first Street against the light and had to jog the last few feet. Coleman reached out and grabbed Reese by the arm to steady himself.

"You got a fire under your ass?"

Reese was walking briskly. He spoke over his shoulder. "You're the one has to work tomorrow night."

"I'm glad you remembered," Coleman said. He was breathing hard to stay with Reese. He grabbed Reese's arm again, to slow him down. "Hey, Kunta Kinte, slow the fuck down. I'm up way past my bedtime and my running days are long over."

Reese stopped to let his friend catch his breath. "Okay?" he asked when Coleman was breathing normally again.

"Yeah, but slow down this time," Coleman said through a yawn. "I'm about twice your age."

Reese nudged Coleman. "I remember right, you used to sleep behind the wheel, too," he said. "You can catch up tomorrow night when you start your shift."

"Very funny. You a laugh riot."

"After this you can take me to the depot," Reese said.

"After what? Where we headed now?"

"Back to the restaurant," Reese said. "I have to meet somebody."

"Meet who?"

"Some brothers," Reese said.

✦ ✦ ✦

When she got home, Janice booted her laptop and then showered for her brother's anniversary dinner. Afterward, while she dressed, she logged into her work server to read her e-mails. There was one from Brad addressed to the entire office. Janice, curious, opened it first.

"Due to a family emergency, I will be flying to Denver tonight to stay with my sister," Brad had written.

Janice laughed at the message. "Yeah, right," she said. She knew Brad and his sister hated each other. He was hiding someplace, and it definitely wasn't Denver.

The light on her telephone machine was blinking. She listened to the messages. They were all from her brother, who had started calling in the early afternoon. He also had called her cell phone, but they were calls she hadn't bothered to return. The last call on her answering machine had come a few minutes before she got in. It showed a 911 emergency code.

Janice called her brother's house. Alex picked up after two rings.

"What happened?" she asked when she heard his voice.

"Some detective came up here looking for Dad today," he said. "About that guy he hired, Johnny Mauro. You know what's going on?"

"No," Janice lied. "Who's Johnny Mauro?"

"The guy Dad put on my payroll. One of his Jersey friends, I guess. Except the detective said he was from the city, this Mauro. I haven't met him yet. The cop was with Organized Crime, he said."

"What the hell is going on?" Janice asked.

"You tell me."

"I don't know."

"Well, somebody does, and it ain't me."

Janice poured herself a vodka martini from a batch she had kept in the refrigerator. "Have you talked to Dad?"

"No. I couldn't find him, either. I just got home myself. And Lydia's stone drunk."

"You're kidding."

"I'm not."

"Will she be there?"

"Yeah, she'll be there. She's upstairs taking a bath. I'll make her swallow a pot of coffee before we leave. I'll never hear the end of it from him, though. Like I need that on top of everything else today."

"Try to sober her up," Janice said. "I'll see you later."

"Right," Alex said.

Janice hung up and sipped her martini. She thought about her day so far and downed the rest of her drink.

CHAPTER
43

"THAT WHO I THINK it is?" Greene asked Belzinger.

They were standing outside the Il Palermo and looking through the big plate glass window that faced bar. Belzinger stood with her arms folded for warmth. Greene cupped his hands and blew into them.

"The con-sa-glerri?" said Belzinger, murdering the hell out of the Italian.

"*Consigliere,*" Greene said.

"Whatever. This round two?"

"I don't know," Greene said. "But if they sit down and order dinner, I'm arresting your bus driver soon as he steps the fuck outside."

✦ ✦ ✦

"Who the fuck're you?" Jimmy Valentine asked the black guy.

They were standing in an open area off the bar. Jimmy had just been handed a glass of scotch. The black guy was holding his glass of beer.

"Reese Waters," he said. "I'm a friend of Peter Rizzo."

"Who the fuck is he?"

"He used to work here. About two years ago."

"Don't know him."

"I think you know his ex-wife."

"Huh?"

"Janice Barrett. She used to be Peter's wife."

Jimmy scanned the bar without moving his head. "What the fuck do you want?" he asked when he was satisfied he hadn't noticed any law enforcement.

The black guy said, "I think we need to talk."

Jimmy was dumbfounded. "What?"

"About my friend and your girlfriend," the black guy said. "He was killed last week. His ex-wife owes him fifty thousand dollars plus two years' interest."

Jimmy said, "This a fuckin' joke? You a cop?"

The black guy said, "Trust me, I'm no cop."

Again Jimmy glanced at the people around the bar, and again he saw no one suspicious. He said, "Follow me, my brother."

❖ ❖ ❖

"You want in," Mufasa Kareem Abdul-Jabbar told Larry Michael Brown, "there's a potential score here."

They had pulled up across the avenue from Il Palermo. Mufasa had pooled together six of his men for Reese Waters. Brown was a seventh man. They watched from the BMW.

At 5 feet, 8 inches and 190 pounds, most of it muscle, Brown had spent the past three years in Angola Penitentiary in Louisiana for assault with a deadly weapon—a tire iron. Four days earlier, Brown had killed a policeman in Alabama with a handgun. He had been on the run since the killing. Today he was with Mufasa, hiding from a nationwide manhunt. When he could find enough money someplace, Brown planned on taking off somewhere nobody would know him.

He had found Mufasa through one of the six fools standing out on the sidewalk looking into some restaurant. Brown shook his head at the fat one on one end, his second cousin on his mother's side. He was a flabby boy with bad acne who had gone away for stealing blank checks. The fool was out on the streets in less than six months, and this was the best he could do, to stand around like some statue. Brown was lucky to find the fool after fleeing the South, but he didn't have to respect him.

"I'm guessing the bus driver is looking to arrange an exchange of some sort," Mufasa said. "Why he wants us around in the first place, to back down any move the woman and her people might make. Her boyfriend is mob, so it could be dangerous. Why I'm glad you showed up when you did."

Mufasa had told Brown about Reese Waters and his situation with a woman who owed some money. When Mufasa told him there might be as much as ten thousand dollars, Brown guessed it was probably more and became interested.

"What if the dude gets the money without an exchange?" Brown asked.

"The man told me he's only interested in twenty-five hundred dollars," Mufasa said. "I guess we help ourselves to the rest."

"'We,' my ass," Brown was thinking. If there were ten thousand dollars or two thousand dollars to take, he'd shoot Mufasa and the bus driver before he whacked it with them.

"First thing you gonna need, though, is a Muslim name," Mufasa said.

"Huh?"

"I keep some in the back of my head for times like these, emergencies. I already picked one out for you. Shalaar. Spell it S-H-A-L-A-A-R."

"Sha-what?"

"Shalaar."

"The fuck does that mean?"

"I don't know. Some boy in Brooklyn called himself that. He was no taller than five-nine, five-ten, could stuff a basketball from a standstill. I remembered the name because he had game."

"I can use the sunglasses and suit for now, I guess," Brown told Mufasa, "but I don't have time to waste. This thing gonna go down soon?"

"The man called me and asked for our guys today," Mufasa said. "He'll get back to me later tonight and we'll know."

"The bus driver?"

Mufasa nodded.

"And if he gets the money quietly, without our help? What then?"

Mufasa turned to the newest member of his flock and winked. "I have his number," he said. "We go find him, take what's ours."

Brown nodded, thinking, "'We,' my ass, motherfucker."

CHAPTER

44

REESE FOLLOWED THE STOCKY man back inside the men's room, where he was frisked for a wire. When the stocky man was satisfied that Reese was clean, he led him through the restaurant to the dining room in the back. There were couples at four of the tables. The stocky man slid into a booth and motioned for Reese to sit across from him.

Reese set his beer on the table and sat opposite him.

"You know who I am?" the stocky man asked.

"Not really, no," Reese said. "Jimmy somebody."

"Jimmy Valentine."

Reese extended his right hand across the table. Jimmy ignored it.

"I already told you my name," Reese said.

Jimmy wiped his hands with a napkin. "Okay, what's your story? You want mine, you can read the papers."

"I was a bus driver fifteen years before I went away," Reese said. "Then I met Peter after a fight inside Fishkill, and he saved my life. We wound up cellmates until we were released. We both did two years."

Jimmy bit into a sesame-covered breadstick. He pushed the breadbasket toward Reese. "You want?"

"No, thanks. Anyway, Peter said his ex robbed him and he wanted to get his money. He asked me to talk to her after we got out."

Jimmy looked away from Reese. "This Janice woman."

"Yeah."

"And?"

"Peter was already dead."

"So, problem solved, no?"

"No. She never paid him."

"What she say?" Jimmy asked.

"I should go fuck myself."

Jimmy chuckled.

"Tonight I told her she'd be the one getting fucked she didn't take care of Peter's cremation," Reese continued.

Jimmy's face tightened. "You some kind of dumbski?"

Reese didn't understand. "What's that?"

Jimmy scratched at the back of his head.

"Look, I'm not looking for the entire amount," Reese said. "I just want what I'll need to cremate Peter. And to pay his family for an authorization to release his body."

Jimmy cracked his knuckles.

"I just spoke to her a little while ago where she works," Reese said. "I saw you leave her in the lobby."

"You were following me?"

"Her," Reese said. "She owes him fifty thousand, plus—"

"Interest, yeah, yeah, you said."

Jimmy ate the last of a breadstick and wiped his hands again. "I'll tell you this much, my friend. You've got balls. Coming in here like this, seeking me out."

"I'm running out of time," Reese told Jimmy. "The city has possession of Peter's body. They hold it for four weeks before it goes to Potter's Field. Your girlfriend can afford it."

Jimmy was wide-eyed. "You're sure she's my girlfriend, huh, this Janice broad?"

"I'm pretty sure, yeah. I saw you kiss in the lobby."

"You saw me come in here, I did the same with the hostess, the girl sits people."

Reese pulled Arlene Belzinger's identification card from a pocket. He flipped it over to where he had written Laney's cell phone number. "You can call this number," he told Jimmy. "I gave it to your girlfriend, but I'm not sure she'll keep it."

Jimmy turned the card over. "A detective's card," he said, then looked up at Reese. "I'm supposed to shit my pants now?"

"The police already think I had something to do with Peter's murder," Reese said. "I didn't, but they think I did. They also think your girlfriend was involved, which she probably was. Probably through you, but there's nothing I can do about that. The other night somebody tried to shoot me. Somebody put three bullets through my apartment door. I was lucky they missed."

Jimmy was back to staring.

Reese said, "I already did two years upstate, my best friend was murdered the same day we were released, and my mother died a couple days after, so there isn't much more that can go wrong for me."

Jimmy spoke without emotion. "I'm sorry about your mother."

"Thank you."

"Where'd you do your time?"

"Fishkill."

Jimmy pointed a finger at Reese. "You only think there isn't much more can go wrong for you. Whoever shot through your door, if he was trying to kill you, he was a fuckin' moron. I don't know if you have other family, but they could get hurt, too. And, quite frankly, there are worse things this life than death. So why don't you do yourself a favor with this black fuckin' macho routine and lose it, okay?"

Reese had seen this routine before. The woman, Janice Barrett, had done it the same way, first the stare-down and then the threats.

"I'm trying to avoid a situation," Reese said. "It's got nothing to do with being macho."

"You wanna avoid a situation? Go the fuck home."

"I came to you so I won't have to deal with your girlfriend."

"Why, did I take it, your friend's money?"

"Your girlfriend did. She still has it."

Jimmy leaned forward.

Reese surprised himself by saying it aloud this time. "I can see where she gets it from, her tough-gal routine. She gets it from you. The mannerisms, the way she stares a man down. It's you."

"Like I said, you got balls."

"And I'm not going away."

Jimmy turned to his left and nodded at someone. "You're sure of that, huh?" he said without looking at Reese.

"You not the only one with meat, Jimmy."

Jimmy's eyebrows furrowed. "Are you fucking kidding me?"

"All I want is twenty-five hundred. She gets to keep the rest of what she stole."

"You want me to shake her down is what you're asking," Jimmy said. "And you're threatening me in the process. How, you're gonna go to the cops and make something up? You really think that'll get you the money you're looking for?"

"I asked first," Reese said.

"Like I don't got enough bullshit in my life," Jimmy said. "You asked? You asked the wrong guy. I'm not the one took your friend's money."

Reese noticed two muscular young men standing in the doorway.

Jimmy pointed at Reese's beer. "You want another one of those?"

"No, thanks."

"Then our conversation is over. Sorry, my friend, but I can't help you."

"You sure?"

Jimmy turned to the two men. He motioned at them, then pointed to Reese. They started toward the table, and Reese slid out of the booth.

"Call off your dogs, mister," Reese said, "and take a look out the window."

The two men were standing in front of Reese now. They looked to Jimmy for further instructions. Jimmy turned to the window but couldn't see without standing up. He waved and said, "Go see."

The two men went to the window, looked out, and turned to Jimmy.

"What is it?" he asked.

"A row of those shines in the suits with the sunglasses," one of the men said.

"Six shines," the other man said.

Jimmy got up to look for himself. He turned to Reese. "You really think this circus act scares me?"

"I think you wouldn't want to go there," Reese said. "The Nation outnumbers the five families by thousands, Jimmy. I definitely think you don't want to go there."

Jimmy exhaled and returned to the table. He said, "If I could convince her to pay you, she gives you the money, would that do it? That satisfy you enough to stay out of here while I'm trying to eat my fuckin' dinner?"

"It's all I'm asking," Reese said. "You have my number."

◆ ◆ ◆

"Now it's getting interesting," Greene told his partner.

He was pointing at a line of black men in dark suits and sunglasses. They were standing in a perfect line on the avenue and facing the restaurant windows.

Belzinger said, "You think they're with Reese?"

Greene was still watching the black men. "Huh?"

"You think they're with Reese?"

"They're not with the Italian-American League. Those are Farrakhan's boys."

They watched the scene until two big white men escorted Reese outside the restaurant. Greene looked to the line of black men who were still standing rigid in front of the restaurant window. None of them flinched.

"I hate to admit it but he's pissed me off," Belzinger said.

"I'll let him get a few blocks from the restaurant," Greene said.

"Who were the two goons brought him outside?"

"Just goons probably," Greene said. He spotted the man Reese had been with earlier. "There's the mystery friend again."

They watched as Reese and the older man crossed the street against traffic.

"Oh, shit," Greene said as he put the car into gear. He pulled away from the curb, but a UPS truck blocked his path. "Fuck!" he yelled.

"I'll go, Dex," Belzinger said. She pushed her door open, and a tenspeed bicycle slammed into it. Belzinger caught an elbow to her head as the courier riding the bike crashed across the hood of the car.

CHAPTER

45

"WHY DON'T YOU MARRY the dude?" Alex Barrett asked his sister.

They were at the restaurant waiting for their father. Michael Barrett was already half an hour late. Everyone was hungry. Janice grabbed at the bread in one of two baskets at the center of the large, round table. Alex was chewing on a celery stick. Lydia sipped at her third white wine.

"Because the dude is more boring than housework," Janice told her brother, then quickly glanced at her sister-in-law. "No offense, Lydia."

"None taken," Lydia said.

Alex and Janice were being cautious in front of Lydia. They'd had a private conversation when Lydia used the restroom. Neither of them could account for their father's absence. Neither of them was comfortable discussing what might be wrong. Alex pressed his sister about her boyfriend. Janice was evasive.

"Are you going into a partnership with him or not?" Alex asked.

"I don't have the money," Janice said.

"Yeah, right."

Janice avoided his eyes. "I don't."

"I'm getting hungry, Alex," Lydia said. "Where's your father?"

"How the hell do I know?"

Janice nudged her brother. "Easy," she whispered.

Alex said, "So tell me more about the boring dude. Isn't he in control of the partnership deal you were trying to get? Dad mentioned something about it."

"He's a dickhead," Janice said. "And he's afraid of the competition."

"I thought you said he was gorgeous," Lydia said.

"He is gorgeous. And short. And he isn't half as good as he looks in bed."

"Ouch," Alex said.

"I'm out of his league. Until me he was screwing desperate clients ten years older than him or else receptionists, word processors, and secretaries. He doesn't like competition of any kind."

"So marry him and get divorced," said Lydia, reaching for her wineglass.

"Now you sound like my father," Janice said.

"Our father," Alex said.

Lydia raised her glass and toasted the end of the phrase as she said, "Who art in heaven."

✦ ✦ ✦

They had just left the restaurant when Detective DeNafria approached them in the parking lot. He introduced himself to Janice and Lydia and suggested that they talk inside the pizza parlor next door to the restaurant. Once they were inside, Lydia excused herself to use the restroom.

"Your father didn't make it?" DeNafria asked Alex.

Alex looked at his sister and said, "Ah, no, he didn't. And we waited for him almost an hour."

"Actually, we're a little concerned right now," Janice said. "I tried calling several times and he hasn't answered."

"I see," DeNafria said. "Do you know where he was supposed to be today?" he asked Alex.

"Not really. Like I said, he might've been getting the work permits for that guy you were looking for."

"Johnny Mauro," DeNafria said.

"Yeah. I don't really know, though."

DeNafria asked Janice, "Do you know where your father might be?"

"No," Janice said. "And I'm worried about him. He doesn't do this, miss appointments. It's my brother's anniversary."

"Happy anniversary," DeNafria said to Alex.

"Thanks," Alex said.

"Because Johnny Mauro is also missing," DeNafria added as he turned to Janice again. "He's missing for two days now."

"I don't know him," Janice said.

"Well, I sure hope your father doesn't either. Not too well, anyway."

"Why's that?" Alex asked. "Should we be concerned?"

"Maybe, if they were involved in something together. If they were doing something the boys didn't know about."

Alex looked at his sister again. Janice looked away.

"Mauro is mobbed up," DeNafria said. "I think your father has a history of knowing these kinds of people from the past. In his business, I mean. Mauro was a two-time loser. I don't think the boys would take the chance of him taking a third pinch. He'd have nothing to lose if he sang and gave a few of them up."

"Jesus Christ," Alex said.

"Excuse me, but my father doesn't have a history of knowing those kinds of people," Janice said. "I think you're mistaken."

DeNafria handed Janice his card. "Give me a call when you hear from your dad," he said. He held up another card for Alex. "You have one, right?"

"Yeah," Alex said nervously. "Yes, I do."

"Give me a call or have him give me a call soon as he turns up. It isn't all that important. Just some routine investigative stuff about the other missing guy, Johnny Mauro. Mauro might've been involved in a shooting the other night in Brooklyn. I just need to talk to your father and check on this Mauro's alibi."

Janice didn't flinch. Alex shuffled uneasily as the detective wished them a good night, excused himself, and ordered a slice of pizza at the counter.

◆　◆　◆

"Where the hell you been, man?" Laney asked Reese over the telephone. "I've been waiting by the phone since I'm home from work."

"I was with Vincent," Reese said. "He went to the city with me."

"To the city for what? To get yourself killed?"

"To get the money for Peter's cremation."

"You're a crazy man, Reese Waters. An absolute fool."

"Here we go again," he was thinking.

"I can't come over tonight. I've papers to grade."

"I'm not home," he told her.

He was lying on the floor of a bus parked in the Jackie Gleason depot in Brooklyn. Vincent Coleman had borrowed a comforter and pillow from a friend. He'd given them to Reese to sleep on. He also had a box from Dunkin' Donuts, a thermos filled with coffee, and half a cup of vodka from Coleman's flask.

"Where the hell are you?"

Reese told her where he was and that Coleman was the person to contact if anything happened.

"What do you mean, 'if anything happened'?" Laney asked. "What the hell are you doing?"

"You'll see tomorrow," Reese said.

"Don't be cryptic with me, man. What's going on?"

"I don't know yet. I'll know more tomorrow."

A long pause followed. Laney wasn't speaking.

Reese said, "Laney?"

"Good night, Reese," she said and hung up.

CHAPTER

46

IT WAS SIX-THIRTY IN the morning when the apartment intercom woke Belzinger. She crawled out of bed, grabbed her robe, and buzzed the person in without asking who it was. She put on coffee while she waited for a knock at the apartment door.

The bruise above her right temple was still tender. She touched it gingerly. When she heard the knock at her apartment door, she covered the right side of her face and held her robe closed with her free hand.

"Who is it?" she asked through the door.

"It's John, Belz."

She immediately recognized DeNafria's voice. "Oh, shit," she whispered as she tied her robe and opened the door a crack.

"Hey," DeNafria said. He looked at her funny. "You okay?"

"Not really."

DeNafria looked over her head into the apartment. "Did I come at a bad time?"

She shook her head and felt an immediate pain. "No, not at all," she said. "I'm sorry, come in."

She was still covering her face when DeNafria entered the apartment. She yawned as she pointed into the kitchen. "I'm a mess. Excuse me."

DeNafria waited while Belzinger closed and locked the door.

"Come," she said, heading for the kitchen. "I just put on coffee."

DeNafria followed her into the kitchen and took a chair at one end of a small oblong table. She set a coffee mug in front of him and took a seat across the table. She let her hand down and turned her head to him.

"What the hell happened?" he asked.

"You should see the other guy."

"Huh?"

Belzinger stopped to yawn again. "A bicycle," she said. "I was rushing to get out of the car and didn't look. I opened the door and ka-boom. Some messenger slammed into the door. Broke his arm in three places. I got this."

"Jesus."

"How are you doing?"

"Better than you, I guess."

Belzinger did her best to smile.

DeNafria looked at his watch. "Couple more hours it'll be two days without booze. Even drunk, though, I managed to stay out of the way of messenger bikes."

Belzinger half smiled. "Dex mentioned you were drinking."

"He did me a favor," DeNafria said. "I hope so anyway." An uncomfortable moment passed. He pointed to her bruise and said, "Other than that, how've you been?"

"Aside from the show, Mrs. Lincoln?" Belzinger joked. She tilted her head back and forth. "Okay, I guess. I can't complain. This case we're working is a little weird. Dex told you about it?"

"Why I'm here, actually. It's a pretty good bet the Peter Rizzo murder in Fort Hamilton Park was a mob hit, or at least sponsored by the boys. It seems to trace back to the Vignieri people over in Jersey, the Perth Amboy crew. Anthony Gangi, his construction people, and maybe Jimmy Valentine."

Belzinger sat up straight. "Jimmy Valentine!" she said. "The one in the papers, right? The con-sa-glerri or whatever he is."

"*Consigliere*," DeNafria said.

"We saw him yesterday. Me and Dex. We were watching the bus driver when we saw them meet. At some high-priced restaurant, Il Palermo." She pointed to her bruise. "This happened right after they split up. I was going to follow on foot."

"Well, then, there you go," DeNafria said. "Your boy is dirty."

Belzinger became suspicious. "Do you know?" she asked. "Is Reese

Waters involved? Is that why you're here? Did Greene put you up to this?"

DeNafria pushed his chair back from the table. "Easy does it. I came here to apologize for being a shit the last few months, the other reason I came. And to fill you in. Greene didn't put me up to this at all, no. We haven't talked yet. I asked, and he told me to call him first. I didn't. I came here to see you. Like I said, to apologize."

Belzinger was uncomfortable again. "There's no need to apologize."

"Well, I did, so now it's over with."

"Is Reese Waters involved?" Belzinger asked again.

"Maybe, if he's dining with Jimmy Valentine, that doesn't look good. If you say you saw them together."

The coffee was brewing. Belzinger inhaled the smell. "Dex is pretty pissed at me about all this. Especially after what happened yesterday. He was probably filling out paperwork all night."

"There's a guy's name came up on a payroll upstate is a known Vignieri associate," DeNafria said. "He, too, is just out of prison. He's supposedly over in Jersey, working out of there, except his name come up on a payroll with this construction company upstate. He's also MIA last night and so far this morning. He's not around."

"Afraid he might've botched a job?"

"Maybe. He also could be down at the dog tracks in Florida spending the money he made off the Rizzo hit."

Belzinger leaned forward with enthusiasm. "You know it was him?"

"I didn't say that. I said he could be down there. He also could have nothing to do with the Rizzo hit. More than likely, he contracted the work for someone else to put distance between the job and whoever gave the order in the first place. Mauro, it turns out, is muscle but not the deadly kind."

Belzinger got up to retrieve the coffeepot. She set an empty cup under the spout to catch the coffee still brewing. "Dex tell you we're at odds about this?"

"He said you had 'divergent views.'"

"That sounds like Dex."

"He makes a good point about the guy being an ex-con," DeNafria said. He watched her switch mugs under the pot. "The fact you saw him with Jimmy Valentine yesterday doesn't do much for his defense. You know, contrary to the American Civil Liberties Union, most cons really are guilty."

"Well, call it a hunch, then. I don't think this con is guilty, not about killing Peter Rizzo, and he certainly didn't shoot through his own apartment door. And that meeting with the mob guy wasn't overly chummy from what I could see."

She handed him his mug of coffee.

"Thanks. You have to understand Greene's position. If the guy is guilty in any way, shape, or form you'll look like a pair of misfits protecting the wrong guy. You'd be cooked if you were wrong. Especially if some wiseguy six months down the road does a backflip, something they're known to do of late, and implicates your bus driver."

Belzinger sat at the end of the table and sipped her coffee. "And if the poor bastard gets killed in the meantime?"

"Why I'm heading into Canarsie from here to talk to somebody else might know Mauro."

"I talked to the ex-wife twice," Belzinger said. "She's a piece of work. She's definitely dirty."

"So, we'll see what turns up. Greene might be right, too. You both might be."

"That would ruin the banter, if we're both right."

"It's just something to think about," DeNafria said. "That's all I'm saying."

◆　◆　◆

Reese called Peter's lawyer a few times, but it was early in the morning and no one picked up. He avoided leaving a message and took the bus back to Starrett City. He walked to Laney's building half an hour before it was time for her to leave for work. He sat in a coffee shop directly across from her building but so far she hadn't left through the front lobby.

Reese tried the lawyer again and was surprised when Neve Rosenblatt answered.

"I need a favor," Reese said after exchanging hellos.

"If I can help, sure," Rosenblatt said.

"Can you draw up papers that will give me possession of Peter's body? His mother and brother won't sign the release, but I figured out a way to get them to do it."

"You want papers for a release but . . . what are you going to do?"

"I'm gonna make them an offer," Reese said.

"Excuse me?" said Rosenblatt with genuine concern.

"I'm going to pay them. I'm going to offer them money for the release."

"Are you serious?"

"Yes, sir."

"Why? How much?"

"I'll try to bargain, but I'll go as high as a thousand. I need to make sure his brother or mother sign something that will hold up in court. If you can handle it, I'd appreciate it."

"Sure," Rosenblatt said. "I'll do it for free if you can get them here. How will you pay them?"

"I have a few bucks left from before I went away," Reese said. "I'll get it to you, whatever amount I get them to agree to, and if you can handle it from there, I can do this for Peter."

"Sure," Rosenblatt said. "How's everything else going? Any more trouble?"

"None at all," Reese lied.

CHAPTER

47

TOMMY BURNS HAD SPOTTED the police car in front of Reese Waters's address and had parked two blocks farther up the street. He'd read the *New York Post* cover to cover before growing tired and finally falling asleep. He was snoring loudly when a private security guard tapped on his window a few minutes after sunrise.

"Yeah, huh?" Burns said as he cleared his throat of phlegm.

"Are you okay?" the guard asked. He was a young Arabic man with thick eyebrows and pearly white teeth.

Burns looked around the guard and spotted the security car. "Oh, yeah," he said. "Thanks. I musta fell asleep."

"Are you okay?" the guard asked.

"Yeah, sure," Burns said. "Thanks."

"Good day, sir," the guard said.

"Yeah, right," Burns said under his breath. "It's a great fuckin' day."

◆　◆　◆

"Like I was telling Belz, if he had dinner with Jimmy Wigs, it's probably a safe bet he's dirty," DeNafria told Greene.

They had met outside the entrance to the Canarsie pier parking lot. They were parked one behind the other on the rim of the traffic circle.

"What she say?" Greene asked.

"She didn't say. Did O.C. spot you?"

"I don't think so. Not our guys, anyway. We spotted some feds, though."

"It'll be a problem if they spot you," DeNafria said. "You'll know soon enough. They'll tell you to back off, the feds will. Why I can't hang around Jimmy, by the way. You and Belz want to follow him, do it at your own career risk. I'm supposed to be on leave. I'm spotted, and I'm history. All the department needs right now is an excuse."

"I thought Arlene was coming around," Greene said. "What else does she need? After that mess with the bicycle, I think she's got her wires crossed again. She thinks he's doing this on his own, the bus driver. She thinks he's just naive. She told me you stopped by. Today she wants to follow him in case something goes down. She thinks he's in danger."

"You know better than me," DeNafria said. "In the meantime, I'm heading back to Mauro's place right now. You're welcome, you wanna come. I placed a pretty good bug up the Barrett kid's ass at the construction site yesterday and then again last night at the restaurant. I'm pretty sure I shook up the daughter, too. The father never showed, and Johnny Mauro is still missing in action."

"You think something happened?" Greene asked.

"I know something happened. What it was is another story. I'll call you later if you want."

"I'm supposed to go straight to the bus driver's place. Arlene is already on her way."

"No problem," DeNafria said. "I'll call you either way."

◆ ◆ ◆

Janice woke up to her telephone. She was anxious and, hoping it might be her father, answered after one ring.

"Dad?" she said.

No one answered.

"Daddy?" she asked again.

"It's me," Jimmy Valentine said.

"Oh, God, Jimmy, I was hoping you'd call back last night. My father didn't show to dinner. He's missing."

"No, he's not."

"What? Huh?"

"He's not missing," Jimmy said. "He's being held in Perth Amboy."

"He was arrested?"

"Not exactly."

Janice was frantic. "What? Jimmy, what happened?"

"It's a long story made short by fifty grand."

"What are you talking about?"

"It isn't good talking like this. I already said more than I need to."

"Is he okay? Is my father all right?"

"Everything is fine," Jimmy said. "But I'll have to get back to you later, okay? I have a bad connection here, if you know what I'm saying."

"Oh, right," Janice said. "Sorry."

She waited for the line to go dead before killing the connection. She waited ten minutes; for ten minutes she stared at her cell phone, but it never rang.

◆ ◆ ◆

Jimmy turned off the cell phone and puffed on his cigar. He turned to the federal agent seated at his lawyer's conference room table and pointed to the pile of losing instant Lotto tickets.

"You can have them for fifty cents each," he said. "You don't even have to scratch them."

The special agent in charge, William Hernig, pushed his chair back from the table. He was a middle-aged man with short gray hair and sharp features. He looked at Neil Lehman and said, "How much does he pay you an hour?"

"Enough," Jimmy said. "Trust me."

Lehman removed his suit jacket and stroked his black silk tie. "Agent Hernig is here for your surrender," he said.

Jimmy looked from his attorney to the special agent. "When, today? Now? Bull-fucking-shit."

"Before this game you're playing with that woman gets out of control, for one thing," Hernig said.

"What game? I'm thinking of going into business with that broad."

Hernig forced a chuckle. "Her husband wasn't a convicted criminal, I might give a shit you had him killed."

"Allegedly had him killed," Jimmy said. "Although the police never even questioned me on that one."

Hernig looked to Lehman, then back at Jimmy. "Yeah, well, guess what? They're about to."

Jimmy puffed on his cigar again. "Huh?"

"The two agents keeping you alive spotted surveillance yesterday," Hernig said. "It was on Peter Rizzo's cellmate, but they no doubt picked you up, too. It's only a matter of time before it comes back to you, whatever you arranged for your new business partner. Janice Barrett, is it?"

Jimmy looked to his lawyer. "You gonna say something, or should I make the checks out to myself?"

Hernig turned to Lehman again. "You want to tell him?"

Lehman cleared his throat. Jimmy said, "Tell me what?"

"It's about Angelo Vignieri," Lehman said.

"Yeah, what about him?"

Lehman couldn't look his client in the eye. He stuttered a few times, and Jimmy slapped the table. "Hey, what the fuck is it? Talk to me! I'm payin' you enough."

"Angelo suspects you made a deal," Lehman said.

"He knows you made a deal," Hernig said.

Jimmy was stunned. "What? How? How's he know that?"

Lehman shot Hernig a dirty look. "He only suspects you made a deal," he said. "He was overheard talking to his attorney and one of his brothers." He motioned at Hernig. "They picked it up at the prison with a listening device."

"So big fuckin' deal?" said Jimmy, suddenly relieved. "They listen hard enough, they'll hear them two guys talk about each other, Angelo and Aldo. And Gene, they'll talk about him, too, the younger brother. It's the nature of the business now. Nobody can be trusted anymore."

"Come on, Jimmy, suspicion these days is as good a bona fides as catching your wife with her skirt around her ankles," Hernig said.

"The Vignieris are guessing you made a deal, and they're not gonna wait to find out if they were right. We want you off the street."

Jimmy was shaking his head. "This is bullshit," he said. "You know how many times, how many discussions, guys like us have about this kind of shit. This guy is going bad, that guy is wired, and so on. It's bullshit. After the things I just did with these Jersey shore contracts and that other stuff upstate New York? Bullshit, they don't think a fuckin' thing, Angelo and Aldo. That was for you morons, to see if you panic and pull me off the street. Exactly what they'd want if they did suspect I flipped. You'd prove them right."

Lehman turned to Hernig. "I told you he wouldn't want to go."

Jimmy pointed at his attorney. "Stop patting yourself on the back. You told him. I'm over here. You talk to me. I'm the one paying you."

"Well, what about Tommy Burns?" Hernig asked.

"What about him?" asked Jimmy, not backing down.

"You two catching up, or he doing work for you again?"

"He's an old friend I haven't seen in a long time. We did time together a hundred years ago. So what?"

Hernig said, "You do it this way on the stand, I'm sure the federal prosecutor will appreciate it, how you don't flinch when you're lying through your teeth."

Jimmy turned to Lehman again.

"My client would like a few days," Lehman told Hernig. "At least a few."

"And if your client gets killed in the meantime?"

"Nobody is killing me," Jimmy said. "Unless you guys plan to."

"Hey, if it was up to me," Hernig said. "But it isn't."

"Fuck you," Jimmy said.

Hernig held up a finger. "One day," he said. "Twenty-four hours. And then we pull you off the street."

CHAPTER

48

WHEN LANEY FINALLY CAME out of the lobby, Reese approached her with a bagel and coffee. Laney looked into Reese's eyes and waited.

"I told you I'd be okay," he told her.

"Excuse me," Laney said.

She started to walk around him. He blocked her way.

"Wait, hold up a minute. What's this about?"

"Where were you yesterday?"

Reese frowned.

"If you can't tell me, then you can't tell me," she said and started to pass him again. He shuffled back in front of her.

"I went to the restaurant like I said," Reese said. "I also went to her office and talked to her. I tried to scare her. I think it worked."

Laney closed her eyes.

"I can't stand what she did to Peter," Reese continued. "I can't stand the thought of sitting back and watching all this, especially after somebody shot at me."

Laney opened her eyes and waited for more.

"I'm thirty-seven years old," he went on. "I don't know how much more time I have, but I'm not gonna do it as a spectator to my own life, Laney."

"Your mother was a very dear friend to me," Laney said. "I want to help you for her sake, but I can't afford to get involved with a fool."

Reese smiled at her. "'Get involved'?"

"Don't be arrogant, man."

"I appreciate all you've done for me, Laney. I have."

"You're welcome, Reese. Now, I have to pass, please."

Reese stepped out of her way.

◆ ◆ ◆

DeNafria stood outside a bar in Canarsie. He stood half on the curb to avoid the people traffic on Rockaway Parkway. A group of Canarsie High School football players wearing their division championship jackets eyed DeNafria as they passed on their way to school.

He was waiting for Fred Walker, a former cop forced into retirement ten years earlier, after he was found guilty of police brutality. Walker had owned and operated the Glenwood Tavern ever since. Because of its location close to the Sixty-ninth Precinct, and because Walker was a former cop, the small bar was a police hangout during the day. It also was a front for a small escort operation Walker ran from an apartment upstairs.

When he suddenly appeared from behind a bus, Walker was hurrying across Rockaway Parkway with a McDonald's bag. He was a large, middle-aged man with a severe case of vitiligo that had blotched his face with blanched pigmentation. He wore a heavy coat, hat, and gloves. DeNafria waved to Walker, and they huddled in front of the bar's front door together.

"I was hoping I'd catch you opening up," DeNafria said.

"Things must be pretty slow, you're out breaking a bar owner's balls," Walker said. He fidgeted with the key and finally opened the front door.

"You get an extra coffee?" DeNafria asked.

"I didn't know I had company."

When they were fully inside the bar, Walker set the McDonald's bag on the bartop and turned on the lights.

"One second," he said as he returned to the front door and bolted the lock. "Anybody sees us in here, they might think I'm looking to work."

"Let them taste your beer," DeNafria said. "It was any flatter, it'd pass for piss."

"Why I drink from cans only," Walker said. He pulled the contents of the McDonald's bag out on the bar. "There's an Egg McMuffin, a pastry, and two home fries. Leave me the McMuffin and take your pick."

"No, thanks. I have a car full of doughnuts."

Walker grinned. "What's up?" he asked as he peeled his coat and gloves off.

"A guy named Johnny Mauro. You know him?"

"Never heard of him."

"He's just out the joint upstate. I'm looking for him, can't find him. Lives two blocks from here."

Walker sat on a bar stool. "Sorry."

"Any of your girls know him? Specially since he's just out."

Walker was chewing on the McMuffin. "I can ask. He around anybody? I noticed the Italian name."

"His priors place him with Benny Luchessi before he bought it on the pier. He was once busted along with Jimmy Mangino, but that goes pretty far back, too. Word is, he shipped out across the river, to Jersey. He just lives here."

Walker said, "I remember that Mangino guy, all right. Jimmy Bench-Press, right?"

"That's the one."

"Crazy motherfucker. The other guy your partner shot on the pier, right? Benny Luchessi?"

"I shot him," DeNafria said. "Yeah."

"On the pier?"

"Mauro was with him in the past, but that's a while ago. He just came out of the joint. Moved back here after he was released. He used to live here as a kid. Not far from here, on Farragut, across from the market."

"I'll ask the girls," Walker said. "This important?"

"Very."

"Then I'll know something later today or tonight, no later than tomorrow. All the girls are around, as far as I know."

"I appreciate it."

Walker picked at his home fries. "How you doing otherwise?" he asked. "The family and all?"

"I'm divorced," DeNafria said.

"Another career casualty. That's too bad."

"I used to think so," DeNafria said. "But it could be worse. It could be a lot worse."

◆ ◆ ◆

Reese watched her walk about ten yards before he chased Laney down. He apologized again and promised he was almost finished with what he had to do. When she asked him what it was, he told her it was something he'd felt strongly about since the Saint Jude statue had saved his life.

"You're talking gibberish, man," she said.

"Maybe," Reese said. "But it's how I feel. I'm supposed to do this. I know right from wrong. It would be wrong for me to walk away. If you can't understand that, I'm sorry."

Laney took a deep breath. "When does it end?"

"Tonight, I hope."

Laney frowned.

"Can I walk you to work?" he asked.

"I already called in. I was on my way to Saint Lawrence."

"To pray for me?"

"You really are too arrogant, man."

Reese leaned over and pecked her on the cheek. He was surprised when she didn't flinch and just stared at him.

"I need to make a phone call," he said. He pulled Laney's cell phone from his back pocket. "Thanks for this, by the way. I'll get it back to you tomorrow."

"If you're still alive," she said.

It took Reese three calls to locate Paul Rizzo's work site. When he finally reached his ex-cellmate's brother, Reese learned that Rizzo worked less than fifteen minutes away. They made an agreement to meet at the pizza parlor in the Starrett City shopping mall when Rizzo went for lunch.

CHAPTER

49

WHEN SHE ARRIVED AT work, Janice locked herself in her office. Chain-smoking cigarettes, she paced back and forth in anticipation of Jimmy's call.

A few minutes before noon, her cell phone rang. Janice sat on the edge of a radiator cover and stared out her window as she spoke in whispers.

"Where are you?" she asked.

"Close," Jimmy said.

"Can we talk?"

"If we keep it short."

"What's going on? Do you know where my father is?"

"Jersey," Jimmy said.

Janice was beside herself. "What do we do?"

"He took fifty grand, your old man."

"What? Why? Why would he do that?"

"You can ask him when you see him. All I know is it's a headache I didn't need. It was a cash deposit left for him to pass on to somebody else, and he got greedy. He claims he never picked up the bag, but somebody saw him. It isn't worth getting into any more than to say he's not getting released until the cash is returned."

Janice was shaking her head. "Why doesn't he give it to them? Maybe he didn't take it, Jimmy."

"My guess, why he doesn't fork it over, is from fear," Jimmy said. "Maybe he figures it won't do him any good. I have no clue. All I do know is if he doesn't come up with the fuckin' money, it's my headache. And I don't like headaches, not like this. Not now."

"What do I do?"

"There's something else," Jimmy said. "Your ex-husband's moolie cellmate came to shake me down last night."

Janice was perplexed. "He went to you?"

"I sent a guy to take care of him last night, but your boy never showed. He didn't go home."

"What do we do now?"

"He left me his number. I'll call him later, and we'll take care of everything together."

"What do you mean?"

"I'll tell him you're paying him."

"I'm paying him?"

"I didn't say that. I said I'll tell him that."

"Oh, okay. What do I do?"

"You go about your business," Jimmy said. "Go to work or whatever else you gotta do and sometime during the day you get to a bank and get fifty grand."

"Jesus Christ," Janice said.

"Hey, he's your father."

"All right, all right. I'm just not comfortable walking around with that kind of money. Can't you come with me?"

"Not in a million years. Especially not today. I might get indicted today. I'm hiding out until I know for sure."

"Oh, God, Jimmy. What do I do if that happens? What about our partnership?"

Jimmy sneered over the phone. "You got your priorities, I'll say that for you."

"What?"

"Nothing," Jimmy said. "I won't get indicted. I'm hiding. Nothing'll happen until I'm ready. Have somebody go with you to pick up the money if you're nervous. Just don't mention what you're taking out."

"Okay," Janice said. "When will I see you? Please tell me you'll be there when I have to turn this over."

"I'll be there," Jimmy said. "Just don't panic or do anything dumb like discuss this with anybody. I don't need my name dragged into more bullshit. Frankly, you're lucky I'm involved with this Croton thing. Your old man is lucky. The guys over in Jersey are pretty fed up with it. When he grabbed the money, he was lucky they didn't clip him."

"Oh, my God!"

"He's fine, don't worry. Just make sure you're ready to go when I call later. I'll pick you up in a cab and we'll go get him."

Janice was crying now. "Will they hurt him?"

"No, not with me involved. All they want is their money."

"I'll get it," Janice said. "I'll get it now."

"And then he can give it back to you."

✦ ✦ ✦

The first thing Janice did when she hung up with Jimmy Valentine was call her brother.

"Did you find him yet?" Alex asked.

"No, I didn't. Do you know anything about Daddy stealing money?"

"No. Should I?"

"I don't know. Somebody told me he did and that he's being held until they get the money back."

"Holy fuck, Janice. Are these the guys from New Jersey?"

"I think so."

"They're mobsters."

"I know. I'm scared. They want it back."

"How much money is it?"

"Fifty thousand."

"Fuck. Do you have it?"

"Yes, I can get it. Can you help?"

"You know I can't. Did they contact you? Is it like a kidnapping?"

"Yes, sort of. I think so."

"Should we go to the police?"

"Only if we want to kill Dad. Maybe ourselves, too."

"Jesus Christ, Janice. I knew something was going on with you two. I knew you were keeping things from me."

"Calm down, Alex, this is important."

"No shit it is."

"I mean if something happens to me. You need to know what to do."

"Me? What the hell can I do?"

"I mean if something happens to me."

"Huh?"

"Just listen. Get a pen and paper and write down everything I tell you."

❖ ❖ ❖

"We can't sit around here much longer," Greene said into his cell phone.

Belzinger was on the other end of the line inside the lobby of the building where Reese Waters lived. "Give it another few minutes," she said.

Greene said, "I'd rather issue a warrant."

"And I'm thinking we should go inside."

"With or without a warrant?"

"I can pick a lock, Dex."

"I didn't hear that."

CHAPTER

50

REESE SPOTTED PAUL RIZZO from across the parking lot. Rizzo was wearing his sanitation uniform and black work boots. He crossed the lot quickly and stopped a few feet from Reese on the sidewalk.

Reese looked around the parking lot and backed his way into the pizza parlor. Paul Rizzo took his time following Reese inside.

They stood to the side of the counter. A group of kids exchanged money for pizza slices served on cardboard plates. A tall man working the counter asked Reese and Rizzo if they needed any help. Reese told the man to give them a few minutes.

"How much?" Paul Rizzo asked when Reese turned to him again.

"Five hundred," Reese said.

"No good," Rizzo said.

"How much you want?"

"Two thousand."

Reese rubbed his face. "I don't have two thousand," he said. He ordered a Coke.

"Fifteen hundred then."

"I don't have fifteen hundred either."

"Then you're out of luck." Rizzo started for the door.

Reese stood in his way. "A thousand," he said. "It's all I can afford."

Rizzo thought about it a moment. "How do I know that?"

"You don't. But it's all I'm offering."

Rizzo took his time before he held out an open palm.

"You'll have to go to your brother's attorney and sign the papers there. I want this legal so it's a done deal once you get the money."

"Where's the lawyer?"

"Brooklyn," Reese said. He paid for the Coke, then pulled one of Rosenblatt's business cards from his wallet. He handed it to Rizzo. "He's on Eastern Parkway. He handled your brother's case."

"I never met him."

"You'd have to have given a fuck to do that."

"When?" Rizzo asked.

"When I give him the money. Tomorrow."

"I work during the day."

"You can pick it up after work. After you sign the paper releasing your brother's body."

"A grand, right?"

Reese said, "How the fuck do you live with yourself?"

"I asked you first," Rizzo said.

✦ ✦ ✦

DeNafria stepped into the back office at the Glenwood Tavern and was introduced to Dorothia Margo Fielder—aka Do-Marge, My-Field, and DMF—by Fred Walker.

"She dropped the last one, though, DMF, because of all the nasty things associated with it," Walker said. "She's a singer. A wannabe singer."

DeNafria extended his hand. Dorothia frowned.

"Right," DeNafria said.

Dorothia was a bulky woman with thick limbs. She wore a gold nose ring and lots of costume jewelry. Today her wig was blond.

"I am a singer," she said. "I just do this other shit, massage therapy, on the side, you understand."

"Sure," DeNafria said. "I'm not interested in that. I need some information on a guy named Johnny Mauro."

"Stonewall's friend? Yeah, I know him. He asked me could I take out my nose ring. I told him no fuckin' way, not unless he wanted to pay extra."

"Stonewall?"

"Irish-looking dude drives one of the car service things," Dorothia said. "I calls him Stonewall because he another racist. He like me to dress like a southern slave girl. Some of the other girls, too, but he settled on me. I'm his steady. Makes me wear a housedress and take off my shoes. All he ever want is a hand job and he goes off just like that once you start." She snapped her fingers for emphasis.

DeNafria looked to Walker. Walker shrugged.

"How are they friends?" DeNafria asked.

"One recommended the other. Mauro give me Stonewall's name the first time. Said Stonewall recommended me."

"And that name is?"

Dorothia turned to Walker. "And if these guys get into it?" she asked. "I lose two customers. One very steady."

Walker said, "I'll compensate till you find new ones."

"And how long is that?"

"A couple weeks," Walker said. "I'm not unemployment insurance."

"Excuse me?" DeNafria said. "I don't need to hear this. You can discuss it later."

"Tommy Burns," Dorothia said. "Stonewall's real name. He live here in Canarsie, too. One of the white holdouts. He down on Canarsie Road, off the Belt Parkway, across the street from that convent."

"Saint Jude's," Walker said.

"I see nuns there," Dorothia said. "I don't know where they from."

"And Mauro?"

"Was his first time the other night. Straight head is all he wanted, like I said. But he a racist, too, the motherfucker."

DeNafria looked to Walker again. "Classy," he said.

Dorothia looked DeNafria up and down. "Suck my ass," she said.

✦   ✦   ✦

"You're sure nobody saw you go in the apartment?" Greene asked Belzinger.

"I'm positive," Belzinger said. "It was a simple lock. Let's just hope he's with this woman."

"It's good you did the star-sixty-nine thing."

"Leave it to a woman."

Greene was about to turn into the Starrett City shopping mall to park when Belzinger spotted Reese Waters and the woman.

"Over there," she told Greene.

Greene pulled up alongside them. Belzinger brought down her window.

"You want to explain it now or in lockup?" Belzinger asked Reese.

Greene said, "Just for the record, I thought you were involved from the get-go."

"Involved in what?" Reese said.

"You wanna get in, or do we need to cuff you?" Belzinger asked.

"We were just going upstairs," Reese said. He turned to Laney. "Can we invite them?"

"This guy kidding or what?" Greene said.

Laney leaned down to speak to Greene. "What exactly are you going to arrest him for?"

Belzinger turned to her partner. "Let's hear what he has to say first."

CHAPTER

51

"WE HAVE ANYTHING ON Tommy Burns?" DeNafria asked Joe Shields, a longtime friend with the Organized Crime Task Force.

"He's a contract killer," Shields said through a yawn. "Usually for the hard guys, but he might've done some private work. He's a gambler. They always need money."

"His name came up with Johnny Mauro," DeNafria said. "While I was looking for Mauro. They recently used the same hooker service. One of the girls says Burns is a little weird. Kinky weird. She calls him Stonewall, as in the Confederate general. Likes her to dress like a slave girl and give him a hand job."

"Me, I prefer they wear boots," Shields said.

Both detectives shared a laugh. DeNafria said, "What about this Burns? He ever take a pinch?"

"Long time ago," Shields said. "He lays low. Only takes something on when it's small or he needs the money. We suspect him on a few things, all low-priority hits. He's not close enough to deal anybody away, and he hasn't been in on anything the task force would consider celebrity status."

"You mean like hitting a boss or something."

"Or a potential witness and so forth. Burns is old school. He drives for a car service out of Manhattan. Whatever he does, it's without flash."

"What he go up for?"

"Manslaughter. He's never really been pressed since, though. This guy getting all the attention in the papers, Jimmy the Blond, he's a friend of Burns. They did time together twenty-five years ago or so."

"Jimmy Valentine?" DeNafria asked.

"Yep, the reigning *consigliere* to the Vignieris. Why?"

"This thing in Brooklyn last week. The guy killed in Fort Hamilton Park."

"The ex-con, yeah."

"A friend with Homicide is wondering was it a mob hit or a contract. He thinks it might be the ex-con's ex-wife, that she might've gone through Jimmy."

"What do you think?"

"I'm Organized Crime same as you," DeNafria said. "We don't get paid to think. The big shots point, and off we go to watch mob guys eat and drink."

"It sounded more glamorous when I was recruited."

"It's a regular rave. Besides, I'm just doing a favor. I'm still on leave."

"Speaking of which," Shields said after looking around the area, "I heard your name come up in discussion twice already today. McMurphy wants to know what you were doing in the Canarsie Lounge yesterday, why you called in for that information on Johnny Mauro."

DeNafria tapped Shields on the right arm. "I appreciate it, buddy."

"No problem."

"You think this Burns is worth talking to, or he's out of the picture already?

"If Burns is active right now, he's flying below the radar," Shields said. "He hasn't come up on anything I'm aware of. Maybe they rattle him, your friends with Homicide, they do us a favor, too."

DeNafria took Shields's hand. "Thanks again," he said. "For everything."

"Just be careful," Shields said. "You don't wanna give McMurphy a reason. Not while you're on leave."

❖ ❖ ❖

"You made it," Jimmy told Tommy Burns.

Burns had taken himself off the radio for a few hours to meet with Jimmy Valentine outside Il Palermo. He had just pulled up at the curb.

"Your wish is my command," Burns told his friend.

Jimmy sat in the back of the town car. He removed the blond wig he was wearing and patted Burns on the right shoulder.

"There's still time, I can have the papers forged, make you Italian, induct you myself," Jimmy said.

Burns winked at the rearview mirror. "Thanks, but no thanks. I read the papers, too. Quickest way to the big house is to get overinvolved with yous guys."

"Tell me about it."

Burns put the car into gear and turned his headlights on as they pulled away from the curb. He drifted in the Second Avenue traffic heading south.

"How long ago was it we did that stretch together?" Jimmy asked. "Thirty years now?"

"A hundred years ago it seems."

"The last time guys didn't rat. And it's nothing but downhill ever since."

"It's a fuckin' shame is what it is." Burns lit a cigarette. "Sorry about last night. The guy never showed. I fell asleep waiting. There was a squad car parked out front, just so you know. I was gonna use the back entrance and let myself in. Good thing I didn't. I mighta sat on the couch and slept right through."

"The car was there because of Mauro," Jimmy said. "Hopefully we'll get another crack at the shine later. If not, fuck it. He's no sweat off my balls. He didn't get mouthy inna first place, he'd be home free."

"It's a sign of the times," Burns said. "A general lack of respect across the board. People don't discipline their kids the way they used to. Nobody touches them anymore. They grow up spoiled."

"I know what you mean. My own daughter's the same way. 'Hands off,' she says. 'Don't you hit my son.' Don't get me wrong, I love my grandson, but the kid's a little shit can stand a crack across the teeth every once in a while. I had him alone once, he give me the finger, I almost broke it off for him."

Burns laughed. "Good for you."

"Yeah, except my daughter throws me out of the house for it.

Imagine? The little prick is giving his grandfather the fuckin' finger for Christ sakes, and I go to teach him something, and I get tossed." He waved his hands. "What's the use?"

"It's the way of the modern world."

They drove in silence until they reached Forty-second Street. Jimmy pointed ahead from the backseat. "Let's grab a spot somewhere down here."

"Sure," Burns said. He veered into the right lane and slowed down for a red light.

"You said you read the papers," Jimmy said. "Speaking of rats, there's one gonna be released in a few days. Someplace over in Jersey along the Garden State Parkway, just past the Raritan tolls. They're letting him go there, Frank Gennaro. At a service area."

"Not bad," Burns said. "Could you be any more specific?"

"All luck, tell you the truth. The broad processes the paperwork for the feds likes to munch on her therapist's muffin. The therapist likes to party. It's a long story."

"I got stories longer'n that one, but nobody'd believe them either," Burns said. "What's it worth, somebody meets Gennaro in Jersey?"

"Considering he took down a dozen guys or so, myself almost included, you do the math. I know what I'd contribute, and he missed getting me. A guy was to take it on, I'm sure it's substantial."

Burns was pleasantly surprised. "You cleared that mess? Good for you, Jimmy!"

"More luck is what it was," Jimmy lied. "But I won't always be this lucky, and don't think I don't know it. Gennaro is getting tossed from the program. He violated something, and the feds kicked him out. I got the release location"—he made the sign of the cross—"I swear to God, because the right broad likes to eat pussy. We don't have an exact date yet, though, when Gennaro'll be at that service area, except they said a few days."

"So life is good again," Burns said. "Except there's no spots around here. I'll have to garage it."

"Garage it then," Jimmy said. "I got a situation downtown later could be a nice little score. Maybe a down payment on that Gennaro thing, you're interested."

"Always."

Jimmy laughed.

"I said something funny?" Burns asked.

"What I have in mind for later," Jimmy said. "That down payment, for one thing, and leaving a gold digger with her thumb up her ass for another."

Burns smiled at the rearview mirror.

Jimmy, still laughing, said, "She's bringing me fifty grand for something can't happen, she gets her father back. The shine shows up thinking he can bury his dead friend, the guy you whacked. He was her ex. She gives me the money, I get inna car with you, she stands there all nervous waiting to see Daddy, the shine stands there waiting for his money, and we take off fifty large the better for it. I could be a fly on a wall I'd give my right arm to see the look on their faces, this broad and the coon."

Burns winked at Jimmy in the mirror and said, "Fifty grand will more than guarantee Frank Gennaro don't buy Christmas presents this season."

Jimmy composed himself. "It's a beautiful thing," he said. "A beautiful thing. In the meantime, I'm hungry and feel an urgent need to celebrate my newfound wiggle room. The Palm Too is around here, right? Forty-fifth, I think. We'll eat and chat and then you should call in sick, because afterward I wanna drink and I'll still want company for that, too."

He pulled a stack of instant Lotto cards from his coat pocket and dropped them over the front passenger seat. "Scratch these off, you get a chance before we eat. We'll split the winners."

Burns was smiling at the rearview mirror again. "No problem," he said. "I'll call in after I park. I hear there's a nasty flu going around."

"You got a phone I can use?" Jimmy asked. "I gotta call a guy."

"Funny you should mention it," Burns said. He reached under his seat and grabbed one of the prepaid cell phones.

CHAPTER

52

REESE TOLD THE DETECTIVES about his adventures the past two days, minus his involvement with members of the Nation of Islam. It went on for more than an hour. Both detectives sat at the table in Laney's kitchen with Reese. Laney remained standing.

When Reese was finished telling them his story, Belzinger started a new round of questioning.

"And what was that all about with the Muslims outside the restaurant yesterday?" she asked.

"Excuse me?" said Reese, putting it on.

"The Farrakhan five plus one," Greene said.

"Huh?"

Greene smirked in his partner's direction. He said, "You're inside the restaurant and so is Jimmy Wigs. Outside, on the sidewalk, six guys from the Nation of Islam are staring in the window of the same joint."

"Yeah, so?" Reese said. "The hell's that got to do with me?"

"They were there for the kitchen help?" Belzinger asked sarcastically.

"You see me leave with them?" Reese asked right back.

Nobody spoke.

"Okay, so what were you doing in the restaurant?" Greene asked.

Reese was tired of telling the story. He answered abruptly, "Trying to get money for Peter's cremation."

"From Jimmy the Blond?" Greene asked.

"From his girlfriend," Reese said.

"And now we're all waiting for Jimmy to call you with some kind of arrangement to pick up the money?"

"That's what he said he'd do."

Greene turned to Belzinger. "If just half of this bullshit story is true, you do understand that this guy has a serious death wish, right?"

Reese pulled the Saint Jude statue from his pants pocket and set it on the table. "I'm safe with this," he said.

"It looked like Janice Barrett shoved you yesterday, from where we were watching," Belzinger said. "What was that about?"

"That's her routine. She can't help herself."

"And what made you go to her again? If you didn't already know her, you're sure getting cozy since you two met."

"I told you, I went there to try and get her to pay for Peter's cremation. I just got out of the joint, I don't have it to spare or I would."

"And what did she say?"

"The second time, she threatened me. Yesterday she just gave me the stare routine. How I know I scared her."

"Or did you threaten her?" Greene asked.

Laney said, "Give it a break already, man."

Reese took one of Laney's hands.

"We're like the Keystone Kops with this already," Greene told his partner.

Reese said, "Look, I saw them together, Jimmy and Peter's ex-wife. I went to the restaurant because a bartender there described Peter's ex to me the day before. So talk about the Keystone Kops. I'm the one doing your job."

Greene flushed red. Belzinger turned on Reese.

"Can the wisecracks, okay? I'm the one that believes just enough of this story to keep him from locking you up. He's working a very short fuse right now. Remember that."

Reese remained silent.

Belzinger turned to Laney. "I'm trying here, but he's not making it easy."

Laney's cell phone rang. Reese held a finger to his lips. "Maybe this is him now."

Laney said, "Would that make it any easier?"

❖ ❖ ❖

She had already picked up the money, fifty thousand dollars in hundred-dollar bills. A large envelope on the bottom of a tote bag held five stacks of ten thousand dollars each.

She chain-smoked through a pack of cigarettes, thinking about her father. It didn't make sense that he would steal fifty thousand dollars. Her father was greedy, but he was not a stupid man. As headstrong and arrogant as he could be in his business, Janice couldn't imagine him stealing from the mob.

She held the handgun her father had brought her. She hefted it in her right hand but found it too heavy to fire that way. She held it with both hands and aimed at a vase across the office. She was afraid to touch the trigger.

Jimmy had once told her, "I'll give you a few street rules you won't learn on *Law and Order*. A couple of things you can always use, especially in negotiations."

He had stopped to make sure she was watching him. He pointed to his eyes. "Maintain this," he had said. "Eye contact. Stare the cocksuckers down. It makes most people uneasy."

Next Jimmy had mimicked a chattering mouth with his right hand. "Let them talk," he said. "You listen. The less words the better."

He had stopped to light his cigar.

"What about cops?" she'd asked. "When they question you."

"You see *GoodFellas*?"

"Sure."

Jimmy had raised a hand to his chin and flicked the bottom of it with his fingers. "*Niente*," he said. "*Nada*. Nothing. You keep your mouth shut. One of the two best lessons in life."

Janice had mimicked the gesture.

It was then Jimmy had made a gun with his right hand and pointed his trigger finger behind his right ear. "And another thing, you ever gotta go this route, two in the back of the head," he had said.

Janice's eyes had opened wide.

"It can be messy, but it works. Two here in the chest, dead center, works just as good."

Janice had quivered.

"Oh, and wear a wig," Jimmy had added. "I'm big on wigs."

It was what she was thinking about now, while she was holding one of her uncle's old weapons. She should've brought more than one of her wigs.

When her cell phone rang, Janice walked to the corner windows in her office. She looked out across the neighboring rooftops and answered the second ring in a whisper.

"Hello?"

"It's me," Jimmy said. "I'm downstairs in a cab."

"Give me two minutes," she said.

"Hurry."

"Right." She killed the power on her cell phone and stashed the gun inside her tote bag.

❖ ❖ ❖

"That was him again," Reese told Belzinger. He folded the cell phone and stashed it inside his coat pocket.

They had traveled into the city after Jimmy Valentine's first call. Detective Greene was parked on a street a few blocks away. Detective Belzinger and Reese were standing outside the Broadway-Nassau subway station. It was the end of rush hour. The streets were still crowded. They moved inside a doorway to avoid getting shoved.

"What did he say?" Belzinger asked.

"Same as before," Reese said. "He wanted my location and told me to stay close to the Seaport. Within ten minutes' walking distance."

"He's letting the crowds disperse," Belzinger said. "So he can see you."

"He's the man with the money," Reese said.

Belzinger shot him a dirty look. "You're pretty cavalier about all this. He takes a few more shots at you later, you might not find it so amusing."

"Where's your partner?" Reese asked.

"Close."

"He still doesn't trust me, does he?"

"He's being careful."

"Bullshit," Reese said. "The guy thinks I'm guilty is backing you up and I shouldn't be cavalier?"

CHAPTER

53

GREENE WATCHED THEM FROM his car, which he'd parked at the corner of Nassau and John Streets. He sat low behind the wheel and kept his right hand firmly on the Glock hidden under a newspaper on the front passenger seat.

DeNafria had called a few minutes earlier to confirm that a professional hit man with prison connections to Jimmy Valentine had been in recent contact with John Mauro. DeNafria was convinced that Mauro's sudden disappearance suggested something professional.

"It's a fairly standard move after a guy botches a job," DeNafria had said. "He gets clipped and left in the streets to serve notice, or he disappears altogether."

Greene was anxious for DeNafria to get there. He was coming from Brooklyn and would be there within the hour, he had said.

A beggar knocked on the driver's side window and startled Greene. He jerked his right hand and momentarily exposed his weapon. He jammed the gun between his legs as the beggar's eyes opened wide. Greene flashed his badge. When the beggar stood there staring, Greene fished two singles from his wallet and dangled them out the window.

✦ ✦ ✦

Jimmy had instructed Tommy Burns to drive to the South Street Seaport and wait for him there. Jimmy then arranged for a cab to wait for him inside a parking garage on Seventy-first Street. When he pulled into the parking garage, he switched from one cab to the other and called Janice to meet him.

"You okay?" Jimmy asked Janice once she was settled in the back of the cab.

"Yes," she said, then did a double take at the red, curly wig Jimmy was wearing.

"You like it?" he asked. "I like yours."

Janice started to cry. Jimmy signaled for the first cab to exit on Seventy-first Street. He waited until he saw the black Impala follow the cab.

"Okay," he told the driver. "Let's go."

He draped an arm around Janice as their cab pulled out of the Seventy-second Street exit. "It's okay," he told her. "It'll be okay."

She was clutching her tote bag between her legs. She wiped sweat from her forehead and turned to Jimmy.

"What about the black guy?" she whispered.

Jimmy didn't hear her question. "You get the money for your father?"

"Yes, of course."

Jimmy set two small gym bags between them. "Put it in there," he said, pointing to one of the bags.

Janice hesitated. "What's that for?" she asked, indicating the other bag.

"That's for the shine," Jimmy said. He lifted the bag and handed it to Janice. "It's got instant Lotto cards inside, about fifty bucks' worth. I already scratched them. All losers."

Janice transferred the fifty thousand dollars from her tote bag to the gym bag. She zippered it shut and started to shake.

Jimmy took her hand. "It'll be okay."

"Where are we going?"

"Downtown. I got a guy waiting there for us."

"Is my father there?"

"He better be."

Janice quivered as she covered her mouth with both hands. "Oh, my God," she said.

Jimmy rubbed her back. "It's okay," he said. "I promise."

The cab turned east and headed for the FDR Drive.

✦ ✦ ✦

Reese killed his connection with Mufasa Kareem Abdul-Jabbar and called Vincent Coleman.

"I'm downtown in a KFC men's room," he told his friend. "I'm heading to the Seaport, where the man said to go. Where you at?"

"John and Water Streets," Coleman said. "I'm driving. They called me in early and I'm fucked. You need me I can get sick real fast, hop a cab, and be there. I tried you earlier but my cell battery was low. I juiced it on the ride in."

"I don't think so," Reese said. "The cops are with me."

"That should go over well with the Mafia guy."

"Tell me about it. When do you swing?"

"My break is coming up. I'll be at the ferry in ten, fifteen minutes. If you're in the Seaport, that isn't far."

Reese flushed the toilet. "Keep your phone on," he said. "I already programmed your number. In case anything happens, I'll call you."

"What might happen? I thought the cops are there."

"If this guy really pays me, maybe I can meet you up on Water Street or something. He said he'd put the money in a small gym bag. I don't know he's for real or jerkin' my chain. Just keep your phone on."

"And you be careful," Coleman said.

Reese held the cell phone against his ear with his right shoulder. He quickly dried his hands with a paper towel and said, "I'll try." He glanced at himself in the cracked mirror and saw he was sweating. He wiped the sweat, took a deep breath, and was on his way.

✦ ✦ ✦

Greene drove to Gold Street and recognized John DeNafria leaning against a parking meter. DeNafria wore army fatigues and hadn't shaved. He sat in the front seat and rubbed his hands in the heat blowing from a vent.

"You drinking again?" Greene asked.

"No. This look is on purpose. In case I need to get close."

Greene put the car into gear and U-turned toward the Brooklyn Bridge. "Arlene just called," he said. "They're doing this near the fish market. Just north of it."

"Where it's nice and dark."

"You know the area?"

"Pretty good, yeah." DeNafria pointed east on Fulton Street. "The Seaport ends at the old terminal building. There's a walkway, though, along the water there. There's always a host of bums camped out along the way. It's cold enough now there shouldn't be."

"Or they're frozen stiffs."

"What is it they're doing tonight? You said something about money."

"What the bus driver told us," Greene said. "He asked for some of his friend's money so he could cremate the guy. He claims Jimmy the Blond told him he'd get it. He's supposed to meet with him tonight."

DeNafria made a face.

"It's what Arlene is believing and I promised to go along with it," Greene said.

"If Jimmy is there, so might half a dozen federal agents be there," DeNafria said.

Greene crossed South Street and drove slowly onto the cobblestones of Front Street. "Which is another reason I should go home and play with my kid tonight," he said. "The feds."

✦ ✦ ✦

Belzinger zippered up her jacket and put her gloves back on.

"You okay?" she asked.

Reese wiggled to adjust himself under the Kevlar vest. "Be a lot easier without this coat," he said. "I can hardly move."

"Just make sure that phone doesn't cut off," Belzinger said. "Keep your hands in your pockets and let them think it's a gun."

"They might shoot me they think that."

Belzinger said, "Your hands are in your pockets, they might think you're the one's gonna shoot."

CHAPTER

54

REESE REACHED INTO HIS coat pocket and killed his connection with Detective Belzinger as he walked north on Front Street. He pressed the code for Coleman's phone and could hear the beeps as the number was dialed. He peeked over his shoulder to make sure he was far enough away from the detective to speak.

"Hello?" he heard Coleman say.

"It's me," Reese said as he took careful steps. "I'm on Front and Dover, just past the market. Tell me you're on break."

"I am indeed," Coleman said. "At the ferry. I'll be right there."

Reese continued walking slowly along South Street until he saw a yellow taxi parked near a corner. He looked across the street and could see the exhaust from a car idling under the FDR Drive. He looked from the car to the yellow taxi and stopped when the cab's lights blinked off and on.

"Now what?" he whispered to himself.

◆ ◆ ◆

"Where's John?" Belzinger asked Greene.

"Circling around from the other side of the bridge," Greene said. "He's wearing worn army fatigues and looking homeless. Anything happens, look out for him."

Belzinger was crouched beneath an empty fish stand on the west side of South Street. She checked her cell phone and cursed when she realized the connection had been broken.

"What is it?" Greene asked.

"I lost the connection," Belzinger said. She leaned out to see where Reese was. A sanitation truck stopped at the corner and blocked her view.

"You give him your vest?" Greene asked.

Belzinger nodded.

Greene quickly removed his jacket, folded it, and set it on the floor. He undid the Velcro straps of his Kevlar vest and pulled it off. Belzinger looked up and waved him off.

"No, don't be stupid," she said.

"Just put it on," Greene said.

"No. No way."

"Put it on, damn it."

Belzinger shook her head. "It's yours. No way."

Greene dropped the vest at his partner's feet. "Here. It's getting cold holding the damn thing, and it's not doing either one of us any good like this."

Belzinger grudgingly picked the vest up. "I'm not comfortable doing this," she said.

Greene said, "Put the damn thing on."

◆ ◆ ◆

They were watching the black guy from the back of the cab. Janice was nervous. Jimmy seemed preoccupied.

"He's waiting for us," Janice said.

"Huh?"

"The black guy."

Jimmy nudged Janice and said, "This works out right, that shine might save you fifty grand."

"How?" Janice asked.

Jimmy held a hand up. "Wait," he said. "Give it another minute."

◆ ◆ ◆

DeNafria used chewing tobacco to build up enough spit to pass for vomit when he bent at the waist and feigned retching. He had circled the area from South Street to Robert F. Wagner Sr. Place and taken the walkway along the East River. He staggered against the railing a few times for effect.

He could see a car idling among a group of vehicles parked under the drive fifty yards ahead. The windows of the car were tinted. DeNafria angled back toward the railing to catch a glimpse of the license plate. He saw it was a radio car and turned to the water again to speak into his cell phone.

"Yeah," Greene said.

"There's a radio car idling under the drive," DeNafria told him. "I can't get close enough to see the plate."

"Burns?"

"Maybe. He drives for a radio outfit."

"What's up with that cab?" Green asked. "We saw the headlights flash."

"There are two people in the back. A man and a woman. The guy could be Jimmy. I'll try and get closer."

"Be careful."

"Right."

❖ ❖ ❖

The black guy was still waiting on the corner. He gestured to the cab, and Jimmy flicked four fingers off the end of his chin. "I'll give you this," he said.

"What are you going to do?" Janice asked.

Jimmy looked past Janice and out her window. Janice followed his gaze; she could see engine exhaust from a car parked under the FDR Drive.

"Who's that?" she asked, pointing at the car idling across South Street.

"That should be your father in the back there."

Janice was staring at the car now. "I don't see him. What are we waiting for?"

"So I know it's not a setup."

"What do you mean?"

"Cops," Jimmy said. He grabbed one of her hands. "Just relax. It'll be fine."

Janice turned toward the car idling under the FDR Drive. The headlights of a sanitation truck turning on the near corner illuminated the area. She squinted as she saw a cigarette drop from the driver's side window. She followed the cigarette down and thought she saw a small pile of butts.

"Oh, shit," she thought.

◆ ◆ ◆

Tommy Burns had already attached the sound suppressor to his Beretta. Now it sat in his lap. He used all three of his mirrors to watch what happened across South Street. When he saw the yellow cab's rear door open, he turned on his seat and opened his window a crack. Smoke from the fresh cigarette he had just lit blocked his view. He tossed the cigarette out the window.

Burns grabbed the Beretta and brought it to chest height when he heard Jimmy whistle. He immediately brought his window all the way down.

CHAPTER

55

MUFASA COULD ONLY MUSTER three of his membership, besides Shalaar, for Reese tonight. They were huddled in the BMW parked on South Street, just off Robert F. Wagner Sr. Place. Mufasa had kept his eyes trained on the stretch of South Street where Reese said he was to meet the man with his money. The tinted windows shielded anyone from seeing inside the BMW, but Mufasa kept the weapons he'd brought in the trunk just in case they were stopped.

Earlier, he had told his brothers, "We up against connected dudes tonight, but we owe Reese for what he did for Rahib. The brother needs our help."

"We packing?" one of his brothers asked.

"They's two shotguns and two Glocks in the trunk under the spare," Mufasa said. "But I'm hoping we don't have to touch those tonight. Our boy said we scared the man off at the restaurant. We scare them off again tonight, our debt is paid and we partying through the night."

"What do we do?" the inquisitive brother asked next.

"Walk the walk when the time comes," Mufasa said. "The man didn't like our formation, we use it again. Stare directly at him this time." He motioned at Larry Michael Brown sitting up front with him. "Shalaar here will get up close to the man and the dude will think he's surrounded."

Shalaar was busy watching the street.

The inquisitive brother pointed out the windshield, and Mufasa saw the woman running across South Street. He wondered what was inside the bag she was carrying.

"Let's go," he told his brothers, then slipped on his sunglasses.

They all put on their sunglasses before filing out of the BMW. Mufasa led them across South Street about fifty yards behind the taxi. He could see a man in the backseat struggling to get out of the cab. He could see Shalaar heading for the cab, and he was holding a gun.

Thinking it was a race now, Mufasa led the formation single file toward the woman with the bag. Then he saw she was holding a gun, too, and he stopped on a dime.

"Uh-oh," he said.

Two of his brothers weren't paying attention and walked into each other.

Then they heard the shots, and they all scrambled back north on South Street. Mufasa was the first to make it back to the BMW.

✦ ✦ ✦

She had grabbed the gym bag filled with money and leaped out of the cab. She'd stashed the gym bag inside her tote bag; she'd pulled the gun. She had started to cross South Street when she heard Jimmy getting out of the cab.

"Wait!" he yelled.

Janice ignored his call and ran toward the car parked under the FDR Drive. She saw the window open. She saw a cigarette drop from the window. She heard Jimmy whistle, and she saw the window of the car go down. Then she saw the silencer in the window. Janice stopped and took aim. She fired two shots. Windshield glass exploded after the second shot.

When she turned around, a group of black guys in suits and sunglasses were running north on South Street. But Jimmy was coming for her. So she turned her gun on him.

✦ ✦ ✦

Jimmy was startled when Janice grabbed the bag with the money and left him inside the cab. Grabbing the other gym bag, he pulled himself out of the cab. Then there were black guys running past him. "What the fuck?" he yelled.

And then he saw Janice shooting at Tommy Burns. He was almost close enough to stop her when she turned the gun on him. Jimmy heard the shot and was knocked to the ground before he knew what happened. When he looked up, Janice was running away again. Jimmy reached under his coat and felt blood. He looked up for Tommy Burns, but the town car was screeching away in reverse.

◆ ◆ ◆

Reese was standing there a few minutes before the woman got out of the cab. He wasn't trying to make a deal with God this time, and he said so in a silent prayer.

"If you're out there, God, I'm not asking for anything special. No deals this time. Just help me do the right thing here. That's all I'm asking for now, a chance to do the right thing."

Then he saw Mufasa and four of his men. There were supposed to be six, but there were just four he could see.

He saw the woman do something with the bag she was carrying before she hurried across South Street. Then the Mafia guy, Jimmy, was out of the cab. He also was carrying a bag. Reese noticed the guy's hair was curly and a different, red color tonight. He heard the guy call to the woman as she approached another car parked under the FDR Drive. When Reese realized she was holding a gun, he crouched. He heard gunshots and hit the pavement.

When Reese looked up again, Mufasa was nowhere in sight. The car under the FDR Drive was leaving rubber as it backed up onto South Street. He turned and saw the cab cut the near corner and race away.

He was getting up from his knees when he saw that the woman was running right at him. He put his hands up when she pointed the gun at him, but she fired anyway. The bullet slammed into the vest at his left shoulder. The force sent him rolling on the pavement. He crawled under the front of a parked car as another car raced along South Street.

He saw the woman running and smiled when the heel of one of her shoes broke. She lost her balance and fell hard onto the cobblestones. She lost her bags and gun. Reese saw the gym bag near the curb and grabbed it.

The woman crawled up and was on her feet again. She had her tote bag and was just reaching for the gun when another shot was fired from somewhere behind her.

"Toss the bag here, motherfucker," Reese heard somebody say. Another man yelled something else, but Reese had turned to his right. One of Mufasa's guys was pointing a gun at him.

❖ ❖ ❖

She saw the black guys crossing the street, and then she saw them scramble when Janice Barrett started shooting. Belzinger ran across South Street with her weapon drawn and her adrenaline pumping. Only she was nearly hit by her partner, who'd bolted away from the curb in the car. She didn't even hear the squeal of brakes a few feet behind her.

The cars up ahead were moving, and Reese Waters was lying flat on the street. She saw Jimmy Valentine get shot, and she was stunned to see the woman run toward Reese and shoot at him, too. Belzinger stopped to take a firing stance, but the woman fell to the ground just after she passed Reese.

Then Belzinger heard another shot. DeNafria had his weapon trained on the woman. Belzinger started running again, this time toward Jimmy Valentine, since DeNafria seemed to have the other situation under control. She had no idea where the black guys had gone.

❖ ❖ ❖

Greene gasped and slammed the brakes when he saw his partner crossing directly in front of him as he pulled away from the curb. He managed to avoid Belzinger, but the two cars up ahead were already racing away when he resumed the chase.

Greene didn't see Jimmy Valentine hit the street, but he did see the woman aim and fire her weapon at Reese Waters.

"Fuck!" Greene yelled.

There were two cars. The cab had turned the corner. The town car was flying north under the FDR Drive. Greene saw DeNafria with his weapon drawn and slammed his foot hard on the accelerator. He followed the town car. He was catching up when a city bus turned onto South Street two blocks ahead. Greene slammed on his brakes. Cursing, he leaned on the horn.

◆ ◆ ◆

DeNafria had started dialing a call to check on the license plate number of the town car when he saw the four black guys crossing South Street. Shots were fired, and he heard glass explode.

He ducked behind a highway column for cover. Another shot was fired. When he peeked out from behind the column, he saw the black guys running north on South Street. Two were climbing inside a BMW.

He heard tires burning rubber as he stood up. Then he heard another shot, and this time he saw its mark. Reese Waters was rolling on the pavement. DeNafria sprang out from behind the parked car and ran in a crouch with his weapon in both hands.

He saw the woman fall to the ground. He fired a warning shot. "Freeze! Don't move!" he yelled, and took small, careful steps across South Street. A bus turned the corner, and DeNafria could have sworn he heard a loud thud before he saw a small bag tossed inside the bus.

◆ ◆ ◆

Shalaar ran low and dove behind the cab after the woman started firing. He scrambled up onto the sidewalk and hid behind a pillar until he saw the woman running with the bag fall in the street.

When he saw the man grab the bag, Shalaar raced across the street and pointed his gun. He told the man to toss him the bag a moment before the flashing light blinded him.

The impact was sudden. Shalaar never knew that it was a bus that had killed him.

✦ ✦ ✦

Coleman turned off his headlights when he was on Dover Street. He heard shots and tried to locate his friend. When he saw the man pointing a gun at Reese, Coleman raced the bus and flashed his headlights on and off. He slammed on the brakes a moment before impact and hit the dude with the gun dead center in his chest. Blood splattered across the windshield. When the bus stopped, Coleman backed up to where Reese was still lying near the car. He opened the door, and Reese tossed a bag up the bus stairs. Coleman saw Reese waving at him to go. He hit the accelerator.

CHAPTER

56

"WHERE'S MY MONEY?" JANICE asked the detectives.

"I didn't see any money," Belzinger said. "Did you?" she asked Greene.

"I saw her shoot a couple people," Greene said. "That's what I saw."

They were seated around a metal table in an interview room at One Police Plaza. The detectives sat on one side of the table. Janice Barrett and her attorney, Phillip Landau, sat across from them. Landau was a stout, middle-aged man. He was wearing blue jeans and a Michigan State sweatshirt. He was still groggy from being woken up so early in the morning.

"Her father was kidnapped," Landau told the detectives. "Ms. Barrett was trying to save him."

"Did you see the father?" Belzinger asked Greene.

"I saw her shoot a couple people," Greene repeated.

"They were going to kill me," Janice said. "And they have fifty thousand dollars they stole from me."

"Not to mention your father," Greene said.

"That isn't remotely funny, detective," Landau said.

"It wasn't meant to be."

"It was in a gym bag, the money," Janice said. "Jimmy made me put the money in a small gym bag."

"There was a bag we found that Jimmy had," Belzinger said. "There were some instant Lotto tickets inside, but they were already scratched off and there were only twenty or thirty or so."

Janice face turned red. "That was . . . damn it."

"That was what?" Greene asked.

"Look, I was acting in self-defense," Janice said. "Both of them were extorting from me, the black guy and Jimmy. I was protecting myself. Didn't you see those other black guys there? Those had to be that convict's friends. They were coming for me. What about that guy with the gun that was hit by the bus?"

"Except Jimmy Valentine is still in surgery," said Belzinger, ignoring her comment about the black guys. "It'll be interesting to hear what he has to say about it, if he survives. Especially after he hears you're accusing him of kidnapping your father."

"Not to mention you shot the man," Greene said.

"And your ex-husband," Belzinger added. "Jimmy might have something to say about him, too."

Janice turned to her attorney. Landau said, "Don't say anything."

✦ ✦ ✦

"You okay?" DeNafria asked Reese.

They were in a curtained cubicle in the Downtown Beekman Hospital Emergency Room. Reese was shirtless. He touched his shoulder where the protective vest had stopped the bullet and left a nasty bruise.

"This is sore," he said.

"Imagine what it'd feel like you weren't wearing the vest."

"She in jail?" Reese asked. "The woman shot me."

"She's over at Police Plaza now, not far from here."

"She shot that other dude, too. How'd he make out?"

"He's in surgery."

"Bad?"

"I don't know."

"Where'd she shoot him?"

"Stomach. It could be bad."

Reese tried lifting his right arm, but the pain from his bruise was too strong. He moaned from the attempt.

"They'll probably sling that for you," DeNafria said.

Reese held his arm across his chest.

"She was making a lot of noise about money she claims she had," DeNafria said.

"Who?"

"The woman who shot you. She claims she had fifty thousand dollars in a small gym bag."

"I wouldn't know."

"I thought I saw a bag get tossed up on that bus," DeNafria said. "Maybe that was it?"

"What happened to that bus?" Reese asked. "That driver saved my life."

"We put out a call but the guy left the bus at the Staten Island Ferry. Went home apparently, called in, and said he was all traumatized from what he'd seen. You know the guy?"

"I didn't see him, whoever was driving that bus."

DeNafria said, "It was supposed to be on Water Street, that bus. It's not supposed to come down to South Street."

Reese remained silent.

DeNafria said, "Just a lucky break, I guess."

"Maybe there was a detour on Water," Reese said. "I used to drive a bus. It happens. All the construction going on."

"Right, construction."

Reese poured himself water and sipped it from a plastic pitcher. "She said it was fifty thousand she lost?"

"That's what she claims," DeNafria said. "But who knows? She claimed her father was kidnapped or something and that was the ransom, the fifty thousand. And she said there was a group of black guys coming for her. Guys she claims were friends of yours. But don't forget she shot you and at least one other person. She needs to say something in her defense."

Reese was biting his fingernails.

DeNafria nudged him. "Right?"

"Huh? Oh, yeah, right," Reese said. "She's gotta say something."

CHAPTER

57

SPECIAL AGENT IN CHARGE William Hernig entered the interview room a few minutes before dawn. He sipped coffee from a Dunkin' Donuts container. He stood in front of the door. Everyone in the room looked tired and disheveled.

"Rough night?" he asked the detectives.

"Long night," Greene said. "And you are?"

Hernig presented his identification and introduced himself.

"And you're here because?" Phillip Landau asked.

"None of your business," Hernig told the attorney.

"Do we need to talk privately?" Greene asked Hernig.

"If you don't mind," Hernig said.

Both detectives stepped outside the interview room and huddled with Hernig in a hallway.

"What's up?" Greene asked.

"Jimmy Valentine is signed up with us," Hernig said.

"With who?" Belzinger asked.

"Uncle Sam," Hernig said.

Belzinger looked to Greene.

"He flipped," Greene said. He turned to Hernig. "And?"

"He's in critical condition. He's got less than a fifty-fifty chance of surviving."

"Then what?" Belzinger asked.

"I'm not sure. But I need to know what you have on the situation. We understand another detective was snooping around, an Organized Crime detective. A John DeNafria? We already know he's on leave. What's going on?"

Greene looked to his partner. Belzinger said, "He's my boyfriend. End of story."

❖ ❖ ❖

Hernig learned that Jimmy was in stable condition but had developed an infection from a lanced spleen. There was no definitive prognosis as yet. Before he was anesthetized, however, Jimmy had identified by name and description Janice Barrett as the woman who had contracted for her ex-husband's murder.

Hernig informed the detectives, and they all rejoined Janice and her attorney in the interview room.

"I'll give you the good news and the bad news," Belzinger said.

"Don't bother wasting your breath, Detective," Phillip Landau said. "Ms. Barrett has nothing to say."

"I'll tell her anyway," Belzinger said. "First, the good news. Jimmy Valentine isn't dead." She spoke directly at Landau. "As of now, there's no murder charge against your client regarding him."

"It was self-defense," Janice said with total indifference.

Landau put a finger to his lips.

"Now for the bad news," Belzinger said. "Jimmy Valentine isn't dead." This time Belzinger looked directly at Janice. "And he just gave you up on the murder of Peter Rizzo."

"Motherfucker," Janice said.

"Then there's the attempted murders of Mr. Valentine and Reese Waters, but I don't think those'll much matter once Jimmy testifies as to premeditated conspiracy. From what I understand, you'll feel a pinch from the needle and not much else."

Landau stood up and turned his back to Belzinger. "We'll see about that," he said.

"Your client was lucky last night," Hernig said to the attorney. "Jimmy gave two of our agents the slip when he picked your client up. Why they call him Jimmy Wigs. Otherwise, I suspect, the second she pulled her gun last night, however she managed it, they would have left her for dead."

Janice was trembling. She started to sob in her hands.

Belzinger pulled a Kleenex from a box on the table and held it out to Janice. "Here," she said, "before your mascara runs."

CHAPTER

58

"I DON'T WANT A dime," Coleman told Reese. "Not from that money. Not after I learned I might have a reward coming."

They were sitting around Laney's kitchen table. The money had been counted, and it now lay on top of the flattened gym bag in five stacks of ten thousand dollars. Reese was staring at it.

"I called in a red tag, told the dispatcher I had a four-five," Coleman continued. "Shots fired. What I did was call in first to say there were people blocking Water Street and some of them looked like they carrying weapons. I said this just to make it sound good. Didn't know when I turned the corner, there actually were motherfuckers ready to shoot somebody."

Reese said, "What they cite you with?"

"Everything," Coleman said. "Once you tossed the bag on board, I took off for South Ferry and left the bus there. Called in when I was on the subway heading home. Told them there was a shoot-out and I was afraid for my life. Told them I thought I hit something, too, but wasn't sure what it was. They wanted me to report to Jackie Gleason, but I told them I was too shook up and needed a drink."

"That couldn't be smart, telling them you needed a drink," Laney commented.

"It's the perfect thing to say in that situation," Reese told her. "Vince know the ropes, it comes to farm talk."

"Farm talk?"

Coleman said, "What they call guys go off for rehabilitation, farmers. I been back and forth so many times, it sounds legit."

"Except you killed that dude," Reese reminded him.

"Cops didn't seem to mind," Coleman said, "even after they picked me up for leaving the scene and all."

Laney shook her head.

Coleman said, "So, technically, I was off-route, leaving the scene and abandonment."

"Not to mention what else they'll figure out before they charge you," Reese said.

Both men shared a cautious chuckle.

"Reese?" Laney asked.

"Oh, I need to get one thousand over to Neve Rosenblatt," Reese said, "so I can buy Peter's body from his family."

"The cremation will cost another seventeen hundred," Laney said, "but you can afford to bury him now if you want."

"You can afford to bury him in a Cadillac," Coleman said.

Reese shook his head. "I told them twenty-five hundred," he said. "That's what I'll take."

"What about the six niggers in sunglasses?" Coleman asked. "You pay them for standing like statues and running for the hills, you paying me to lose my job."

Coleman had been suspended without pay for several violations. The man he had run over was wanted for killing a policeman in Alabama. Coleman was looking at a possible fifty-thousand-dollar reward.

Reese said, "Those brothers are likely to be in hiding the next several years after what happened. Mufasa's not the type to push it. I suspect you did him a favor running down that boy. Police'll be more than happy to have a cop-killer. They won't care about Mufasa and his crew." He turned to Laney. "You can bring the rest of the money to the church, you want."

"Just make sure I'm good and drunk when you do it," Coleman said.

"Are you sure, Reese?" Laney asked. "You can buy a set of drums with some of it. I'm sure your friend would want that."

Reese smiled. "Peter'd want me to open a restaurant or nightclub. But even fifty grand isn't enough to do that."

"He might want you to have a night on the town," Coleman said. "Maybe invite a good friend or two. Do it up, you know. Some Johnny Walker Black, maybe some Courvoisier."

Reese pulled the Saint Jude statue from his pants pocket. He kissed the statue before setting it on top of the middle stack of cash.

"Twenty-five hundred," he said. "That's what I'll take. I'll pay the balance of the cremation on my own. Take the rest to the church, Laney. Split it, you want. Give half to Saint Lawrence and half to Saint Jude's over in Canarsie."

"Are you positive?" Laney asked.

"Positive," Reese said. "Peter'd be happiest knowing she didn't get over. Not on robbing or killing him. He's smiling on this, what we did."

"What we did was get lucky," Coleman said. "Especially you, motherfucker."

Reese looked to the Saint Jude statue and said, "I'm not so sure about that, my man. I'm not so sure about that at all."

✦ ✦ ✦

Alex Dale Barrett learned about his sister when he received a call from her lawyer a few minutes after noon. He looked for his wife but couldn't find her. He left a message for Lydia on her cell phone to call back.

A few hours later, Alex stood alongside two New York State troopers and two detectives with the Organized Crime Task Force from New York City, at the Poughkeepsie construction site. One detective looked over maps of the Barrett Construction properties in Westchester.

The other detective focused on a patch of freshly upturned dirt jutting out from one end of a blue tarpaulin.

✦ ✦ ✦

A warm front crossed the Northeast the following morning when "Fat" Tony Gangi's crew was rounded up in Perth Amboy. Several teams of federal agents, as well as local law enforcement, were involved in the arrests.

Gangi was brought to Manhattan in a dark van with four of the agents, including Special Agent in Charge William Hernig.

Gangi sat with a frown on his face during most of the trip. When Hernig mentioned a possible deal for future testimony, Gangi said, "What's the point? I'm living this life more than forty years. I probably have less than ten left. I couldn't sleep nights, I gave anybody up now."

"You already know somebody gave you up," Hernig said. "Or why would we be here, right?"

"I also heard the guy might not make it," Gangi said. "Why you guys are so pressed to flip somebody before it's too late."

Hernig was silent.

"Right?" Gangi said.

"And if you have twenty years left?" Hernig asked. "Or maybe more? You could probably sleep a lot better in a bed in a house than you will in a cell."

"Says you," Gangi said.

"Says me," Hernig said.

Gangi laughed. "Where, in Arkansas someplace?"

"Or Phoenix or Salt Lake City," Hernig said. "Could be anyplace."

"I'll take my chances," Gangi said. "What the hell am I gonna do in Phoenix?"

Epilogue

TOMMY BURNS HEARD ABOUT his missed opportunity in New Jersey while driving along a state highway in Georgia. The execution-style murder of Frank Gennaro at a Garden State Parkway rest area was a news highlight the day it happened.

After dumping his town car on the Lower East Side the night of the shoot-out under the FDR Drive, Tommy had stolen a Honda Civic parked on First Avenue and used it to slip across the George Washington Bridge into New Jersey. He later boosted another car in Fort Lee and eventually made his way west to Pennsylvania.

In Pennsylvania, Burns had robbed an all-night convenience store and later a liquor distributorship. A few days later, after purchasing a car cheap off a lot under a phony name, Burns had weaved his way back east and south until he found himself low on funds again, this time in Georgia.

Now he grew tired from driving. He spotted a farmer's market that might be a good place to pick up some cash. He had five prepaid cell phones left. If he couldn't sell those, he still had his weapon.

Burns pulled into the market where an old-timer was wiping down his fruit display with a paper napkin. Burns grabbed two of the cell phones and slipped his Beretta inside his pants. He let his shirt hang over his pants as he got out of the car and approached the old man.

"Top of the morning," Burns said.

"Morning," the old man said.

"Can I interest you in some prepaid cell phones? I'm on my way to visit some family down in Florida and my brother-in-law give me a box of these things, and don't you know, the first time in his life the guy comes up with something, I'm on my way out of town? I'm not a big fan of him, my brother-in-law, but the guy come through and there's nothing else to say about it. Prepaid cell phones, the next big thing in technology. They're great you're out here by yourself all day. Even better you're on the road a lot, what you must deal with here all the time, people on the road."

"Prepaid what?" the old man asked.

"Cell phones," Burns said. He pushed one across the table.

The old man examined the phone while Burns continued to talk. "I got a few with a hundred bucks of prepaid calls on them," Burns said. "I can let you have them for sixty bucks apiece. Fifty-five you take three or more."

The old man walked to a pickup parked behind his stand. He turned the sideview mirror so he could see himself.

"You're right," he told Burns. "I do look like a fool today, don't I?"

Burns couldn't help but chuckle.

"No, thanks anyway," the old man said. "I got a grandson run his mother's phone bill to three hundred dollars on those girlie lines. He'd probably go for one of these but then I'd be the one lending his mother to pay for it."

"I know what you mean," Burns said. "Kids today."

He noticed the old man was selling cigarettes for eighteen dollars a carton. Burns pointed from the cell phone on the table to the cartons of Camel regulars. "Fair exchange?" he asked.

The old man pointed to the cell phone. "That and a twenty, sure," he said. "I'll even give you two bucks change."

Burns laughed again and plucked a twenty from the diminishing roll of cash he was carrying. He set the twenty on the counter and picked up the cell phone. He watched where the old man stashed the cash, inside a pocket in his overalls.

"Anything else?" the old man asked.

"Matches?"

The old man produced four books. He tossed them on the table.

"My grandson managed to steal a carton of matches from my daughter's basement where I kept them," he said. "What the hell he's gonna do with all those matches, I have no idea."

"Neither probably does he," Burns said.

"I guess I should be grateful the silly bastard didn't burn the place down."

"That's one way to look at it."

"He's seventeen years old with no direction at all. Quit high school and he don't have a trade. Don't know north from south, either. Kid found himself a piece of tail and that's all he cares about anymore."

Burns had slipped his right hand inside his pants to grab the Beretta. He flipped the safety on and removed his hand. He waited for eye contact with the old man, winked, and said, "It's the way of the modern world."

Acknowledgments

THERE ARE SEVERAL PEOPLE in the chain of thanks for *Cheapskates* . . . Eddie Rodes (twenty-one years a New York City bus driver) for his expertise and advice . . . Jim Nyland (an expert marksman and dear friend) and James W. P. "Kimo" Andrews (born and raised in Hawaii, a direct descendant of the last two kings of Oahu; Kimo also was a highly decorated Marine aviator who flew more than a thousand Vietnam combat missions in helicopters, transports, and fast attack jets) for their help with *the guns, the guns, the guns* . . . Uncle Pete Cerami, because he's my type of guy . . . Cecilia Tardo and her Web site (*haminahamina.com*) for the Ralph Kramden quote . . . my core group of readers for this one (Dave and Ross Gresham, Craig McDonald, Nicole Hope Stella, Trevor Maviano, and, of course, the Principessa—my heartbeat and wife—Ann Marie) . . . and always the man I look to for the most help, my editor, Peter Skutches.